War brews among vampires. Facing extinction at the hands of an ancient one, the Vampire Council plods along with a secret strategy. Jaret Bachmann, both vampire and witch, fears the Council elders move too slowly. He has the power to assist them in defeating their enemy, but the longer they keep him at arm's length the more defiant he becomes. He's already pushing the boundaries to assert his will when tragedy strikes, devastating him and compelling him to become even more rebellious.

A young vampire alone in the world, Jaret struggles to find his true self and discover how he wants to spend the remainder of his eternal life, even as the vampire war intensifies and the rogue vampire strikes again. To compound his problems, he's faced with the allure of a hot renegade vampire, not sure if he is friend or foe.

Who will win the war, and where will Jaret's soul-searching lead him?

THE VAMPIRE'S WAR

THE REALM OF THE VAMPIRE COUNCIL, BOOK FIVE

DAMIAN SERBU

A NineStar Press Publication

www.ninestarpress.com

The Vampire's War

First Edition, December 2022

ISBN: 978-1-64890-601-5

Also available in eBook, ISBN: 978-1-64890-600-8

CONTENT WARNING:
This book contains sexual content, which may only be suitable for mature readers. Depictions of murder, kidnapping, death of a prominent character, graphic violence, grief, and a scene of attempted date rape.

To Elisabeth, for including me on your journey

PART ONE

IMPENDING WAR

CHAPTER ONE

CONFRONTATION

20 JANUARY 2019
Estes Park, Colorado

Jaret hugged himself as if to fend off the frigid air blowing across Lake Estes on a winter's night. His long, brown curly hair blew into his face, blurring the image of the man sauntering away. The muscular hunk faded into the distance, his rock-solid body and sandy brown hair nothing but a memory.

Of course, Jaret wasn't cold. A vampire's body was immune to the elements, always a perfect temperature. He clutched his arms around his slight but powerful body to contain the emotion vying to burst out. The lust for Charon, a narcissistic vampire Jaret loved to flirt with, always made his head spin. The forbidden alure frazzled his mind because Jaret was completely loyal to Anthony, the most powerful and oldest vampire in the world.

More than desire confounded him at the moment, however. The dread of a looming vampire war, over five years in the making but brewing beneath the surface, had his emotions on edge. He had met Charon and started their flirtatious relationship because of the impending war, seeing the powerful warlock vampire as a needed ally. But Jaret felt guilty for courting Charon and his harem of hot men to join the cause without the Vampire Council's knowledge.

Jaret, a strong vampire and even more powerful witch, feared little in terms of humans or other vampires. He felt certain of his own justification for defying the Council and even more confident he had never betrayed Anthony. But containing his rage and terror threatened to undo him.

It was becoming too much to balance outward obedience to the Council with his secret intentions about the war. Jaret's magic pushed him to make his own plans to fight, despite the Council ordering him to stay out of the way.

Both conflicting agendas whirled in his head.

When another being materialized before him, as if dropped from heaven, Jaret launched himself twenty feet backward in one swift motion and took a defensive posture. Lost in his thoughts, he'd failed to sense the approaching danger.

Jaret remained rigid, even as the person before him stepped forward, transforming from an unknown threat into a very familiar vampire. The long blond hair. The bright blue eyes. The hot muscles. The height. Everything about Anthony's appearance thrilled Jaret as much as during their first encounter along the shore of Lake Michigan when Anthony saved Jaret from a gang of football players wanting to rob and bash him.

Usually, Jaret would run into those inviting arms, but tonight the full moon shone down on the infuriated face Jaret never liked to see on his lover. The telltale thrum of a vein in Anthony's forehead gave away the rage. Anthony pressed his lips together and glared.

Jaret's body trembled. After losing his entire family when an enraged ghost had killed them, Anthony and his friends had saved Jaret. Jaret loathed the thought of losing his vampire family, but this episode would come of his own doing because, without a word being spoken, Jaret knew Anthony had caught him with Charon.

"How long has this been going on?" Anthony spoke in a measured tone, stepping forward with a slow, deliberate movement.

Jaret remained crouched in a defensive posture. "What?"

"Don't play innocent," Anthony sneered. "I didn't want to believe my eyes. Even when confronted with the evidence. How long have you been cheating on me?"

Jaret shook his head. "Never. I never cheated on you." His heart sank as he ignored all the questions except the accusation of infidelity. All the temptation, the repeated and earnest attempts by Charon to fuck Jaret, but he never betrayed his lover. Never.

Anthony rushed forward and grabbed Jaret's crotch. He spat his words into Jaret's ear. "Your erection says otherwise."

"No." Jaret whispered. "Nothing ever happened. I went to him for help. We need him."

Anthony released Jaret's cock and stepped away, facing the frozen lake with his back to Jaret. "Explain, or I leave." Anthony stood straight as an arrow before taking two steps farther away from Jaret. "When I do, I'll bring the full wrath of the Vampire Council down upon you. It will be as if you and I never fell in love."

Jaret gasped out his despair. "Without knowing the truth,

you'd throw me into the wind?" A blood tear trickled down his cheek.

Anthony turned and clutched Jaret's arms in his fists before yanking him forward. He spoke in a whisper, his rigid façade evaporating in the cold night air. "Talk to me. Explain this before my world crumbles around me."

Jaret leaned into Anthony and flung his arms around his waist. They embraced for several minutes before Jaret stopped shaking and looked into Anthony's eyes.

"It's not what you think." His voice quaked. "I met him about four years ago. Right after we learned some renegade vampire was plotting a war against the Vampire Council and threatening to exterminate vampires. You know I disagreed with the Council's caution. I discovered Charon through magic. He's a vampire, yes, but his maker created him with a spell to conceal him from all other vampires, including the Vampire Council."

"How is that possible?" Alarm sounded in Anthony's voice. "What maker? Why?"

"I don't know. But Charon's also a witch. Like me. A vampire and a witch. Hidden from everyone. He created his own harem of vampire guys, and they live separate from other vampires. He's not a threat. Charon only wants to live without interference. But his power and ability could help us. We have to plan for this war. We'll need every force available."

Anthony walked along the path circling the lake. He gripped Jaret's hand as they continued, like a couple on a warm summer's evening.

"Do you love him?"

Jaret laughed despite the situation. "No. He's not very loveable. Not my type of personality."

"But he *is* your type in terms of being in command, hot, and domineering. So maybe you fucked him for fun."

Anthony's bitter words wiped the smile from Jaret's face. "No." He shook his head. "I mean, I hear you. He's hot. Like if a college-aged dude with long hair, full red lips, hazel eyes, and a slight build came running by right now." Jaret pointed to himself. "You'd watch his tight ass run by and admire the beauty. You'd flirt like hell if he stopped to ask for directions. But you wouldn't go seduce him, even if he came at you first. It's the same for me. Yeah, he's hot. I lust for him, but I love you. I would never betray you for a quick fuck with another man. I couldn't survive losing you." Jaret choked out a cry with the last words.

The silence between them as they sauntered over a bridge that crossed the Thompson River almost undid Jaret as Anthony considered his words. Anthony tightened his clutch on Jaret's hand, causing Jaret to stumble at the signal Anthony may have believed him.

"I wouldn't survive either." Anthony released Jaret and wiped a tear from his face but his anger returned too soon. "That doesn't explain your defiance of the Council. I have a duty to the vampire ethic, regardless of how my service to the Council affects you and me."

Jaret sighed. Their same argument. "We've been over our disagreement a million times. The Council keeps me in the dark." Jaret bit his lip before raging against the Vampire Council, an ancient entity with power to enforce vampiric laws. The members possessed a sorcery to detect defiance of their edicts, and they could punish those who disobeyed, including a death sentence. The Council spent most of its time regulating the one hundred or so vampires worldwide so that everyone kept their existence a secret from humanity. The possible war meant they needed to shift their focus, and their slow movement toward the battle infuriated Jaret, especially because he had no voice there, despite knowing all five members on an intimate level. "And I think you're being too passive. The Council needs to act, fast. It's been over four years since we learned about a possible war. We know the enemy's getting ready to move."

"You're too powerful a witch. We've talked about your magic too. Trust the Council. We're keeping abreast of the situation."

"Magic, magic, magic. You throw my power in my face all the time. It's a part of me, which you also knew as soon as you met me. So how about we get over my power already. Let me in on the meetings. I feel like a total dweeb—all my friends sit on the Council. You. Xavier. Thomas. Catherine. Harriet. All the important people in my life. But I sit on the outside like a fucking asshole because my jewels give me power. It's fucking ridiculous."

Anthony stopped and frowned at Jaret. "Maybe we keep you at a distance because you're young and impetuous."

The truth of Anthony's words made Jaret laugh. "Okay. But *maybe* we need some of my spice to get the war going. To protect ourselves. Caution may very well kill us. Have you ever studied Europe's reaction to Hitler in the 1930s?"

"Listen, Mr. Historian, I lived it." Anthony continued along the path. "I understand your frustration."

"Yeah, right."

"I do." Anthony gripped Jaret's hand tighter to emphasize his point. "I've been worrying about the war for the same four years. Keeping informed. Trying to track the vampire down. Seeing the signs of a war but nothing concrete enough to enable action. Pouring over the magic at our disposal to find a way to win. Please, Jaret. Your working against us distracts us. Now I'm here investigating a rogue vampire you secretly meet with. Tell me about him so we can move on."

Jaret stared at the power plant to his left, as if gray walls might provide a way to dodge Anthony's request. "He's an ace up my sleeve. I can't tell you more. Even if you arrest me."

"I'm afraid." Anthony whispered, melting Jaret a bit. "This feels like the first war, so long ago. The war almost destroyed every vampire." Jaret knew the rest before Anthony continued. "One sadistic vampire took on the Council, created a counter army, and hundreds died. I alone survived from the Council. He killed my lover." Anthony stopped as tears streamed down his face.

"And you're afraid I'll be next." Jaret leaned into Anthony. "But I won't be. I can protect myself. And, unlike then, when he killed his maker and issued a surprise attack, we'll be ready. You're not the lone vampire on the Council anymore. Ever since you brought on Catherine, Thomas, Harriet, and Xavier, it's not the same as before. This is different."

They walked in silence, once again at a stalemate.

Jaret pressed on. "It's not like you have the corner on the tragedy market. My family past has a fucked up elder who died when a lover murdered him before he immigrated to America. What's he do? Henrik haunts his family, killing off the witch born to every generation because we're all fags. I had to fight him, remember? Won, until he came back and killed my whole fucking family, not to mention my previous boyfriend. All of them. Dead." Jaret trembled with rage at the memory.

Anthony stopped and snatched Jaret into his arms, then pressed his face into Jaret's hair. "Why are we going down these roads again? We have each other. I believe you didn't do anything with this vampire. We both have plenty of sorrow in our lives for every living creature combined. Let's forget."

Jaret nodded against Anthony's chest. "Even Charon? Forget I know him?"

Anthony pushed Jaret away so they could look in each other's eyes but kept his hands around Jaret's shoulders. "I'm not being flippant. Or too cautious. Or protective. Whatever label you want to place on my reactions to the upcoming war, I think you misread me. It isn't about latent fear I could lose you or psychological damage from last time." Anthony squeezed so hard the pressure hurt. "This war vibes *exactly* like the last one. The buzz in the air. How the circumstances have even confused the magic and its messages. This isn't a false parallel I've drawn to the war of old. This war mimics the first one in every way. Every...single...way. Even the method used to conceal this vampire's actions from us."

The idea hit Jaret like a bomb. The vampire who made Charon, who was completely nuts and had invented a way to conceal Charon from the Council in order to provoke chaos. Charon said his maker seemed off and angry, a total loon bird. What if the impending war sparked alarms and danger mirroring the past because the same vampire was inducing the alarms? Charon's creator told Charon he had survived the first war to seek revenge for a lost lover, but in truth he hid himself and spent centuries to complete the war he began.

"But I thought you killed him?" Jaret asked Anthony, hoping to hear something to refute his dread.

"Apparently not." Anthony started walking along the path again. The serene mountains surrounding them seemed so out of touch with the bombshell news.

"What does this mean? What should we do? This is why I wanted to act much sooner!"

"And it's why we kept you in the dark. It's why the Council, and the Council alone, must decide what and where to fight him. His return is precisely why we need caution and deliberate action."

"He might have made Charon."

Anthony stopped. "Which explains the concealing magic. Another reason to keep you out of this. He may be manipulating your relationship with Charon."

Jaret's mind whirled in a thousand directions. The jab about keeping him in the dark infuriated him, as usual, not to mention the inference about being manipulated. Fear shot through his spine at the thought of such an old and powerful vampire coming for them. And his heart melted at Anthony's concern. No matter what Anthony had said about knowing the difference between this time and last, Jaret knew the thought of losing another lover terrified him. Anthony still missed his first lover after centuries of mourning.

Jaret tilted toward sympathy instead of continuing the fight. "But you'll include me at the right time? You won't always push me to the side?"

Anthony paused. "We'll all be involved, whether we want to be or not."

CHAPTER TWO

SAVANNAH PARTY

25 JANUARY 2019
Savannah, GA

Jaret patted his dog on the head. He owned the only vampire dog in existence. After a deranged ghost murdered his entire family, spiraling him into despair, Xavier turned Darth so Jaret would never need to say goodbye to her.

"Darth, we need to talk." She eyed him but appeared uninterested since Jaret made no move to leave or to give her a treat. "See,

Anthony and I chatted last night. Agreed to keep me in the dark because, well, he and the Council want to, and I have no recourse. Right?"

She tilted her head. Except he was certain she wanted a treat or to go on a walk, not to commiserate about the Council cockblocking him.

"But, you know I disagree with their slow, passive response. I mean, they're going to get us fucking killed!" Darth wagged her stub of a tail in agreement. "See, you get it. Murdered. Wiped out. So to keep Anthony happy, I had no choice but to agree to his secrecy. However, I never technically promised not to operate my own plans on the sly. With you in the know, of course."

Darth leapt to her feet when Jaret reached for the treat jar. She still wanted her dog biscuits, even though, like a human vampire, she needed blood and nothing more. He threw one to her.

"We're heading out for a little party, you and I. Charon and I need to talk. On the downlow." He pointed a finger at Darth. "So zip it. No telling Anthony. Or anyone else on the Council. We can have secrets too."

When Jaret grabbed Darth's leash and headed for the door, she spun in excited circles. He almost never used the leash because she obeyed as a vampire dog and could never get lost from him. But sometimes he needed the leash to keep up appearances when around humans. They hit the street and headed out.

Before they both became vampires, Jaret and Darth jogged

together almost every day. In their undead state, they continued the ritual but instead of a thirty-minute jaunt up and down a mountain or along the Chicago lake front, they sprinted thousands of miles in a matter of minutes. One second they were in a Chicago house, next they stood on a deserted street corner in Savannah, Georgia.

Savannah haunted Jaret with its old-world feel and charisma. The historic houses and layout of the central tourist area hinted of a bygone era, one of both wonder and horror. The scenery spoke of ancient rituals and exquisite clothes. But the aura also reflected through time on slavery, human cruelty, and unsettled spirits. Modern Savannah included a vibrant arts scene, a college atmosphere, and a lot of little touristy places, not to mention a ghost tour on every corner.

Jaret loved the atmosphere and its complications. But tonight, he had little time to act as a vacationer enjoying the sights and sounds because of his mission. He would rather meet Charon in a more formal setting, one-on-one and away from distractions. But, alas, Charon seldom agreed to anything professional or too staid. He reserved intimacy for the possibility of being laid, not for official business.

Jaret sensed his way through the streets, following the magical trail of perception Charon had provided to find his location. Charon had promised a southern bacchanal. He gathered his little harem of vampire boys, added as many hot Southern men as they could entice in an evening, and put on a big bash. The occasion? Charon and his minions were bored and wanted "fresh meat," as Charon charmingly described their desires to Jaret.

Despite Charon's insisting the details were a huge secret, Jaret took little effort to figure out the right house. He could have located the revelry without any of Charon's magic, because the "discreet" party rumbled through the walls of an old Georgian brick mansion right in the middle of town.

Jaret smiled at the view from across the street. Every light in the house illuminated the interior for passersby. The music and laughter burst out the open windows. And Jaret saw hot guys mingling, dancing, and sucking face. He would bet a shitload of money the one hanging out the window and waving to people was also getting fucked by the tall blond vampire mashed into him from behind, a former basketball player, Jaret recalled. A classic Charon party, indiscreet, full of sex, partying hard, and flaunting the fact the Vampire Council had no control over him. Jaret had already met Charon's boys, the vampires in the crowd easy to spot as they acted human and embraced the festivities.

Jaret hesitated, needing to see Charon and continue to urge him into the war but not wanting to dive into a party scene. Introverted by nature, even with vampiric power and charisma, Jaret was self-conscious and nervous in large gatherings. Jaret leaned against a light pole, more comfortable as an observer than participant.

A couple minutes later Charon appeared in the front doorway, winking and laughing as he grabbed some guy's ass. The human, tall but very slight, with all the looks of a college twink enraptured by Charon's charm, smiled from ear to ear, hopped down the three steps off the porch, twirled around, and waved goodbye.

After blowing the young man a kiss, Charon spotted Jaret across the street and grinned. True, Jaret would never cheat on Anthony, but his loyalty never stopped his appreciation for someone so gorgeous, and Charon pushed every one of Jaret's buttons. His was chiseled with spiked sandy blond hair, tall, confident, and oozed sex.

"You can't get enough of me, can you?" Charon asked as he strode across the street. "Are you going to come in or gawk like some old troll?" Charon brushed his hand across Jaret's cheek.

Jaret grabbed Charon's hand and lowered it as Charon moved them toward the house. Ignoring Charon's jabs, he redirected the conversation. "I see you wanted to try something new for a change. A party full of sex and drinking."

Charon giggled. "My boys demanded nothing less."

Jaret arched a brow. "I thought you were in charge of your little harem? You kidnapped them, converted them all into vampires, but with magic so you control their every move. Now you pretend they tell you what to do?"

"Ah!" Charon held a finger in the air. "They came of their own will to my *harem*, your words, not mine. And they *chose* to remain under the constrictions I implemented. But their continued compliance goes much better when I indulge them. Otherwise, they pout and bitch, which annoys me to no end. A castle full of whining fags becomes unpleasant rather fast."

"So the sex and all those young men tonight have nothing to do with you? You're a martyr here?"

Charon laughed. "Did you come as some puritanical preacher to scold me? Remember what I do to pastors who pontificate and annoy me."

Jaret laughed, despite his disapproval for Charon's reference. Charon had started an annual tradition at Christmastime of stalking a conservative antigay pastor and murdering him in his church. The nation dubbed him the Christmas Eve Serial Killer. "You know I don't approve of your little serial killer game." Yet his grin gave away how he did not lament losing an asshole or two every year.

"You think my serial killer side is sexy." Charon licked his lips and grabbed Jaret's ass. "Follow me. We need a beverage." Charon guided them past a parlor full of naked men playing charades, through a dining room of chatting gents, and into a kitchen with every drink imaginable spread before them. "You better drink something or it'll look funny."

Jaret glanced around and eyed the wine. "What haven't you spiked with a drug?"

Charon mocked offense. "Moi?"

Knowing better than to trust a thing coming out of his mouth,

Jaret grabbed an unopened bottle of Pinot Noir, uncorked the wine, and poured himself and Charon a glass. He swirled and smelled the bouquet before taking a sip. "Very nice."

"Of course it's nice. I don't serve shit. Now, tell me why you're here."

"Can we talk someplace private?"

Charon peered around the crowded kitchen, into the packed hallway, and toward the open back door to the throng of men there. "Private doesn't exist here. Trust me, the bedrooms are full of naked men and reek of come. Your innocence wouldn't be able to handle the fun. We can go outside and find a corner. If we whisper, we can hear each other, but no one will hear us."

"Except all your vampires lurking about with their preternatural senses."

Charon waved a dismissive hand in the air. "They're much too busy getting drunk and laid to care about the very serious vampire who appears in their midst. He looks dour and frightened."

Jaret smiled and punched Charon in the arm. "You're an ass."

"You just want to lick my ass. Come on." Charon led them outside, past chatting men, a drinking game of some sort, and over to a magnolia tree in the corner.

Charon leaned against the trunk, while Jaret stood a few feet away from him, clutching his wine with two hands.

Charon smiled, then a laugh escaped. He reached out and pulled Jaret to within a couple inches of himself, which Jaret allowed, though the proximity intoxicated him. Charon wound a finger through Jaret's hair. "Your man doesn't deserve your devotion. I would make you my top lieutenant if you joined my harem, and you know you want me to fuck you."

Jaret shook his head as he chuckled at Charon. "I've no interest in bowing down to you, nor is lust the same as devotion. Speaking of not deserving something, you already have a perfect number two. Jordan serves you to perfection and is more than happy in his role. So you and I will remain friends who give each other blue balls. Besides, you need someone in your life to tell you no."

Charon roared a laugh and pinched Jaret on the cheek. "You enthrall me. So, what brings you on such serious business? Is this alleged war you've been carrying on about actually going to happen?"

"The war will start soon." Jaret sighed, knowing he sounded ludicrous because he had enlisted Charon some time ago and nothing had ever come of his repeated dire warnings. "I sense a new urgency. You *have* to assist in the fight. The magic— I can't explain how, but the air tingles with anticipation. Things have changed. Again, I have no concrete evidence, but everything in my magical ability portends cataclysmic war—a war between vampires to extinguish half our people."

Jaret waited for Charon's witty retort, about the language he used, about his seriousness, about nothing happening. Instead, Charon squinted his eyes and pressed his lips together before speaking. "I know."

"You know?"

Charon nodded. "I feel the alarm for the first time. The magic communicated to me. I'm involved somehow, whether or not I want to be."

"This started since we saw each other a few nights ago?" Jaret asked.

"Yes." Charon nodded. "First in a dream, then as glimpses of magical electricity issuing a vague warning."

"What are you talking about?"

"I'm not sure." Charon shrugged then laughed to himself. "For a long time, I thought you were off your rocker or something strange. Cute. Smart. Seductive. With magical ability, but crazy. Scrambled paranoia in your head about wars and danger. Yet you were so convincing I loved keeping you around. And I do intend to fuck you someday." Charon paused to gauge Jaret's reaction but continued when nothing came of his flirtation but Jaret's slight grin. "But now *I* have become the crazed shaman. The past day or so, I get visions. They tell me to watch out. A war to end all vampires commences. And—" He stopped to think.

"What?"

"I think my maker might have returned from the dead."

Jaret stood in silence, considering how Charon's theory matched what Anthony and he suspected. Charon became a vampire when his maker, Styx, created a contest to choose the ultimate narcissistic vampire: governed by his own desires, hidden from the Vampire Council by magic created by Styx, a vampire to prey on humans and bend the world to his will. He proclaimed himself Styx in response to Charon's nickname. Charon, born Blade Haden, had earned the nickname "Charon" in college because the mythological figure paddled people across the River Styx, from the world of the living to the world of the dead. The Charon standing before Jaret had served as the ferryman of young men's dreams of a relationship to the brutal reality of a one-night stand, all to benefit himself. Since Charon rowed people across the river Styx to their demise, Styx proclaimed himself the river, transporting Charon and his vampire life to its own brand of hedonism and conquest. Why did the history lesson blare through Jaret's mind? Because Styx committed suicide after training Charon as a vampire, but Charon just said he thought Styx had returned. And the news confirmed that the one who created Charon was also the rogue vampire, and quite possibly the one who generated the first war.

Charon laughed after an awkward silence. "Right? Nuts. I sound like you."

"You do, which convinces me we're both right. Something is happening. If Styx plays a role, I've no idea. But maybe now you want to join me?"

"Maybe. I'm worried, though, because if Styx returns, what else might he do?"

Jaret squinted at Charon. "You're afraid he might still have power over you?"

Charon pressed his lips together and gulped his entire glass of wine. His lack of an answer told Jaret a lot because Charon never admitted vulnerability. Jaret contemplated how to press his case when Jordan hurried over to them.

Jordan, Charon's number two in command, was young and gorgeous. Right after Charon set off on his own as a vampire, he converted Jordan after finding him prostituting himself in Denver. With long, straight black hair, slight build, a pierced eyebrow, and tattoos of fire running up his arms, he commanded attention with his allure—his youth on full display when he talked. He was the perfect worker for Charon. Loyal to a fault, sex charged at every turn, and in love with a decadent life as much as Charon.

Tonight, however, Jordan's wide eyes gave away his panic even before the blood tear trickled down his cheek. He glanced sideways at Jaret before licking his lips and taking a deep breath and staring hard at Charon. "Got to talk to you. Now. Alone. Now."

Charon stepped toward Jordan. "What is it?"

"Bad. Very, very bad." Again Jordan looked toward Jaret. "Private. Now."

"Tell me." Charon grabbed Jordan by both shoulders.

"Kevin's dead." Speaking the words prompted a flood of blood tears to stream down Jordan's face.

Charon stared at Jordan in disbelief. "Vampires don't die. How could he have died?"

"Take us to him," Jaret instructed.

"You're not one of us." Jordan spat the words and glared but appeared more at a loss for what to do than angry at Jaret.

"No, but I can help."

"Not if he's already dead. He's dead. By another vampire. Stabbed in the heart with a stake that erupted into flames and burned out his chest. Right upstairs. Right in front of people. I got the witnesses out of there and closed the door to avoid total panic. And you don't need to be involved."

Charon stepped between them, wrapping an arm around each one and moving them toward the kitchen. "My place. My command. Jaret, go. I'll fill you in. Jordan, take me to him. Now."

The three vampires stormed through the first floor, but when Jaret turned to go upstairs with them, Charon waved for Jordan to proceed but halted and blocked Jaret with his hand. "You'll only upset him more, and we already know what's going on. Get out of here." Charon turned and leapt up several steps.

Jaret obeyed, patting his leg for Darth to follow him after she had spent the entire time running around the yard and first floor sniffing everyone. Every part of his being wanted to see the scene firsthand in order to learn what had occurred and perhaps take evidence back to the Council to spur them into action. But his inkling about the war held as strong as the impulse to storm upstairs: his side needed Charon and his boys, without which they may lose. Jaret walked into the night, shocked and dismayed. Instead of portents and insinuations, instead of magical feelings and vague warnings, the first battle in the war had just occurred.

CHAPTER THREE

THE VAMPIRE COUNCIL

28 JANUARY 2019
Chicago, Illinois

Jaret sat in the living room of the Boystown mansion Anthony and he kept in Chicago, twitching his leg as he waited for two of his friends to arrive. Anthony had gone, the previous night, to their home in the Cotswolds of England to gather information about the impending war, though he once again refused to tell Jaret any of the details. Jaret dismissed his annoyance at being left out because

Anthony's absence allowed Jaret to make his next move.

He was more anxious than ever before, after Charon confirmed through magical correspondence that another vampire had killed one of his boys during the party. Charon suspected it was Styx.

As for Anthony, Jaret knew he would never convince Anthony to follow his advice and engage the war, let alone enlist the assistance of Charon. And Anthony would never barrel into a conflict—the fact they had known for a few years about the impending war without taking action was because of Anthony's caution more than anyone else's on the Council. Jaret would take his argument to other people: one who listened to him all the time because of his deep sensitivity, and the other who represented the most impulsive of the Council members.

Edgy and impatient, Jaret jumped off the couch and landed in front of the window, his vampire power making the inhuman action effortless. Darth raised her head from where she was taking a nap nearby but went back to sleep when Jaret stood staring out the window.

Xavier and Thomas strolled down the street a few minutes later. How Jaret envied their relationship. The two had met during the French Revolution, when Thomas courted Xavier and won his heart, converting him and establishing their now two-plus centuries old marriage. He was jealous of them because they shared everything and appeared to read each other's minds, nurturing and helping the other—doing what a perfect couple would do. Anthony and he were too new for the same level of intimacy, and Anthony's fear of Jaret's magic being too powerful to allow him on the Vampire Council kept a further distance between them.

Thomas roared a laugh at something Xavier had said, his long black hair flying all over the place when he tossed his head back. Even after a few years of knowing them, their beauty stunned Jaret. Xavier with his slight stature, short dark hair, and hazel eyes, about the same average height as Jaret, versus Thomas, tall and muscular with piercing brown eyes and long black hair. Everything about them soothed Jaret as they climbed the steps and entered without knocking.

After hugs and kisses on the cheek, the three vampires settled into the living room. Darth trotted over to greet the new arrivals, sitting next to Xavier because she had always been attached to him. He petted her as they talked about mundane matters for a couple minutes, as if nothing were amiss in the vampire world.

An awkward silence descended upon them. Jaret was afraid to continue despite summoning them. Ever polite, Xavier always waited for people to feel comfortable before he engaged.

Thomas flipped his hair over his shoulder and rolled his eyes. "You two drive me nuts. Out with it. Why are we here? We all love each other and will feel the same way even if we disagree. We're vampires, it's what we do, century after long century. But instead of making this one night feel like an entire century, tell us why we're here."

"Thomas, for God's sake." Xavier clutched Thomas's knee and stared a warning at him, no doubt concerned about Thomas's direct approach.

But Jaret laughed, relieved at Thomas moving them forward. "No, he's right! I'd delay forever before getting on with why you're here. Besides, you two know this is about the war."

Xavier held up a hand to stop him. "Possible war. There isn't a war yet."

"Wait until you hear everything I have to say. Because the first battle has started, whether we want to admit the truth or not. We're at war."

"What happened?" Thomas asked.

"Since the signs of a threat to vampires began appearing," Jaret explained, "the Council, and me separately, have monitored through magic and waited for a clear indication the rogue would start a war. I tried to use my spells to figure out who was plotting but failed. The Council said we shouldn't alert the person as they might spot our magical trail. But the Council can't find him either. Well, nice work with the caution. Because whoever is doing this struck the first blow. He killed a vampire."

"Are you sure?" Xavier asked, stunned. "He never acted with bold force and the Council magic didn't alert us."

Jaret took a deep breath, already annoyed with Xavier's cautious approach, predicting more delays, more pondering, and nothing assertive. But if Jaret wanted to move the Council toward action, he needed both these men on his side.

Jaret took a moment to decide where to begin. Part of the story started with the long-ago war, when a renegade vampire acquired magic and struck at the Vampire Council. After he annihilated thousands of fellow vampires, including everyone on the Council except Anthony, Anthony defeated him and restored order. The distant echo of the first war sounded here because the ancient Council, too, noticed disturbances in the magic and worried about a problem.

But because Xavier and Thomas already knew the tale, they remained unconvinced.

Jaret thought about stressing to them how the Council and Jaret had been alerted to the current problem almost five years ago because of magical alarms. When the Council kept insisting on a slow, methodical approach, Jaret had stalked and begun his enlistment of Charon. While Jaret concluded Charon was not the perpetrator, he learned Charon possessed strong magic and would be an asset in the upcoming war. But no doubt anthony had filled Xavier and Thomas in on this news too.

"Hello?" Thomas waved his arms in the air toward Jaret. "Where did you go? Did aliens abduct your brain?"

"Sorry. I was thinking. The war will be here soon. I went to visit Charon in Savannah. He was having a huge party—nothing out of the ordinary for him. His boys and he gathered a gazillion hot, young men for a gigantic orgy. While I was there, one of them was killed. And after I departed, the magical warning shot through my head as never before. The Bachmann jewels I carried almost burned through my clothes from the heat of their alarm."

"What were you doing there?" Xavier asked.

Thomas grinned. "Were you participating in an orgy?"

Jaret stifled a grin because he did not want to add levity to the seriousness of the moment. "No." But he smiled anyway. "What they were doing isn't the point. I was visiting Charon. But you were supposed to focus on the death of a vampire. Only another vampire could execute a vampire. Charon thinks his maker, Styx, committed the murder."

Xavier shook his head. "Humans have murdered us in the past with magic, so how do we know this vampire did it? People have accomplished a killing with nothing but fire. And your presence there matters because you were again trying to get Charon to fight, weren't you? You were orchestrating behind the Council's back. Which is also why you wanted to meet with Thomas and me while Anthony was away. Because he wouldn't approve of this venture. Jaret, we're on this. We're studying the threat and preparing to combat whoever initiates the fight. But we don't want to stab in the dark at nothing. Our studying is vital, and Anthony is working to prepare for the fight. We can't lash out against unseen enemies and give away our plans when we don't know who to strike. You have to be patient. Sometimes caution is the best approach, no matter how frustrating."

Jaret sighed. "Have any of you ever listened to Anthony's story from the first war? As I recall, the Council stuck their head in the sand until the rogue struck, wiped most of them out, and almost succeeded. So this time you think we should wait again? Fucking brilliant."

Xavier grimaced at Jaret's outburst, but Thomas grinned, then exploded in laughter. He held up a hand in surrender when Jaret frowned at him. "I know. Nothing you said is funny. And I believe you. Jaret, you know I make your argument to the Council all the time? I hear you. Your point of view has merit. Anthony and this one," Thomas jabbed his thumb toward Xavier, "would want to chat about whether or not to fight if a vampire had them in a head-lock as he thrust a torch down their throats. I get you. But what would you have us do? If a vampire or some other being plans to attack us to bring about vampire genocide, we have no idea who's behind the plot. We would use Council spells all over the world and hope they reveal a source, but the enemy could divert some-place else with ease. The Council's magic, like yours, has warned about the seriousness of the threat. We're lost. We should fight, Jaret. You're right. Caution is bullshit. But we still don't know what to do. We can't locate a target. I know you don't believe us, but we've looked. We're searching. If Styx is behind this, if he has started the war, we must be careful because of his power."

During his monologue, Jaret and Xavier took turns shooting

Thomas looks of bewilderment and annoyance as he had pleased neither of them. In reaction, Thomas laughed again. "I see I have enchanted the entire room with my brilliance."

"What about the killing? A vampire died. So we're going to dance around with caution because we're lost?" Jaret remembered the pain in Jordan's voice as he told Charon about the murder.

"The Council can't help with a dead vampire concealed from our authority, can we?" Xavier shot back. "Charon wants his own fiefdom, so Charon will have to handle the situation on his own."

Jaret hated when the other side had a point, though scoring one failed to appease Jaret. "The next victim might not be one of Charon's boys."

Thomas began to answer when the front door bashed open, surprising them as they looked over to see Catherine and Harriet storm into the room. Catherine, Xavier's sister, wore her long blonde hair in a bun as her piercing blue eyes stared in terror. She began to speak but choked on the words, so Harriet stepped forward. Harriet composed herself but a slight twitch in one brown eye gave away her nervousness.

"Thomas, Xavier, follow us. Urgent Council business." Harriet spun around and grabbed Catherine's arm, pulling her toward the front door.

"What is it?" Xavier stood and walked toward them.

Without a word, Harriet continued walking and pointed toward the door.

Xavier hurried after them, motioning for Thomas to follow, so Jaret got up too. "I'm coming," Jaret announced.

Outside the front door, without stopping, Harriet commanded him. "You are *not* coming. This is Council business."

Before Jaret could protest, the four vampires vanished. He could attempt to follow but they would scold him, order him away, and never change their mind about excluding him. Something big had happened, and while the Council dealt with a number of matters all the time, Jaret sensed the war had pushed them into action. Pissed at being ignored and certain of his own plot, Jaret determined a drastic step was needed—he had to get someone else on his side. He picked up his cell phone and dialed his best friend, Brady.

"Hello, Van Helsing residence. Do you have a vampire problem?" No matter the circumstances, Brady always made Jaret laugh.

"You wish I was coming to drink your blood."

"Nah, I know you seek my come."

Jaret laughed out loud. "Stop. I'm calling about something serious."

"You sound serious. What's up?"

"Do you remember our last conversation, after we had too much to drink and it loosened my tongue? I told you what I wanted to do?"

Brady paused a long moment before answering. "Yeah."

"And you were interested?"

Another delay. "Correct. What about the ethic thing?"

"The vampire ethic can go fuck itself. This is urgent."

"Shouldn't we talk? Like, this isn't the same as deciding to meet at a bar for a drink."

"We can talk, but in person. Tomorrow night. Your place." Jaret hung up on Brady, knowing his friend's concern would attempt to talk him out of his latest plot. Jaret knew he could persuade Brady in person and was tired of all the caution and doing the right thing.

If the Council wanted to piss him off, he'd return the favor.

Jaret woke the next evening on fire about the Vampire Council. Fuck them. Fuck their rules. And fuck Anthony, too, since he never responded to Jaret after he had sent both a text and then magical communication to see if Anthony had returned to Chicago along with the other Council members who had been at Jaret's last night.

Tonight, Jaret was going rogue to start living a little more like Charon. The Council could try to stop him if they wanted, but Jaret's witchcraft gave him a potent weapon. Time to please himself, which started with trying to get more vampire friends on his side. He reached for his phone to call Brady when a magical tingling surrounded him before an orange orb floated before his face. Fuck. A Council summons. He grabbed an emerald bracelet from his magical jewels and swiped at the glowing ball in front of him to dismiss the request.

A text came through from Xavier:

Did you get the message from the Council?

Jaret first typed *Fuck You* but felt bad because Xavier deserved better than his petulance. So instead, he typed:

Yes, but I'm not coming. Very busy on Jaret business.

You don't have a choice.

"Oh, yeah?" Jaret called for Darth and headed for the front door when an unseen force grabbed hold of him and pulled him into the air. Darth barked and ran in circles around him as he floated out an open window and above the trees.

Jaret felt for his gems and began to counter the spell when he sensed the Council's magic and realized they had captured him. Fuckers. He decided to comply and go along for the ride without trying to counter their magic. He sailed over Chicago like a bird, wondering how all their caution about human discovery allowed for a flying vampire over the city at a slow speed. Maybe they had made him invisible?

A moment later, he was set down on the sprawling estate Thomas and Xavier kept in the Chicago suburbs. He walked up the front path as if arriving for a dinner party, entered the front door, and found Thomas, Xavier, Catherine, and Harriet assembled in the parlor. And he could cut the tension with a knife.

"I see the Politbüro awaits my arrival," Jaret said, but not even Thomas grinned. Did their annoying magic alert them to his plans for tonight? Were they there to sentence him for crimes against vampires? He prepared to use his jewels in case of a problem and wondered why Anthony wasn't there.

He sat in an armchair. The Council had assembled in a circle of chairs. Jaret rubbed his hands on his legs, looked around the room to avoid eye contact, and wondered if any of them would speak.

As was often the case, Harriet, who could state things in a matter-of-fact way without seeming cold or uncaring, began. "Before I tell you the news, you must promise to remain calm and listen to us. This will try you as never before. It's essential. Do you understand?" Jaret wondered if her life as a slave in the American South prior to her conversion gave her an ability to deal with harsh truths instead of dancing around them like her peers on the Council.

Jaret's alarm skyrocketed. "Tell me," he demanded.

Harriet took a breath. "Last night, the second strike in the war came." She pressed her lips together and stared hard at Jaret. "Anthony was kidnapped."

Impossible. Jaret sat frozen, unable to marshal a response. No one could *capture* Anthony. The oldest living vampire. A member of the Vampire Council with all its magic at his disposal. Of all the news he may have anticipated, Jaret never would have thought Anthony could be a victim. Jaret shook his head in answer.

Xavier jumped out of his seat and raced to Jaret, kneeling before him and grabbing both his hands. "The Council has a plan."

At last, Jaret reacted by yanking his hands away and standing. He smirked in disbelief. "You think you should act now, do you? No more caution? Too bad you didn't take the situation with such earnest action say, oh, two or three or five years ago. I wish someone had warned you to fight and not sit around thinking all was well."

"Jaret, please." Xavier stood and pleaded with outstretched arms. "Nothing benefits from rehashing the past. We need to work together."

Jaret wagged a finger at them when the others stood, too, and began walking toward him. "No, no. You lost your opportunity to include me in your ineffective and stupid strategy. Stay back."

Thomas held up his hands in a gesture of surrender. "We're not here to punish you for your actions regarding the war. We want to help. Please."

Jaret knew to move fast, before they realized his intention and attempted to marshal their own magic in response. He reached into his pants pockets, grabbed hold of all the gems he carried with him, and tossed them in the air. Before the four Council members could react, the jewels whirled through the air and protected Jaret as he rushed out of the house at vampiric speed. He raced away, commanding the gems to lift him into the air and move him farther and farther away. He had no way to know if they pursued him, but either they let him go or the jewels hid him because he escaped and landed in the middle of a park near Brady's house with no sign of the fuckers following him. He regretted having to flee before learning more from them, but remaining was too risky.

Jaret raged. And he panicked. How he wished to hear Anthony scolding him for defying the Council, to have his lover warn against acting in a rash manner. Jaret started toward Brady's flat but realized he needed better control of himself before meeting his friend and proceeding with his plan, a plot more urgent than it had been even one hour ago.

He consulted his jewels to see if they offered any explanations about what had happened to Anthony. He found a secluded spot in the park behind a dense grove and tossed the gems into the air as he watched them whirl in a frenzy and await his command. He first checked through them to see Darth sleeping at home, safe and sound. He asked them to locate Anthony but they slowed and signaled no answer, so instead, he requested they send Anthony a magical message. Again, the gems failed to act. Which meant the being who captured Anthony possessed as powerful a concealing magic as the Council or Jaret. Instead of calming him, his search for answers ramped up his alarm. Jaret cast a new spell with his family heirlooms, searching for any trace of magic similar to that which concealed Charon from the Council.

At last, the jewels alerted. The gems spun so fast they became a blur of colors before a scene manifested before his eyes. He looked at the outside of a church before his view went inside. Jaret saw Anthony, captured, stern and angry, sitting before an odd group of humans. Jaret ordered his sorcery to read one man's mind, which revealed someone with a radicalized form of Christianity who believed that Anthony was the Antichrist. They all stared in awe at Anthony as if both terrified of what he might accomplish and proud to see him incarcerated. No chains or visible restraint held him in place, but Jaret could see Anthony's inability to act.

Jaret hoped for a sign to give away their location, but a shadowed figure entered the image at the church, his face concealed but his power evident in how Jaret's magical trail went cold, and the scene vanished.

Jaret had learned a little more about the situation but not enough. He attempted other spells but nothing else helped him, so his blood boiled anew.

Still too angry to go to Brady, Jaret decided a solid murder would do him good. He first needed to purge his anger then formulate a plan when he could better focus.

Jaret walked around the neighborhood seeking his prey, with every step becoming angrier, nothing but blood and vengeance available to calm him. After several minutes of no luck with his hunt Jaret ramped up his effeminacy, swishing back and forth, staring at every guy he passed, and letting his hair flow everywhere. One hottie hit on him. A guy with his girlfriend winked. But no victim.

A well-built man with his baseball cap on backward walked by Jaret with a scowl, then muttered, "Fucking fag," as they passed. Jaret turned around to watch but the guy kept walking.

A few steps later, Jaret spun and trailed the dude for a couple blocks until he turned down a more secluded residential street. Jaret caught up to him with his vampire speed, grabbed him by the arm, and jerked him around.

"What the fuck?" The guy yanked his arm from Jaret and glared.

"What did you call me?"

"A fag who needs a beating."

He reared back to punch Jaret in the face, but the vampire caught his hand and crushed every bone. The guy's eyes went wide with terror, and he yelped in pain. Jaret wasted no time in latching onto his neck and draining his blood, the sweet taste nourishing him.

As the man died in his arms, Jaret relished his defiance of the Council. He never investigated before the kill to see if his victim deserved death, instead going on impulse, and murdering the asshole. As the blood flowed down Jaret's throat and the victim's life passed through Jaret's mind, Jaret could see he was a complete turd, but not worthy of death according to vampire law. He bullied people. He harassed women. But always short of what the ethic allowed though it met Jaret's standard for death. The news pleased Jaret. And as hoped, his rage subsided even as his panic about Anthony continued.

He flopped the body onto the ground and kicked it under a tree. Knowing the Vampire Council's magic would soon be alerted to his transgression, Jaret hurried to make his point. He conjured a piece of paper and a pen into his hand and left them a note:

Oh, my. I violated the ethic. Try to catch me. Try to put me in your iron prison over the fire. He deserved to die, despite not matching your law's preponderance of expected evidence. He hurt people. He would do so throughout his life. Better off without him. Still a naughty vampire flouted your rules. I would worry about the consequences but already know it will take you years of deliberation to decide what to do. You won't find me again unless I want to meet you. Fuck off.

As Jaret walked away, he clutched a handful of jewels to ward off any Council surveillance. He had never even told Anthony he could hide from the Council. Maybe Anthony had been right to worry about Jaret's power as a witch before he made him into a vampire. Or maybe the Council would be lucky to have Jaret on their side since their feeble attempts in the war had failed so far.

Pleased with himself and giddy about his new course of action, Jaret sprinted to Brady's apartment and knocked. He took deep breaths to control his nerves and keep his mind from cycling over and over about Anthony's kidnapping. Then he waited a few seconds as he heard their favorite musician, Mika, blasting away. Brady opened the door with a big grin and grabbed him into a hug.

"I'll have you know I'm completely sober," Brady announced without a hello. "Not a drop of alcohol in my system because I know what's coming from you, and I need to be the voice of reason. Which was never your strong suit. Come in." Brady motioned for Jaret to follow him into the living room.

Brady launched himself onto the couch while squinting at Jaret. Brady was one of the cutest guys Jaret knew, with his medium-length, dark-brown hair, piercing brown eyes, and baby smooth skin. A classic looking twink, much like Jaret, Brady and he became best friends soon after meeting in an English class their freshmen year of college. They shared a love of Mika and other music, academic conversations, and laughing their asses off. Brady had learned about Jaret being a witch early in their friendship and never flinched at the news, nor did he freak out when Catherine informed him about vampires or when Jaret himself became one. Loyal and true, Jaret knew no better human being on earth. And better ally.

Jaret sat next to Brady on the couch and stared at him, wondering how best to proceed. While his stomach rolled over with worry, he determined to hide his fear about Anthony from Brady.

"You're kinda close. Are you hitting on me?" Brady smirked. "I'm serious. *No bueno* on defying the fucking Vampire Council. No matter your reasons."

Jaret continued to stare at his friend without a word as Brady squirmed and began to giggle.

"What the fuck?" Brady laughed and punched Jaret on the

arm. "Why aren't you talking? A loss for words never defined our friendship. You're making me fucking nervous. Witchy vampire bullshit. Spill it. Out with why you want to transform me into a vampire and doom me to a death sentence by the Council."

"I already trained you on vampire rules and abilities. I never hid anything from you, even when Anthony scolded me for telling you too much. I promised from the beginning I would convert you. You'd make a good vampire. The Council has even pondered allowing you to join us. Catherine followed through on her promise and planted the seed with the others. You're compassionate but realistic. Minimal ties to your human life since your mom died of breast cancer and your dad threw you out of the house."

Brady reached over and placed his hand on Jaret's mouth. "I know the history. It's about me, remember? But we pledged to wait for Council approval. I asked you already what changed tonight, not to go over my biography. You're fucking with me."

Jaret nodded. "The war has started." He took a deep breath to keep his emotion in check, changing his mind and going for the total truth with Brady. "The enemies have captured Anthony and killed at least one vampire. The Council has finally moved into action but has kept me out of the loop. We need a more forceful response. I recruited Charon, but I need a stronger ally."

"You want me to play Robin to your Batman?"

Jaret grinned. Typical Brady, throwing a joke out there to avoid the serious conversation. "Something like that." He shook his head. "How can you make me laugh even at the most serious moments?"

"Because we're both funny and use humor to survive. And my ass would look great in tights."

"We're not wearing superhero costumes."

"Maybe on Halloween."

"If we survive to participate in the next one."

The room fell quiet. Jaret resisted the urge to pin Brady to the couch and force the transformation, knowing even at his most desperate he could never inflict a conversion by rape. The humor on Brady's face slid away and gave way to resolve, but he stayed quiet.

"I can't promise to protect us forever from the Council but we—"

Brady again held up his hand to silence Jaret before his groveling plea went further. "Do it. Now."

Jaret grabbed Brady behind the neck and pulled him close, smelling his musky cologne and sensing Brady relax as Jaret's arm wrapped around him. He resisted a close look at Brady's past as his life flickered through Jaret's mind when the blood flowed down his throat.

Part Two

Summoning Henrik

CHAPTER FOUR

THE BACHMANN MANSION

1 FEBRUARY 2019
Fremont, NE

Jaret strode through the streets of his family's hometown. He felt nostalgic about family reunions and growing up with visits to Gramps at the Bachmann Mansion. Yet a pit of despair gnawed at his stomach at having lost his entire family when the enraged ghost of his ancestor, Henrik, killed them here. Though the town had changed over the years, part of Fremont reminded him of a simpler past. A happier time, when love and an unknown future allowed Jaret to play and mature at his own pace. Henrik's being imprisoned in a spellbound iron box and further secured within a hidden vampire prison allowed Jaret to push him from his mind and think about happy Fremont memories instead of the misery. The town provided a pleasant moment of distraction from his current problems.

Jaret arrived in Fremont after determining a risky move to find Anthony. The idea had popped into his mind earlier in the evening, after Xavier appeared and stole Brady.

After Jaret transformed him, Brady took to his vampire nature fast, having had a number of years to dream about immortality and already knowing the rules of the Vampire Council because of his friendship with Jaret. The two friends roamed Chicago while Brady acquainted himself with his new powers. Brady fed on a murderer. He tested his strength by carrying boulders around the Chicago lakefront. And he liked to observe people with his vampire eyesight.

Jaret shadowed Brady and never interrupted unless Brady asked a question or, more often, needed to embark on a monologue about something he experienced, saw, or thought randomly. Because Jaret needed Brady focused and on his side, Jaret never hurried him or reminded him about Anthony's capture. Besides, as much as Jaret wanted to engage in the war, he needed to figure out an exact means of doing so.

The next evening, Brady became more solemn and focused on the war. He asked Jaret to fill him in on the details, pledged to help Jaret however possible, and sat with him in Brady's apartment while Jaret used a spell to conduct further research to find Anthony.

Tonight, they woke and first undertook a fast hunt to ensure Brady's strength.

Jaret believed he was getting close to a solution to his problem. They gathered at Jaret and Anthony's home to continue their work because of his fabulous sound system to listen to Mika. Brady spent most of the time dancing and playing with Darth while Jaret worked. A couple hours into the night, Jaret's senses alerted to an approaching vampire but without any danger. Moments later, Xavier sauntered into the living room.

Jaret prepared for a fight in case the Council wanted to incarcerate Brady because of his illegal turning, but Xavier shook his head and smiled. "You've been a very bad vampire, Jaret. We're not taking the bait of the asinine note you left with the suspect killing. And now you've turned Brady. We'll deal with your behavior soon enough. I knew you'd turn Brady someday, though now seems like a horrible time. The Council is taking him. You have no choice."

"You're kidnapping me?" Brady asked.

Jaret leaped between Xavier and Brady to protect his friend, but Xavier held up a hand of surrender.

"Yes and no," Xavier answered Brady. "Relax. I'm going to complete your training. Brady, you're in no danger or trouble, even if Jaret, your maker, has serious issues. We're not leaving you with him. Jaret, I know you could fight me but don't. Please. I'll take good care of him. Let us train him and help him understand our protocols without your skewed take."

Jaret decided to fight one battle at a time, and now struck him as an opportunity to let the Council win. He stepped aside and nodded at Brady, who followed Xavier out the door but turned around before he left to smile at Jaret.

Even though he would need Brady in the future, being alone with Darth provided Jaret the opportunity to discover his next move. And he knew, no matter what Xavier attempted to teach Brady, his friend would believe Jaret over the fucking Council. A combination of playing with his gems, consulting the vampire laws, and listening to his instinct brought him to a potential solution.

Jaret's tremendous power as a vampire combined with his formidable magic garnered him a great skill, true. But the one Jaret sought to find possessed the same ability, and he wanted to remain hidden. If the Vampire Council worked with him, they may accomplish the task, but going to them would result in another dead end. Instead, Jaret figured out he needed to tap into a mystical source, a place containing a history of magic and supernatural powers, a vortex to merge with his own abilities and overcome the rogue's power.

Such locations resided all over the globe, but Jaret thought of one spot in particular because it met the criteria and perhaps could give him a special boost of power because of its significance in his life.

And thus, he stopped outside the Bachmann Mansion in Fremont.

His grandfather's house, which Jaret still owned but allowed to sit vacant, both haunted and endeared him. The large white Victorian home, including the yard, took up an entire city block. It sparkled as if built a short time ago and reminded Jaret of cherished times growing up when they visited his Gramps, or the Bachmann clan gathered for celebrations. Yet the memories also included the enraged Henrik, who was killed at the hands of a gay lover in the 1800s and thereafter haunted the homestead. Jaret once defeated Henrik and locked him in an enchanted iron box, but Henrik thwarted those defenses by manipulating Jaret's former boyfriend, Steve, into letting him out. Henrik then killed Steve, traveled hundreds of miles back to the Bachmann home, and slaughtered Jaret's family in retaliation.

All of which created the perfect vortex—deep love and strong positive emotion combined with the harshest despair imaginable—to enhance Jaret's power. A house where generations of witches had lived and practiced the magic afforded them from the Bachmann family gems. Jaret could feel the power oozing toward him.

He allowed Darth to run around the yard, feeding on a poor innocent bunny before Jaret threw a stick for her to fetch.

A moment later, Jaret entered with Darth through the back-door and into the kitchen. He paid for a cleaning service to maintain the property because he sometimes visited. He checked room by room to feel the energy, finishing in the attic, the scene of his most ferocious battles against Henrik. The unfinished room, with the gables and rafters and boxed heirlooms lining the sides, felt like the ideal place to gather paranormal assistance.

Jaret sat in the center of the room on the floor and crossed his legs. After sniffing around the entire perimeter, Darth plopped down next to him and laid her head on his leg. Jaret placed one hand on his knee and the other on Darth's head, closed his eyes, and concentrated. He meditated. He relaxed every muscle. He let his mind wander through the atmosphere in search of whatever he came upon.

Knowing he still sat on the floor in the attic, Jaret's mind transported itself, along with all sensations in his body, out above the roof, where he hovered in the air as a spirit, seeing the mansion and surrounding property below and all of Fremont. He noticed the gems in his pockets, electrified and pulsating with an energy like never before, followed then by a surge of power within his very being. In addition to feeling like he could fly anywhere, he sensed a force to seek people or items otherwise concealed by a spell. As he stayed in place and took inventory of his ability, he sensed the attic's vortex of magic and realized his body called the power forth and absorbed it. While the location's maelstrom amplified his ability, he alone controlled the situation. Almost intoxicated by the power, he renewed his search for Anthony's captor.

He saw the rogue in an instant, alone, pacing back and forth in the narthex of some church. He recognized Styx from both Charon's description and the time Charon showed him a vision of his transformation. Moreover, he knew Styx was also Anthony's nemesis of old, the vampire who fomented the original war. Unlike the story Styx told Anthony at the time, or related to Charon later, in which his lover participated in the war while attempting to stay outside the conflict, in reality, he had orchestrated the entire event. He had sacrificed his lover to save himself. Afterward, he'd hidden and plotted for centuries to recommence his plan. Jaret marveled at how the information flowed into him without having to do anything but think the question.

Styx had gathered these Christians at the church with a promise of empowering them as his spokespeople when he conquered the world. Who knew what mental gymnastics they performed to justify killing on Styx's behalf or to concoct a system of repression and violence in the name of Christ? But Styx pretended to be a divine presence called down from heaven. Did they see Styx as an angel of the Lord? Or worse, as Christ returned? Lunatics. But dangerous ones.

Jaret transported himself to the church and walked down the center aisle of the sanctuary. Styx realized his presence at once and walked into the large room with stained glass windows lining each side. Jaret stopped several pews from Styx as the vampires glared at one another.

"You're holding Anthony here."

Styx grinned. "Am I?"

"Release him. Do you believe you can defeat the Council? You failed last time, and you'll fail again."

"Such big words." Styx laughed. "Little newbie with his magical jewelry waltzes in and thinks himself more knowledgeable than me? Stop. You're nothing but an apparition."

"The Council and I could kill all of these humans. Then what would remain for you?"

"Be my guest." Styx gestured toward the front door as if the people waited outside for their demise. "I find them useful and amusing, but they serve as little more than a subterfuge. Something to get your gander up and people to worship my power, as everyone will eventually. If they survive, I can build off their faith, but their death would prompt nothing more than a need to locate new people. I get humans to do my bidding with ease. Look at Charon, for example, hoodwinked by me and now a source of consternation for the Vampire Council. A lone wolf."

"But not on your side."

Styx raised his eyebrows. "Do you know for sure?"

Jaret felt confident Charon would act in his own self-interest, not for Styx or the Council or anyone else. Getting Charon to assist with the war meant convincing him to align with Jaret and the

Council or face an eternity of obeying Styx.

Jaret did wonder what he sought tonight. Styx knew he had little ability to accomplish anything as a spirit. Jaret searched for Anthony, but some spell kept him from imagining every part of the church, the blocking being no doubt a sorcery devised by Styx. So Jaret knew Anthony was kept here but little else. "Let me see him."

Styx laughed again, playing the perfect evil villain. "No. Now go."

Styx thrust his hands toward Jaret, unleashing a wave of energy that flew through the air and punched Jaret in the stomach. Jaret felt the impact physically as a blow to the gut. He lost control of his apparition, sending his spirit high in the air, and snapping his image back to Fremont where he floated above his Gramps's before slamming back down into his body, and gasping for breath.

He called his energy back to himself and opened his eyes in the attic, sitting on the floor with Darth by his side, though she had lifted her head and stared at him with concern. Jaret took a moment to gather his senses before he left the attic and sank back on the living room couch to think.

Mission accomplished. He located the church outside Montgomery, Alabama, and confirmed Styx, aka the rogue of long ago, had renewed his war against the Vampire Council. Jaret also figured out he could use particular places to heighten his power.

True, Styx dispatched him with ease but could not stop Jaret from gathering information. Jaret's sense of panic about Anthony and about the war morphed into confidence in his ability to fight.

Rather than delve into another visit with no plan the next night, Jaret stayed in Fremont and assessed his skills to learn more about what the mansion's power plus his own magic could do for him. He moved his spirit to Africa and then Asia and catapulted into the atmosphere so high he saw the Earth's curvature. He practiced zapping in and out of places with extreme speed and learned how to spring back into his body in a split second. Most of all, he enjoyed taking his spirit form and wandering through cities, interacting with people as if he were a human on a sight-seeing tour or heading home from work. He could maintain the appearance of a body for over an hour without even straining. Last, he worked to sharpen his senses and see through any magic concocted to conceal something. He spied on a few Council members, though their defenses kept his vision cloudy and without sound. He strolled through New Orleans and detected the witchcraft of many sorcerers. And he swooped over the Montgomery church and peered into its basement to see where Styx had entrapped Anthony in a mystical prison to strip the vampire of his potency and hide him from everyone. Except Jaret, who thrilled at his new power to see Styx's magic.

Though his spirit form rendered him unable to do anything but observe, at least Jaret could spy on Styx and the situation at the church. Styx could not capture him in this form. Even if he failed to free Anthony, he could learn a great deal before going there in person for a direct clash.

He took time upon waking to play with Darth and went with her into the Nebraska fields for a quick hunt. She fed on a few animals while he drank from a murderer hiding in an abandoned house. He attempted to remain calm and focused, to clamp down when rising panic worried him about Anthony's future. Barreling into a response would ensure failure. Didn't the loser in every historical battle succumb because of overconfidence or panicked moves? Placing his energy on preparation made him feel useful and practical while he bided his time. Unlike the Vampire Council, he would act with the power he had obtained.

Jaret and Darth raced back to Fremont. She sprinted ahead, sometimes for up to a mile, before spinning around to return to him and start the game again. They walked the last few blocks to the Bachmann Mansion so Jaret could gather his thoughts for his next move.

While he doubted any ability to free Anthony or combat Styx while in the spirit form, he still felt the need for another foray to Montgomery for reconnaissance. He had to learn more about Styx.

Comfortable with Jaret's out-of-body adventures, Darth chose to sniff around the attic and hunt for mice while Jaret sat on the wooden floor in the middle of the room. He closed his eyes, concentrated, and in a matter of seconds drifted over the ancestral home and crossed the country to fly over Montgomery. As he drifted down and into the sanctuary, he sensed Styx's presence before seeing him seated on top of the altar and kicking his feet back and forth while whistling a hymn.

"I expected a return much sooner," Styx said when Jaret stood in the aisle between pews. "You left me at the altar the last few nights." He laughed at his own stupid joke.

Jaret scanned the atmosphere and sensed a shadowy witchcraft, Styx's energy, and a tremendous amount of Styx's internal rage. No humans lurked nearby.

"Cat got your tongue?" Styx asked. "You came for another little visit but won't talk. It's rude enough you barge into my sanctuary without an invitation or even knocking first. Your antisocial behavior makes me feel like you have ill intentions." Styx hopped off the altar and paced back and forth. He raised an eyebrow. "Still nothing? Here, let me try. You know, you have more in common with me than you do with the Council. Don't think I don't know a great deal about you, Jaret. You remind me of Charon. Hear me out. Like him, you possess immense power, both in your witchcraft and your charisma. Had I instigated my game to create an off-the-grid vampire before Anthony got his clutches on you, I believe you would have won and accepted the offer. You became the mirror image of Charon, saddled by the Vampire Council and its rules but never satisfied with them. Oh, I know your feelings for Anthony cloud the situation. I do. But otherwise you'd join me. Why resist? I've waited centuries to reignite the war because I wanted to ensure my victory. No Council member comprehends my power except the one I hold in prison, and believe me, I spent most of these decades perfecting my magic against him. After I defeat the Council jackasses and purge all vampires from the world except Charon and his little boys, at least the ones I don't kill—I have to keep him in line you see—I'll make many more like him, so vampires take their true place in charge of the world with me at the head. You could be like Charon. Come over, and two vampires plus his boys will survive. I'd let you build your own harem! Full of tops to plow you every night!" Styx stopped pacing and turned to Jaret with a grin.

"You should sell used cars. You'd be good at it." Jaret noticed a crackle in the atmosphere. He'd suspected something happened during Styx's monologue, but the disturbance grew stronger, coming off Styx as if he were struggling to control his magic. Jaret wanted to keep him going to further analyze the situation.

"So are you agreeing?" Styx asked.

Jaret smirked. "Also like a used salesperson, you don't inspire much trust."

"I could say the same about you! Going from one side to the other. Flirting with my friend Charon and running back to the Council."

There, Jaret sensed the buzz again. Styx juggled too many spells to keep his scheme together. He had succeeded so far because of total secrecy. If Jaret and the Council challenged his magic, they could push his ability to control himself.

"Even if I wanted to follow you," Jaret answered, "which I don't, I could never sentence Anthony to death."

"Oh, well, I'm afraid we can't negotiate the matter. Even you must see the danger he poses to me."

"Let me see him one more time."

Styx contemplated, pacing again. "I'll allow a visit on one condition. You report to the Council what you see."

"Sure. If they want to see me. They're not big fans right now."

As if Jaret existed in actual form, Styx led him around behind the altar through a side door, down a set of stairs to the lower level, and back to a closet door. A strong magic pulsated from within. The door swung open, and a red glow emanated out. Anthony was standing immobile in the middle of a small janitor's room. Anthony squinted in recognition but otherwise remained still, either unable or unwilling to move or speak.

The door slammed shut. "That's it! You've had your visit." Styx announced. He stepped in front of Jaret and waved him away.

Jaret complied by flying straight up into the air, his spirit jetting through two floors and out the top of the church, over the United States, and back to Fremont. Once returned to his body, he called forth a Council orb to communicate with them.

He described meeting Styx, minus the detail about using a vortex to boost his power. He explained his theory they could overwhelm Styx if together they orchestrated their magic against him. Seeing Anthony and the energy Styx expended to control him exposed Styx's vulnerability to Jaret.

Jaret knew the key would be working with the Council, which

would take more work and diplomacy because the Council distrusted him. And they would need Charon, another complication. But the information he sent took the next step toward inching them into his camp. However, even with all the magic at their disposal, Jaret and the Council needed more ammunition.

He called for Darth to join him as he raced across Nebraska, requested admittance to Charon's underground fortress in the Colorado Rockies outside Nederland, and soon enough sat with Charon in a private lounge with a cocktail in his hands. Jordan had greeted him and led him to the room, settling him in before Charon entered, poured drinks, and sat without uttering a word.

"Last time I saw you, one of my boys died." Charon grimaced.

"I didn't kill him. Nor was I responsible for him finding you and your boys. I don't understand why he targeted you because Styx sounds like he wants you on his side."

Charon narrowed his eyes at Jaret. "You spoke with him? You know for sure Styx is behind this?"

"You already confirmed his presence for yourself." Jaret nodded. "And yes, I went to him. He's as crazy as you described. And dangerous." Jaret explained his recent interactions with Styx and included his theory about Styx's weakness. "I've recruited you for this war a million times because I believe we have to, in order to win. Listen, Styx promised to keep you alive but how do you know he's telling the truth? He lies all the time. He's unstable and may change his mind. Besides, even if he wins and keeps his promise to you, you'll live under the authority of a vampire king. You think keeping clear of the Council is hard? You think you'd suffer if you had to obey them? What do you think life will be like under Styx? You'll be like a flying monkey for the Wicked Witch."

Charon had grown morose as Jaret spoke but smiled at the *Wizard of Oz* reference. He sipped his drink once, swished the liquid in his glass, and tossed back the rest before getting up for a refill. He sighed and fell back onto the sofa.

"I don't like feeling impotent or at a loss. Not my style." Charon stared into his drink for several seconds. "But I'll be honest with you because I doubt anyone sees through me better. I don't know what to do. You make a strong case. So does he. I don't want any of this. None of the turmoil and nonsense. My boys and I have created an ideal life. I'm not a saint. I'm in the vampire world for me. This war"—he waved his hand in the air as if the battle raged in the middle of the room—"has nothing to do with me. I don't care who wins."

"You will if the wrong side prevails."

"How do we know which one is wrong?" Charon asked. "You think you do because you're knee-deep in Council business. You can tell me all you want about defying them, pissing them off. About their sanctioning you and pushing you to the side. But you're friends with them. Despite your disagreement with their tactics, you trust them. And you fuck one of them. You're not an impartial observer."

Jaret took his turn to gulp his drink down. Charon got up and refilled Jaret's glass without his asking, and Jaret shot the whiskey back again to quicken the buzz. "I think you're scared."

Charon smirked. "I'm never scared."

"No? Then why did Styx's assassination of Kevin send you back to your mountain hideaway. Have you left here since then? Ventured out for your hedonistic life?" Jaret knew the silent response affirmed his suspicion. "So you already live under his thumb. You already live in fear."

Charon glared at Jaret. "You don't know a thing about me or what I'm capable of doing."

"You're not as complicated as you like to believe." Jaret set his glass on a table and stood to leave. "Staying here forever won't protect you if Styx wins. Maybe Kevin was a warning he sent to you about his power. But if he wanted to warn you, then his murdering could also portend your future under his reign. Keep thinking about joining me. I'm not a simple pawn of the Council, no matter who I fuck."

Jaret left at a human pace, making a point to remain poised. They had reached another impasse, true, but Jaret felt signs of Charon weakening. Jaret sensed Charon's quiet fear would transform over time back into the otherwise brash and confident vampire. But Jaret also understood when to let up on his high-pressure campaign to recruit Charon. Time became more and more of the essence but pushing Charon too far could result in the wrong outcome.

Jaret plotted a battle of Styx and his minions against the three-pronged attack of the Council, Charon's army, and Jaret. He would need to orchestrate with great care to bring them together at the precise moment to seize victory.

CHAPTER FIVE

HELD CAPTIVE

6 FEBRUARY 2019
Montgomery, AL

The Bachmann mansion faded away as Jaret's spirit roared into the atmosphere with a force even Jaret had never before marshalled. After calling forth more power and using every gem at his disposal, Jaret initiated his boldest move so far but knew speed was of the essence as he dove back toward earth a split second later and shot his spirit through the Montgomery sewer system and up through rusted pipes before landing in Anthony's locked janitor's closet-cum-cell.

The putrid smell put forth by Styx's magic reeked even worse than the sewer and the red glow added a macabre atmosphere.

Jaret's image materialized before Anthony, who remained bound by magical chains as if dangling from a cross but instead suspended in midair. Unlike the vision of Anthony that Styx had allowed him to see, Anthony appeared alert and in full control of his senses. Before Jaret uttered a word to check, the pulsating vein in Anthony's forehead and his stern expression cued Jaret to the fact his lover was indeed there and comprehended the moment. The signs also pointed to Anthony's ire before he spat the words at Jaret.

"What the fuck are you doing here?" he hissed through a whisper. "If one of those humans hears, we're doomed. Not to mention if Styx catches on. Get the fuck out of here."

"I came to check on you," Jaret spat back. He struggled to contain the mixed emotions of anger at Anthony's being pissed and hurt at his lover's nasty demeanor. "You're in trouble. We have to do something."

"I'm fully aware of the trouble I'm in. It seems rather obvious." Anthony glared at Jaret. "And you're arrogant and impetuous." Anthony pressed his lips together before taking a deep breath. "I'm trying to protect you. I'm trying to protect all of us. You always think you know better than everyone else. You don't. Go, before this gets any worse."

Jaret clenched his fists tight to control himself. "The Council better clue me in, and fast. I have ability none of you can imagine. We have to work together to defeat Styx. Pushing me out won't stop me."

Anthony sighed in frustration. "You know I can't tell you anything. Trust us. Trust *me*. What in the hell do you think you can do as a spirit except piss him off and set his sights on you? Get out of here. Get control of yourself. Go."

Jaret attempted again to reason with Anthony, but he shook his head without speaking.

Jaret's voice rose as Anthony became a petulant child, refusing to speak. "You and the Council have done such a fucking splendid job. I'm overwhelmed with your success. Why, without your careful planning and decisive action maybe all five of you would be caught in Styx's clutches instead of you hanging here like a fucking helpless Christmas ornament. Years you've dawdled and fucked this up. Time for a new strategy. Tell me. Now."

Like Jesus on the cross, divine but submitting to human will, Anthony stayed there in the air and would not speak.

"Will you fucking talk to me?" Jaret continued to whisper but shoved the words out with force to make his point. When the lock on the door jangled, Anthony's eyes grew wide with alarm, and Styx stepped into the small closet, everyone inches from one another.

"Well, well, well, back for a visit, are we? Your magic gives off a distinct aura I recognized at once. How delightful to see you." Styx grinned as if greeting a friend who stopped by for a quick hello. "But still nothing more than a spirit." He shook his head. "Not much threat in your form, is there?" Styx passed his hand through Jaret's chest to emphasize his point. "Unlike him." With his long fingernails, he scratched Anthony in the chest hard enough to rip a hole in his shirt and draw blood.

Anthony winced. "Leave him alone. He has nothing to do with our quarrel and acts on his own behalf. He's a renegade as much as you."

Styx shot his eyebrows up in mock surprise. "Oh, my. Did I interrupt a lover's quarrel? How awkward."

"You can't divide and conquer us." Jaret's confident words did not match his inner fear.

"I'll most certainly conquer the lot of you. However, your division has nothing to do with me or my desires. You accomplished the separation all on your own. Now, what *are* you doing here, since I didn't invite you, and it would appear Anthony didn't either?" Styx pretended to grimace. "Ouch. A lover not happy to see you. I can feel the hurt myself."

Charon had warned Jaret about how Styx often seemed unhinged, telling stories with no sense to them, like one about farting butterflies as he searched for a formula to disguise vampires from the Vampire Council, or like bad villain humor in the midst of serious problems and conversations. Yet confronting the demeanor first-hand unnerved Jaret into silence. How could one negotiate with a madman? Anthony fell quiet again too, leaving them looking back and forth at one another like trapped rats.

Anthony hung midair. Jaret's spirit remained motionless as he glared at Styx. And Styx glanced about the room as if searching for an answer out of thin air.

"Awkward," Styx said after a minute. "Should I tell him, or do you want to?" Styx turned to Jaret and asked the question as if Jaret knew what he meant or the two had planned an announcement, neither of which was true.

"No one knows what you're talking about," Jaret answered.

Styx frowned. "Oh, but I think you do. Or maybe you don't know how much I know. My friend Charon tells me everything. *Everything.*" Styx pierced Jaret with a hard gaze. "And I believe in telling the truth. Secrets are not good."

Jaret thought about exposing Styx's lies. Styx was a typical maniacal narcissist who lied but proclaimed his love for the truth. Without knowing what Styx would say, Jaret knew Charon had never told Styx anything. They had never spoken again after Styx feigned his own death once he had transformed Charon into a vampire. As many issues as Charon had, and he had a lot, lying was not one of his vices. He was more than comfortable with the truth, no matter what, and given their conversations about Styx's reemergence and the impending war, Jaret doubted Charon would have concealed any contact with his maker.

Jaret held his tongue, however, because he would never win a verbal argument. Styx would weave more complex and greater lies on top of lies.

"So, shall I tell him?" Styx asked the question of Jaret and pointed to Anthony as his intended target.

"Leave him out of this," Anthony spoke to Styx. "He shouldn't be here. He should *leave*!" Anthony shouted the last word at Jaret. "Which would allow us to focus on *our* business. No one cares what you have to say about anything but your attempt to destroy the world."

Styx swayed back and forth, then held a hand to his chin as if deep in contemplation. Jaret had learned an attack on Styx required a very powerful location but started to think he and his allies could also take advantage of Styx's insanity and hubris.

"Did Charon ever tell you about the game we played to create him?" Styx asked a non sequitur.

"Yes," Jaret answered with an arched brow.

Styx had kidnapped three people, including Charon, to force them to compete against one another for the right to become a vampire. And he promised to execute the losers. Charon won and Styx made him murder the other two to complete the competition. Styx then transformed Charon and included a spell to conceal Charon from the Vampire Council. Charon had also tricked Styx. Charon stole Styx's knowledge about magic at the moment of his conversion, making Charon even more powerful. At the same time, Styx manufactured the appearance of his own suicide so Charon thought him dead. Only Styx knew what any of the complex story had to do with Anthony and Jaret. Unless it was simply another manifestation of his insane mind.

"Then you know I like games." Styx smiled.

Jaret rolled his eyes. "Would you get to the point?"

"No. Let's play a game. Jaret, you first. I'll ask a question, and you answer. If you refuse, I torture him. Here we go. Jaret, tell me what would devastate Anthony more than anything else in the entire world."

Jaret glanced to Anthony to see if he should answer. Anthony mouthed the word *leave* to Jaret.

Sensing an escalation of the insanity and realizing he could learn nothing else, Jaret obeyed. He pushed himself into the air and looked up toward the ceiling when Anthony screamed in agony. Jaret shot back into the room and saw Styx's finger implanted in Anthony's chest.

"I thought I could persuade you not make a rude exit."

"Losing me," Jaret answered. "I think we knew before you asked the question. Losing me would devastate him beyond belief."

"Oh," Styx exclaimed. "You answered with the truth already. Bravo. Though I expected a longer game. Oh, well. I doubt I could ever top the one I invented that led to creating Charon. Yes, you're correct. Losing another lover. Poor Anthony, with so much sorrow and loss in his long lifetime."

"You can't kill Jaret's ghost form," Anthony spoke in a

monotone. "He's not really here."

Styx narrowed his eyes at Anthony. "No. But you are. Do you know what Jaret's been up to these last few years? You thought you entered a happy monogamous relationship. You thought your lonely centuries after I killed your lover in the first war ended with Jaret. You should know, however, how someone else plugs Jaret's precious hole. Jaret gets fucked in private by Charon." Styx hunched over so he could stare Anthony in the eyes. "You know it's true. You feared such a thing already. Jaret has a little action on the down low with a bad boy."

"Anthony, he's lying." Jaret stared hard at Anthony to try to communicate the truth against Styx's lie, thinking Anthony must already know but worried in the context of an upside-down world what might be misconstrued.

Anthony squinted as if puzzled, his glance moving back and forth from Styx to Jaret. No one spoke, Jaret because he had already proclaimed the truth, Styx presumably because he wrought the desired turmoil. Had the tension between Anthony and Jaret over the last few years about the impending war created doubt in Anthony's mind? Could Styx throwing out a preposterous lie sway Anthony against Jaret? Anthony was smarter than to take the bait.

Even if Styx had succeeded in planting doubt in Anthony's mind, what had he gained? Nothing over Jaret, who stood there in spirit alone. He had Anthony incapacitated by some extreme magic because otherwise Anthony would flee or fight. So why the plot?

Another way to create chaos? Jaret remembered a lecture from one of his college classes on the history of Russia. His professor proclaimed Russia failed and muddled along for centuries and never accomplished much except for exceling at the creation of chaos, often at their enemies' expense. Maybe Styx was like Russia.

Jaret turned his attention back to Styx. Styx straightened up and walked behind Anthony. He reached around his back and pulled out a long golden knife with strange markings etched on the blade. The knife glinted in the light as he raised it high and thrust the point into the back of Anthony's neck and twisted.

Jaret's heart lurched into his throat when Anthony slumped forward, the magic chains evaporated, and a lifeless body lay before them.

Styx laughed and clapped. "You helped me! I tried to kill him before, but he held so tight to the Council magic all my efforts failed! You distracted him enough to let loose! Dead! The most vile vampire in all history is *dead*!"

Jaret lost control. With no idea how he arrived back in Fremont, he snapped back into his body and stared into Darth's worried eyes as the world went black around him.

CHAPTER SIX

FUCK OFF

7 FEBRUARY 2019
Fremont, NE

Jaret experienced a wave of surreal emotions. Styx had killed Anthony. Jaret's lover, dead.

Styx had lowered Anthony's guard with the stupid distraction of insinuating to Anthony that Jaret had fucked Charon. Too easily, Styx had manipulated their responses to gain the power to kill Anthony.

When Jaret woke, an enchanted missive from the Vampire Council laid next to him on the floor. The message confirmed Anthony had died and pled for Jaret to come to them, his friends, for help. Next Jaret cast his own spell to search for Anthony, but it also led to the conclusion Anthony was gone.

Given the grim reality, Jaret sat surprised because he anticipated despair, a complete blackness at the loss of his lover, much like the turmoil which had engulfed him after Henrik had killed first his former boyfriend and then his entire family. He remembered grief, unbearable sadness, and a complete loss of the will to live. Those emotions became his constant companions for years after their deaths. But no. Total and utter desolation did not consume him.

He marveled at the power of his vampire dog, the most loyal and true friend Jaret had had for his entire human and then vampire life. Darth and he would do anything to protect each other. Jaret remembered passing out in the attic when his spirit had slammed back into his body. Yet he woke the following sunset in the basement of his Fremont mansion, tucked away in a safe and dark corner with Darth curled up next to him. He figured a Council member had come to protect him, but no one else was in the house. He texted the Council to see if anyone was nearby, but they all said no. After investigating the route to the attic, he then concluded Darth had dragged him down here to protect him. No one else could do the job and there were bite marks and tears in his shirt, likely from where she'd latched onto him. And as a vampire animal, she possessed more than enough strength to carry him to Europe and back.

Jaret anticipated agony and grief surfacing but one feeling alone dominated Jaret's being at the moment. Rage. Pissed off, out of control, wild anger coursed through his veins. Profound hatred of Styx. Ire at the Council. Seething at Anthony. Jaret was furious at the world, every person, and every being. He did recall anger as a stage of grief, so perhaps he had moved there already.

Sensing his distress, Darth nuzzled up to him. Her efforts melted him a bit.

"Darth, let's go play."

She followed him with her typical enthusiasm as Jaret led her around Fremont on a spree to release his pent-up aggression. He allowed her to murder several squirrels in a park for sport. He found a couple random people and murdered them, though making sure the executions complied with the vampire ethic so he would not have to deal with the Council and because of a nagging sense of morality. Still, he left the dead bodies in the open to defy Council rules a little.

Darth and he chased a bunny until she killed the poor beast.

But Jaret tired of the killing spree and wanted something more entertaining for his new evil persona. He searched a wealthy section of town, invading various homes and pricking their inhabitants to taste their blood and see their life stories until he found a suitable victim.

A degenerate lawyer, at home alone because his family had gone on vacation without him, served Jaret well. He tied the guy up to his office chair on the first floor of a large house. The dude sat in nothing but his underwear, trembling with fear. Jaret had carried him around with ease and allowed Darth to bite at his ankles for a little snack to heighten his dread.

Jaret had no desire to listen to his pleas for mercy so stuffed a bandana into his mouth to stifle him.

"All those people you bilked out of money. Innocent folks coming to you for help, needing to trust someone, and you lured them in with false promises and faux empathy, never looking back when they lost everything but still paid your handsome fees. You knew the last client's husband would assault her if she returned to him, but once you fucked up her case you left her forlorn and thinking she had to go back. Did you even feel a little guilty when he killed her? I haven't even touched on the corruption and other scandals."

Jaret stopped himself, bored of his monologue. "Forget it. I sound like Henrik or Styx, ranting and raving at no one but the air. Let's be done."

Jaret sliced a fingernail along the man's forearm, causing him to squirm. He then leaned over and bit into his neck to suck down some of the delicious blood but ceased before killing him. For five or ten minutes he tortured the man, long enough to inflict anguish and for the Vampire Council's magical alarms to blare with a warning about a vampire taking sadism too far. Satisfied they would get his message, Jaret drank the rest of the blood. He staged the killing to appear as if a disgruntled client murdered the asshole. He used his own blood to heal bite marks and scratches, then stabbed him with a letter opener. He slapped the dead body on the cheek and called Darth. The two took their leave.

The cold February air invigorated Jaret when the wind hit his face, causing him to contemplate more fiendish possibilities as his anger spiked and he fought to forget about Anthony. Darth sprinted ahead, a typical sign she spotted something to hunt so Jaret let her go as he ambled along near a wooded preserve on the outskirts of Fremont. When she failed to return after a couple minutes, Jaret called for her. She failed to respond so he sprinted ahead to find her.

Before he spotted her or the visitors, his senses tingled a warning of other vampires in the area, but their ability to conceal their identity meant one thing: the Council had found him.

He rushed ahead around a bend in the trail and found Xavier and Thomas sitting on a bench with Darth between them, licking their faces and happy to see them. No wonder she had failed to return, having other people available to fawn over her.

"What do you want?" Jaret asked as he walked toward them but stopped several feet away. "I'm dancing close to the edge but never disobeyed a hard rule. Besides I have no intention of letting you take me."

Thomas smirked but Xavier stared hard at Jaret. Darth jumped off the bench and trotted over.

"Aren't all your theatrics a little cliché?" Xavier asked. "Pushing the envelope, stopping short of total defiance, but doing enough to trigger an alarm, you've become a caricature like Charon but without the chutzpah. Being an asshole to make a point doesn't suit you. We're all in mourning."

Xavier's words stung but shocked Jaret more than anything. He expected sympathy and the Xavier who nurtured him back to health after the murder of his entire family, the caring vampire who took him under his wing and treated him like a son.

Jaret shrugged. "I'm over the drama."

"What do you mean?" Xavier asked with a disgusted expression.

Except Jaret had no answer. He wanted to respond to Xavier's question by flipping him off and turning around, except silly antics would confirm Xavier's suspicion. But he wasn't out of control. Just pissed off.

"I'm done." Jaret spun around, commanded Darth to follow, and sprinted back into town to the Bachmann Mansion. He enchanted several spells to protect himself and to alert him if Xavier followed, but several minutes passed with nothing. He prepared to go on another hunt when flashing colored lights lit up his living room to warn of approaching vampires. Jaret looked out the window to see Xavier and Thomas returning with Brady following behind.

Jaret laughed because Brady made a funny face when he saw Jaret in the window. He acted scared to come inside. Of course, Brady would find humor even in the worst situation.

When they got inside, Thomas stayed by the door, once again mute, while Brady jerked his head toward Jaret as a greeting.

Xavier glared. "You need to stop the childish defiance. Will you at least listen to Brady? We'll go."

Xavier turned around and grabbed Thomas's arm to force him to come along before storming out.

"They're in a mood," Jaret said to Brady.

Brady shrugged. "So are you, mi amigo." He jumped onto the couch and laid back. "They're worried about you, but you're pissing them off, and they want to focus on the war and what happened to Anthony, but you distracted them. I'm concerned too, you know. Not because you're acting batshit fucking crazy. I already knew you were. But losing Anthony I know is killing you. I don't want to lose you to insanity or to a Council jail."

"I'm fine." Jaret sat on the floor next to Darth.

Brady arched his brow. "Yeah, you seem peachy." He took a deep breath. "We're too close for me to spew a bunch of bullshit at you. They brought me because they thought you'd listen to me. They knew you'd tell them to fuck off. I'm not in some secret deal with them. I agreed to come because I wanted to be here for you. I love you. And if our conversation helps things with them, great. Whatever. But you gotta cut the bullshit because you're not okay. You're not fine. You're acting wiggy."

Jaret laughed. Brady always humored him with the way he framed things. "No. I'm devastated. You're right." Jaret nodded. "But more than anything I'm raging pissed off and done being a good little boy. The Council can go fuck themselves. For years they let this asshole Styx build his empire in preparation to attack them. They pondered how to respond to him and dismissed the knowledge my magic gained about how to fight him. As far as I'm concerned, Anthony killed himself. So I'm done with the obedient dog routine and will do things my way."

"Cool."

"Cool?"

Brady giggled. "You still sound pretty messed up. But I trust you. I'm here when you want to talk. They aren't going to come after you unless you really go off the rails because they aren't sure about your magic and what you'd do. Besides, and this is the truth, they're knee-deep getting ready for the war and don't have time for you. I think Xavier is all pissy because of everything going on."

"Did they tell you their plans?" Jaret asked.

"God, no." Brady shook his head. "They were so cool after I went with them. They trained me, helped me adjust, and were super nice. They knew we're good friends so never bad-mouthed you or warned me against seeing you. They focused on training me until they asked me to tag along tonight."

"Good. Anything else?"

"Nope." Brady sat up on the couch. "I wish you'd obey because I want everyone to get along and hang. I get what pissed you off. And you can deny whatever you want, no judgment from me. But don't you think part of your defiance is how you're mourning for Anthony. Promise this, and I'll leave you alone. Before you do anything too crazy or dangerous, come to me. Okay? Let's talk. I won't stop you. You're my BFF, no matter what. So keep me in the loop."

Jaret jumped off the floor. "Agreed. Here's my next plan, if you want to tag along." Jaret told Brady what he intended, making his friend laugh. Except Brady pleaded with Jaret not to follow through on the plot. When Jaret insisted he had to complete his intended mission, Brady followed but told him a number of times he sounded nuts as they meandered through Fremont.

"You know in the superhero movies when the villain loses his shizzle? Like he's all smart and devious but hits a wall and the full-on crazy emerges? We're super close to the line, my friend. Getting ready to watch you dance right over the line. I think you need to stop and cry instead."

"Stop yammering and watch. You can record if you want. Then take the footage to them."

Brady nodded and got his phone out. As Brady began to record, Jaret stepped in front of the camera, turned his back to his friend and facing the Catholic church in front of him. He held his hands in the air, called forth his jewels from every pocket of his pants, and ordered them to spin around the steeple. The frenzy of color lit the night sky like a rainbow until the heat and friction built enough to explode the bell tower as if someone had planted a bomb and ignited the fuse. The church crumbled in on itself and flames leapt into the air.

Hurrying away from the scene, Jaret laughed and pointed to Brady. "See you soon. I gotta split. Show them the video, and tell them that's my answer."

Brady nodded. "Pretty sure you've stepped over the line, Joker. Or Riddler. I'll figure out a better name and let you know." Then his grin turned into a frown. "I love you. Please hang in there."

Part Three

Unhinged Villain

CHAPTER SEVEN

ENLISTING CHARON

8 FEBRUARY 2019
Nederland, CO

Since the circumstances demanded caution, and Charon had created a powerful charm to protect his underground lair in Colorado, he refused to meet Jaret anywhere but his castle deep inside James Peak.

Jaret followed the adorable chief of Charon's boys, Jordan, as he sashayed through various rooms to find Charon. Jaret kept staring at his tight ass because Jordan wore nothing but a sling. Jaret wondered why he bothered with the little cloth because even a frontal view left little to the imagination. Only in Charon's palace could wearing jeans and a sweatshirt make one feel overdressed. Jaret felt self-conscious about wearing so much clothing in a place dedicated to a perpetual bacchanal.

"Bossman told me you were on the way. Wicked, what happened to you." Jordan turned around to peer at Jaret with a genuine look of sympathy. "Like how we lost Kevin."

"Is that why he's keeping you locked up here?" Jaret asked.

Jordan nodded as he started up a stairway and entered a quiet study with a faux fireplace and decorated in Louis XIV fashion. "Gotta protect us. He won't admit as much to me, let alone all of us, but Charon isn't sure what else to do. We enjoy ourselves enough. We have tons to do and could stay a long time." Jordan's face lit up. "If you need to forget, you won't even guess how many of us would love to fuck you! Or be fucked!" Characteristic of Charon's lair for Jordan to think of sex as the solution to any problem.

Jaret scrunched his brow to search for a response when he heard Charon behind him. "If anyone gets his ass, it's me." He turned to see the gorgeous vampire wearing a pair of sports shorts and a tight T-shirt.

Jaret smirked. "My ass is fine by itself."

Jordan nodded. "Well, let me know if you change your mind.

I get why you might want someone other than him." He jerked his head to indicate Charon. "Though he *is* good. I mean, *really* good."

"Out!" Charon pointed toward the door, and they watched Jordan scurry away.

Without asking, Charon made them both an absinthe cocktail and then motioned for Jaret to sit in one of two chairs in front of the fireplace while he took the other. Despite the sex chat, Charon appeared subdued and too quiet.

"I'm no good with emotion so forgive my avoiding speaking of your loss. Even if you wanted, I'm not sure I know how to help you."

Jaret shook his head. "I'd appreciate avoiding the topic as much as you."

"Then I imagine you came to enlist me in your plot again. As if anything in the last few days had changed my mind."

Jaret sipped his drink. "Kind of, yeah. I mean, yes—but I have more specific plans."

"We're safe here. Nowhere else. I'm still not convinced you can win. My boys and I don't care who's in charge if they leave us alone. Sure, Styx could go bonkers. But I'm also on the Council's radar now. It's not like they'd want me doing my own thing without their oversight."

"Will you hear me out?"

"Sure." Charon shrugged. "I don't have much else going on these days. If I didn't want to see you, I wouldn't have answered your request to meet. You offer your proposal and then listen to mine."

"I'm not agreeing to a *quid pro quo* with you."

Charon grinned. "Afraid you might like it? I want you to hear me out. Nothing more expected of you."

"Agreed. So about the war. Yeah, I keep trying to recruit you, but I have more information and a specific plan. See, I studied Styx and the situation. I know some of his vulnerabilities."

Jaret explained about using the Bachmann Mansion as a vortex and the weakness he felt in Styx's ability to control his magic. "Some of what you had told me about him cued me into how to go after him. You play an important role. If we figure out a place to confront him, the combined magic of the Council, you and I, along with the power of a good location, will overwhelm him. We win!"

Charon swirled the liquid in his glass. "Plausible. Maybe. Let me think about it. You make the strategy sound simple when we know such a fight will be anything but."

"Yeah, well, we don't have ages to ponder our action. The Council took their sweet time and one of them died."

Charon's typical attitude of superiority softened, his face an expression almost of sympathy. "Not a random Council member. Your lover."

"Yeah." Jaret drained his absinthe and handed the glass to Charon for another. "Him. And I thought we agreed not to go there."

Charon refilled their drinks, uncharacteristically in silence, then returned with the full glasses. They watched the fire until Charon spoke.

"Your idea is plausible. Better than the general, 'Let's attack' battle cry you've come to me with so far. I worry about the final outcome. I may be better off sitting this one out. Watching from the sideline to see who wins. Like I said, I need time. I won't dither around like the Council. Promise."

Jaret nodded and felt he had made some headway with Charon. "And what's your proposal?"

"You're a free man now." Charon glanced sideways at Jaret but said nothing else. Charon acted nervous.

"All the buildup and you come at me with something so trite?" Jaret shook his head and smiled. "Another bland solicitation to get me in bed?"

Charon turned with an expression Jaret never remembered seeing before. Still lustful, yes. The same carnal desire of his other offers, his penetrating eyes oozing sex. But he appeared earnest, almost desperate, as if his desire took on a different depth than ever before. Jaret was aroused. Charon began to speak but stopped himself and tilted his head.

Jaret squinted. "I don't think we want the same thing. You flatter me. Really. But I'm not there. I never was good at one-night stands." He laughed at memories of himself. "I fall in love in two seconds and want to spend eternity with someone. And I miss

Anthony. I'm not ready for sex with anyone else."

Charon reached over and ran his fingers along Jaret's cheek. "I can't explain what you do to me. I could be more for you. I won't lie—monogamy probably isn't in my future. But we could be more than an occasional fuck. Something passionate without the boring commitment for eternity of the Council idealists. You're leaving them behind so discard their outdated notions."

Jaret's mind warred between his ideals and his feelings, between needing trust and commitment and wanting to rip Charon's clothes off right then. Sex could distract him from the pain for a little while. He reached down to adjust his erection.

Charon smiled. "Part of you likes the proposal."

"I guess." Jaret smiled. "My turn to say I'm not ready."

Charon leaned between the chairs and grabbed Jaret's crotch. "You feel ready.'"

Jaret took Charon's hand off his lap and pushed him back into his chair. "As they say, you didn't even wait for the corpse to get cold." Jaret winced at his crass analogy, the memory of Anthony erasing all sense of lust and bringing him back under control. "I'll contemplate your proposal while you ponder mine."

Charon sipped his drink, once again back in his chair and surprising Jaret with how easily he had relinquished his effort to fuck Jaret. "Fine. But I'm serious." He stared Jaret in the eyes. "We can do more with whatever you decide. A compromise. We have a bond, whether you admit so or not."

Jaret took a drink to distract himself. He almost blurted out the truth that he liked being with Charon and about their sexual tension igniting the air whenever they got together. But the admission would bring them too close to Charon's bidding and Jaret knew caving to the sexual whim was a horrendous idea. He recognized himself enough to see his vulnerability after losing Anthony. He knew he would long for a relationship with Charon, one Charon would never enter. No doubt the sex would be wonderful. But the long-term emotion would suck as much and for longer than the moment of pleasure.

"Too soon," Jaret dodged his own confusion.

"About that." Charon furrowed his brow. "I expected more pouting. More grief. Your emotion always fills the atmosphere with passion about anything from a little dog walking by to the impending war of the worlds. Yet no tears. No pining for your lost love." Charon softened his expression when he saw how the jab hurt Jaret. "I'm sorry. But I anticipated intense mourning."

Why he entrusted the truth with Charon escaped Jaret, but he needed the release and let the words flow. "I've been trying to figure out what gives for a while myself. I thought I'd be sad. I keep expecting the sorrow to hit me in the head. Instead, I walk around totally pissed off. I mean, his death makes me want to blow up the fucking world and every soul walking around. Starting with the dumb fucking Council and their taking two thousand years to decide what the fuck to do." Jaret failed to notice until the end how he yelled the last two sentences.

"So anger consumes you. I get the message loud and clear."

Jaret finished his second drink. "Yeah. Fucking irate. I miss him, but he never listened to me and ended up dead because of ignoring what I told him." Jaret got up, grabbed Charon's glass, and refilled their drinks.

The drunkenness hit him and first accelerated his anger until a soothing intoxication gave way to melancholy. They sat in quiet for a long time.

"I find your candor refreshing. You used to be more dodgy." Charon drew in a deep breath and sighed. "Do you believe the Council will leave me alone after the war?"

Jaret considered the question. Because he needed Charon on their side, he wanted to blurt out an emphatic yes. But Charon would see through the lie, which could damage any chance Jaret had of convincing Charon to join the Council and him.

"Let me say this." Jaret contemplated for a moment. "Styx played you for a fool with his act and fake suicide. He dominates anyone around him and has declared his intentions to rule not only the vampire kingdom but all of Earth. If he wins, you'll be under his thumb. No way he leaves you alone. He can find you. See? Unlike the Council, *he* can find you. You don't have a choice between the life you lead now or a change. Change of one sort or another will be here soon. Unlike Styx, the Council doesn't know how to find you because of the concealing magic. You'll retain the ability to hide."

"Not from you."

Jaret snarled at the affiliation of himself with the Council but then smiled. "I'm not on the Council, and I don't do their bidding. I'd never rat you out. Besides, you like when I find you."

Charon smiled in return and reached over to pat Jaret on the arm. "Truth."

Jaret finished his drink and got up to go. Charon escorted him to the exit tunnel but grabbed his arm and spun Jaret around before he started toward the surface. He clutched Jaret by both shoulders. "You okay?"

Again, the lust overpowered Jaret as the strong arms and luscious lips ignited his passion. He swayed a bit but held steady because of the powerful grip holding him. "I hope to survive," Jaret whimpered. He bit his lower lip.

Charon leaned forward and gently, as if Jaret were a newborn, swaddled and kissed him on the forehead. Charon stepped away. "I'm sure I'll see you soon. You know you can't resist me." The lustful comment returned them, thankfully, to their normal repartee.

"You sure you got the concept right about who can't resist whom?"

Charon laughed. "I never denied the mutual attraction. I've been pretty clear about what I want to do to you."

Jaret turned to leave but stopped a few steps up the tunnel and turned around. He grabbed Charon's hand and pulled it to his lips where he placed a kiss on the top knuckles and then without control, slid a finger into his mouth. He let go and looked at Charon, who had closed his eyes and reached down to rub his cock.

"You're cruel," Charon said as Jaret spun around and left.

The freezing mountain air hit Jaret hard in the face when he got outside, cooling off the heat and returning him to reality. He found Darth close by, feasting off a large animal.

"Seriously? A moose? You're about forty-five pounds. You don't need to drink an entire moose."

Darth wagged her stub of a tail and bounded over to him. They walked through the deep snow as if a human and his dog were on a hike despite the frigid temperatures and difficult mountain terrain. When the hint of an approaching sunrise beaconed them to bed, Jaret and Darth sprinted across America, tucked themselves into the hidden chamber inside their Chicago home, and fell asleep.

CHAPTER EIGHT

THOMAS

10 FEBRUARY 2019
Chicago, IL

Jaret returned to a powerful snowstorm blanketing Chicago and sending everyone indoors. He and Darth walked the abandoned streets and enjoyed the serenity. A block over, Jaret spotted a snow-plow attempting to control the uncontrollable weather, and Darth leapt through the snow with the excitement of a puppy.

Jaret reached the lakefront, where Darth and he sauntered

along. Jaret didn't even bother with the disguise of winter clothes, instead wearing a comfortable sweatshirt, tight jeans, and flip-flops. Similar to their mountain hike after Jaret met with Charon, the two walked like it was a perfect summer evening and not as if forging through a brisk wind in a blizzard. Jaret risked exposing his vampirism if a human saw him trudging through the conditions with these clothes and the footwear, but no one was around, and he could run away fast enough if needed.

He spotted Thomas ahead, sitting on a rock and staring at the frozen lake. Thomas's long black hair blew back but his chiseled body was hidden because he wore appropriate winter attire.

Thomas smiled when Jaret got to him and sat down. He pointed to Jaret's feet. "I can see the reason for a sweatshirt and jeans if you want a bit more defiance in your life." He grabbed his coat for emphasis. "We don't need clothes and I doubt anyone will saunter along tonight to see you. Still, flip-flops? Are you kidding me?"

Jaret wiggled his toes. "Probably another little tweak at the Council."

"Probably?" Thomas grinned. "I do like how you took most of the heat off me. I was always the rogue, naughty vampire, flouting the rules. They put me on the Council anyway and somehow, I work out there. I challenged them and exasperated them until you came along. Compared to you I must not seem so bad."

"You have no idea."

Thomas grew serious. "I think I do."

Jaret kicked his feet back and forth, amused with himself for having exposed feet. His actions showcased the defiance he wanted Thomas to see. "Why aren't you more upset?" Jaret asked by way of approaching his reason for meeting Thomas. "Anthony was your best friend. I know everyone expects me to be overwrought because he was my lover. *Is* my lover. But you loved him too. Why does everyone think because my sorrow comes in the form of being pissed off, I'm an outlier?"

"I'm glad you're acknowledging the sorrow. You haven't seemed to admit your pain."

"Yeah." Jaret nodded. "Because mostly I'm fucking pissed." Jaret let his anger hang in the air without further comment and waited for Thomas to respond.

Thomas took forever before he said, "Of course, I miss him. But a lot is going on. A war heating up. Like you, I think I repressed my feelings because of the danger."

Jaret frowned. "Again with pretending you four are worried about a war all of a sudden. I don't get the Council. We knew for a long time something lurked, and why you never suspected Styx is beyond me. Okay, so you thought he was dead. You at least knew something as dangerous as the first war was happening. You fucking knew we were all in jeopardy. I told you. I investigated, and I know damn well if I could gather as much information as I did then you at least could find as much knowledge. You let this shit build until

Styx killed Anthony. Maybe my sorrow is buried beneath how fucking stupid I think the Council is. So I can't mourn losing him as long as I'm a lot more irate at his fucking stupidity."

Again, a silence descended between them. Thomas had held his tongue around Jaret of late, but he had never before been at a loss for words.

"You remind me of myself in my young vampire days." Thomas paused, giving Jaret time to think, but he stopped himself from saying *what the fuck does that have to do with anything?*

Thomas got up and walked along the edge of the shore, plowing through the snow. Darth ran after him, excited to move and do something besides sit there. Jaret followed by kicking up snow and letting his flip-flop fly off his foot so he could catch it before putting the footwear back on.

"Did you ever think the Council knew more than they let on about Styx? You know Anthony better than anyone, even better than I did. You think he dithered around without understanding the full scope of the matter? Without a concrete plan?"

Jaret shook his head. "He's dead, Thomas. Some fucking plan."

Thomas touched Jaret's shoulder and stopped them on the path. He looked down into Jaret's face, their long hair blowing around and entangling.

"Authority bothers you. Me too," Thomas said. "Trust is hard for you. I get it. But the Council has protected you for a long time.

The members pushed hard for Anthony to bring you over against all his doubt about you being a powerful witch. They nurtured you. They love you."

Jaret squinted. "What are you trying to tell me? To be a good little vampire for them?"

"I'm trying to open your eyes and get beyond the rage to see a bigger truth. To trust them somehow. Trust us. Trust Anthony."

"He's *fucking dead!*" Jaret screamed. "And why have you become such a Council tool? You're more like me, not all Council goody-goody."

Thomas continued to walk them along without reacting to Jaret's outburst.

Thomas spoke with a calm voice. "Xavier changed me. Time matured me. I resist the Council, believe me. Too many rules. A lot of nonsense. I'm conflicted about their war strategy but think we can pull off a win. Your point of view makes sense. Given what you know combined with how the Council conceals its knowledge, I don't know how you could feel any different. I know. But as one renegade to another, *listen* to me. I can't tell you everything. And I'd be as pissed off as you if someone threw the same thing in my face. But I can say, and believe me they want me to keep this quiet: more is at work here than you see. I argued for them to tell you, but they have their reasons. Will you listen to me?"

Jaret clenched his jaw and bit back his response. "Do I have any choice?"

"What did you want to meet me about?" Thomas deflected.

"I know how to beat Styx." Jaret held up a hand to stop Thomas from saying anything when he sensed the rebuttal. "I do. I practiced and studied and experimented. Two things are key. Speaking of being pissed off and irate, Styx struggles to control himself and his emotion. When he gets overwrought, the feelings threaten to burst so he clamps down on them but concentrates so hard he loses focus on his magic. In those moments he becomes vulnerable. Not to everyone, but to the combined magic from the Council, Charon, and me. And, this is even more important, we have to lure him to a magical location. If we go to the right spot, we can combine forces with the elements around, weaken him, and then overpower him."

"Tell me more about the idea of a spot. What spot?" Thomas's engagement surprised and pleased Jaret.

"A place magic resides, where something extraordinary has happened, maybe bad, maybe good, many times both. Forces and energy collect there. Oh, and the location might be spiritual and old. These places exist around the world, but you must know magic to find them."

"Do you have an example?"

Jaret nodded. He laughed when Darth sprinted by, playing in the snow before he answered. "My mansion in Nebraska. A few generations of Bachmann witches practiced their magic there. The gems were housed there for a long time. Henrik haunted the house for over a century, and my family died inside. There's lots of energy swirling around the place."

"So you want to get Styx to go there for the fight?"

Jaret contemplated the idea for a second. "No. We'll find an even more powerful place. I can't believe you agree with my theory."

"Are you trying to talk me out of believing you?" Thomas smiled. "You make a good case. And I'm going to tell you something else I should keep quiet—Council business they concealed from you. Anthony was working on a similar theory. I assume they still are seeing how to use a vortex to their advantage."

The revelation stung Jaret with the reminder of how much the Council kept from him, including Anthony. But Jaret felt hope for the first time when thinking about fighting in allegiance with the Council because they knew too.

"You assume? Don't you know?"

"Let me do this," Thomas continued, again sidestepping Jaret's inquiry. "The Council should meet with you. I'll demand they keep their minds open to hearing your argument if you promise to control your temper and at least try to trust them. I can't promise how they'll respond, but if I push the matter they'll listen."

"Okay."

"That's all you got?"

Jaret laughed. "Let's try. Wonder—"

Thomas held up a hand to stop Jaret midsentence at the same

time Jaret felt an approaching presence. Before they saw anything they felt the approach of a vampire. Darth returned to Jaret's side when she noticed the sensation. Thomas and Jaret froze in place as they watched ahead of them for the visitor.

Nothing alarmed Jaret even though a meandering vampire in a blizzard seemed off.

First a dot appeared ahead. The vampire plodded through the snow with no apparent hurry. As the vampire came closer, Jaret saw a body concealed in a snowsuit complete with skiing goggles. Every inch of the person was covered with the heavy winter clothes a human would wear if going on an adventure high atop the Himalayas. Even for blizzard conditions in Chicago the attire looked absurd.

When about fifty feet away, the vampire waved with enthusiasm, causing Darth to lurch forward and bounce into the person by way of greeting. The mummified vampire petted her, and Jaret could tell Darth knew the person.

When Darth and the being got to Thomas and Jaret, Jaret first recognized the ridiculous giggle before Brady took off the goggles and ski mask to reveal himself.

Thomas and Jaret burst into laughter at their friend.

"Dude, what are you doing?" Jaret asked.

"Acting human!" Brady laughed too. "I'm a newbie without magic so I obey the Council."

"Um, no humans are out in these conditions." Jaret pointed at the outfit. "And I've never seen a person in Chicago wandering around in a snowstorm looking like you. You look insane."

His next couple of comments made clear Brady donned the uniform more as a humorous statement than true assessment of how to blend. He had concocted his own version of wearing flip-flops but without the open defiance of the Council.

"I need to meet Xavier, so I'll leave you two to enjoy the weather," Thomas said. He hugged each of them goodbye and hurried away.

Jaret, Brady, and Darth walked down the lakefront path toward downtown Chicago, where they continued their blizzard jaunt through the city streets. They chatted like old times, joking about themselves, laughing about past exploits, and for a little while forgetting the cares of the world. Jaret was deliberately trying to forget Anthony.

"Dude!" Brady looked at the clock above Macy's and slapped his forehead. "I gotta go. Catherine's teaching me how to explore museums and monuments and shit without being caught. I don't want to miss a lesson from her."

Jaret giggled. "She did the same for me. Had me almost naked on top of the Eiffel Tower."

Brady grinned. "The other night, I wanted to climb the side of the Hancock and hang out at the top, but Xavier said no because people might see us. After he left, Catherine promised to teach me. So I gotta go because tonight's the lesson. But, listen. I'm on your side. When this goes down, I may not be a member of the Council, and I don't know any magic, but I'll be on your side. Whatever you need."

Jaret hugged his friend in a tight embrace. Then, Brady leaned over to say goodbye to Darth before wandering off, still in his ridiculous snow suit.

CHAPTER NINE

COUNCIL CONCLAVE

15 FEBRUARY 2019
Fort Lauderdale, FL

It had been five days since Thomas promised a meeting with the Council, but Jaret had heard nothing from the vampire gods on high. He wanted to forge ahead with his own plan, with or without them, and perhaps see if Charon would join him since the "authorities" were nowhere to be found. Unfortunately, Styx's power demanded more caution.

The last few days his anger had opened a portal into his sorrow, though the emotion ironically pissed him off even more. He felt alone. Lost. Uncertain.

The house in Chicago reminded Jaret of Anthony and their lives together at every turn—their long-term plans, the way they decided on décor with one another, and the patience Anthony had when Jaret became petulant or wanted to lash out against authority. Though his demeanor had often irritated Jaret, Anthony had known how to calm him and refocus his energy on a different issue.

Without Anthony, and while the Council ignored him, Jaret saw two paths. Either fight alone—unless Charon joined him—or wait around for a Council summons or the war to begin with nothing to occupy his mind in the meantime. Jaret hurled an expensive vase across the room and reveled in obliterating one of their shared purchases into a million pieces. A second later he regretted the fit of passion and knew he'd better change his environment before going insane.

So he and Darth wandered down to Florida to get away from pretending to be cold and to find a spot without memories of Anthony where he could consider his next move. Jaret wandered Fort Lauderdale, nearby Wilton Manors, and the beaches for several nights, no more certain about how to act than before but at least away from constant reminders of Anthony. He and Darth rented a condo and acted like tourists.

Almost every night, Jaret encountered some complete hottie

on the beach and longed to flirt and lose himself in a one-night stand, but also he lost his nerve every time and could not shake complete loyalty to Anthony, even after his death. One gorgeous hunk followed him all the way home and pleaded to at least let him buy Jaret a drink, but Jaret declined, instead going inside alone to watch old movies.

Tonight, the crashing waves soothed Jaret by reminding him of the vast nature of the ocean and entire world. Despite his vampiric strength and immortality, the beach made Jaret feel small and insignificant. The notion felt good because he realized the futility of his compulsion to save vampires from obliteration or the entire world from Styx's tyranny. What could one tiny vampire-witch do to save humanity or even vampires? Nothing.

As so often occurred when Jaret found peace for an evening, something intruded into his life.

"Fuck me," he muttered under his breath as Xavier strode toward him from the opposite direction.

Xavier smirked when he got to Jaret. "Nice to see you too."

"You weren't meant to hear me."

Xavier pointed to his ears. "The curse of vampire senses."

"Am I in trouble again? More attempts to save my soul? Or another threat from the Council?"

"None of the above, though I admit your continued charming attitude makes me want to walk away and leave you to your own devices. I've come because your Council emissary brokered a meeting between you and the Council. Given your lack of anger management, I find the idea ill-advised, so you can take the offer or leave it. Your choice. If you want to make your case, follow me. Otherwise, wallow in your anger and self-pity."

Xavier spun around and walked away, and Jaret waited a minute before he sprinted to catch up and follow.

"Why are you being such a dick all of a sudden?"

Xavier lurched to a stop and glared at Jaret. "*I'm* being a dick? Are you serious?" He walked forward again.

Jaret took a breath. "Well, I know I'm an ass too. But you always rose above the nonsense. And I have a good excuse for my behavior."

"No, you don't. You've invented an excuse so you don't have to deal with reality. As for my ability to rise above something, even I have limits. You want to be testy and mean, you have the choice. But I don't have to take the abuse."

"Sorry," Jaret whispered.

"You sure?" Xavier motioned toward a large beach house with a huge deck surrounded by tiki torches, upon which sat the other three Council members and Brady. Everyone gave Jaret a slight nod, except Brady who smiled and waved with enthusiasm.

"I can stay and listen in," Brady exclaimed to them. "Cool, huh?"

"You have no idea how fun these folks are. A real riot." Jaret spat the words without thinking.

Catherine roared a laugh, prompting Thomas and Brady to join her until Jaret cracked and smiled in return. Typical of Xavier and Harriet to remain placid.

"You have a proposal for us?" Harriet asked when everyone calmed. "Some idea about going to a magical place like Disney to defeat Styx?"

Jaret started to respond then stopped and shook his head. "Okay, I get you. Snide comment about Disney. Xavier with the cold shoulder. Listen, I deserve your attitude. I earned it. Okay? Really, I know. Though I can't shake the feeling that the Council let my husband die. And Anthony must have known he went on a suicide mission, which should give me certain license to question your wisdom. Can we move beyond the past to get to the problem? Because Styx threatens all of us, and I know how to defeat him. I know how to avenge Anthony by making sure Styx loses."

Catherine nodded. "Tell us what you think. No more smart-ass shit from anyone."

Jaret allowed a moment of silence. "We need to fight. Soon. No more waiting around and studying and plotting and being all secretive. Styx is vulnerable when he loses control of his emotions. If we lure him to a vortex of magic and get him riled up, we can murder him. Don't pretend you don't understand. Thomas already told me Anthony was planning the same thing."

Harriet wagged a finger at Jaret. "He theorized something similar. Not the same."

"But you recognize what I'm saying, don't you?"

"We do." Xavier nodded. "But you make the idea sound simple when a lot more is at stake. In time your plan may make sense, but not yet. I vote no."

"Me, too." Harriet gave a thumbs-down for emphasis.

"Wait!" Jaret screamed in astonishment. "I talked for one second and you vote me down?"

"Not everyone." Catherine held up a thumb. "I agree. We move. Fast."

Jaret nodded. "Right. Good."

Thomas reached over to hold Xavier's hand. "Jaret has my vote. I agree with him."

Fuck. A Council tie. How the hell did they resolve the mess, Jaret wondered.

"We don't have the votes to proceed," Harriet announced. "I'll continue to study what Anthony had planned. He left a good trail to follow in the Council's magical vault. We'll figure out what to do soon enough and call you back if appropriate." Harriet stood and motioned for Jaret to leave.

They were dismissing him. He obeyed like a dejected puppy until he arrived near the steps to the beach when he lurched around. "You guys didn't even listen. How can you study this any longer? We know what Styx is capable of. We know his scheme."

Xavier came over and touched Jaret on the arm. "We do. Which is why we're being so deliberate. I know you don't understand our caution. But think like a vampire. Since we live for eternity, what's five years if we get the response right? We have quite a bit of information and will act soon enough. Sooner than you think."

"But you don't trust me to participate?"

"You'll be part." Xavier kissed Jaret on the cheek and turned around. "In time."

Jaret clenched his fists so tight they sparked magic and orange flashes shot toward the beach.

"Those shenanigans don't help." Thomas hurried over and walked Jaret down the steps and onto the sand, though Jaret could tell he held back a smile. "We made progress tonight. We're close. Don't give up or get bitchier, please." Thomas pointed toward the blackened patches in the sand where Jaret's magic terminated. "You feed their reluctance when you get so mad. I'm speaking from experience with them, by the way. They piss me off all the time too."

"I *am* pissed!" Jaret lurched to a stop, feeling as if he couldn't breathe. He clutched his neck and then tears burst forth. He gulped in air and fought against falling to his knees on the ground. "Royally pissed," he sputtered. "I don't know how to convince them. Am I supposed to wait until he kills the rest of you? Until I'm the sole survivor left to fight him? If he killed Anthony without effort, how can you still meander along with business as usual?"

Thomas stopped Jaret by pulling him into a tight embrace with both hands on his shoulders. "Hold yourself together. *Hear* me. You have more of a voice than you think, and plans are further along than you know."

Jaret shrugged out of the hold and walked away without comment, sick of the same old assurances. He wiped the tears from his face with an angry swipe of his arm. Sorrow turned to more rage at how they continued with the maddening refusal to let him in on the secret. He needed to get away before he lashed out even more.

Jaret wanted to scream loud enough to topple nearby buildings when he walked a few blocks away and heard another one of the fucking vampires chasing him. He spun around in a rage and clenched his fists tight again so the magic flared into the sky.

Brady lurched to a halt a few feet away and held up two hands in surrender. Despite his anger, Jaret burst into laughter. Brady stood before him in nothing but a skimpy little speedo of rainbow colors.

"Can I approach without you shooting me with orange shit?" Brady asked.

Jaret nodded. "But don't try any Council bullshit or come as a good cop or secret diplomat."

"Nah." Brady came up and placed his arm around Jaret's shoulder. "I told you they leave me out. In a good way, I mean. Don't muddy the waters. You were right about being at the meeting. Not fun."

After they walked a little way Jaret giggled again. "You look ridiculous."

"Dude! It's the beach! Florida! My vampire-ness gave me a hot little body to show the world. You look sillier with your shirt and shorts on. Here, let me help." Before Jaret could react, Brady took a fingernail, ripped Jaret's shirt down the center of the back, and tore it off. "Better. Show off your fabulous vampire bod."

"I'm not sure you help me." Despite himself, Jaret grinned.

Again, Jaret reacted too late and before he knew what happened, he looked at his shorts in tatters in Brady's hand before he tossed them into a trashcan. In his boxer briefs, even as a vampire, Jaret felt horribly self-conscious out in public.

"Relax," Brady winked at Jaret. "You look adorable."

"I'm in public in my underwear. Nothing else."

"True. But in the middle of the night in Florida. From afar, you probably look like you're wearing a swimsuit."

"Why are you here? To undress me?"

"Oh, yeah." Brady yanked Jaret toward the shoreline and plopped down in the sand. "I should explain."

Jaret deflated. "I knew they sent you on a mission."

"No." Brady half-yelled. "I swear they keep me out. But I don't have to stay out. I want you to know I'm with you, like I pledged before. No matter what they say or promise. I want to work on your side. I don't understand why they have to be assholes or whatever. I don't like how they treat you by keeping secrets even after Anthony died. Yeah, I like them. But they're assholes when they refuse to trust you. I appreciate how they brought me along. You're my closest friend in the whole world, the only family I have left. I followed to tell you. I'm not much help without magic or whatever as a newbie vampire, but I'm on team Jaret."

Brady's pledge touched Jaret. His best friend had hit a nerve, causing Jaret to cry. "Thanks."

"Yeah. We always got each other's back. So I know what else you need."

"What?"

"A diversion."

Jaret shook his head. "No matter what, no matter where, no matter the circumstances, I always know to avoid your diversions. *Always* a bad idea."

Brady grinned with a wicked expression. "You say as much and then love every minute. All those distractions from boring coursework. Or bad boyfriends. Or life's problems. Blah, blah, blah."

Jaret narrowed his eyes. "What do you have in mind?"

"A surprise. Stand up." Brady leapt to his feet and motioned for Jaret to follow.

"I don't trust you."

Brady leaned over and grabbed both of Jaret's forearms to yank him up. "Nor should you. Ever."

Nonetheless, Jaret obeyed. He regretted his compliance a second later when Brady ripped off Jaret's underwear and scampered down the beach. As Jaret caught up with him, Brady tore off his own swimsuit and ran naked and laughing until he stopped before they got to the more public beach away from the private homes.

"Uh, we better go get some clothes." Brady grinned and laughed.

"Now you're worried about public nudity?"

"Well, it seemed like a good idea at the time. But you're getting a woody." Brady pointed to Jaret's growing erection.

"Something about being naked in public excites me. Fuck me." Jaret ran toward his condo, knowing Brady would follow. Before he even greeted Darth, he grabbed a couple towels, putting one around his waist and throwing the other at Brady. "Let's have a drink on the deck and chill."

"Cool." Brady smiled. "Good idea. But you have to admit I distracted you."

"Go." Jaret pointed to the lounge chairs and swatted his friend on the ass as they headed toward them.

CHAPTER TEN

THE DUKE OF MARLBOROUGH TRUCE

28 FEBRUARY 2019
Woodstock, Oxfordshire, England

Jaret sat in the back seat of the Jaguar listening to Charon and Brady banter back and forth. He knew before introducing them that their being together was a bad idea. Brady was going to love the awkward tension between Jaret and Charon because of their weird relationship. Add in Brady's sexual energy and Jaret was sure to be embarrassed. Once Brady and Charon figured out they could make Jaret uncomfortable they were off to the races.

Their theatrics included renting a car despite not needing such a mode of transportation. Jaret decided not to fight their desire to appear as wealthy travelers in England—he needed to pick his battles. He concentrated on the English countryside by way of ignoring the shitheads, particularly fond of the stone fences.

"Oh!" Brady exclaimed. "Did Jaret ever tell you about the time he banged a fifty-year-old in the back seat of a car? After Jaret broke up with Steve but before he met Anthony, Jaret hooked up with a dude when we were shit-faced drunk and away they went. He's not as pure as he makes out."

"You're not telling an accurate story," Jaret said.

Charon laughed. "I *knew* you were a little minx with all your teasing. You do like older men."

"I have never denied my tastes." Jaret could not suppress his grin. "But the guy was more like forty, and we made out. No dicks even emerged from our pants."

Charon and Brady both choked on a laugh and said at the same time, "Right."

Before their hilarity went further, thank the gods, Charon turned onto the long drive toward Blenheim Palace. Typical vampires to secure meeting at one of the most historic spots in England where a duke still resided. They donated an obscene amount of money toward the palace preservation in return for an evening on their own there. They parked the car and walked down the grand path toward the building.

"Do vampires ever meet in a simple pub?" Brady asked as they stared in awe at the fortress before them.

Charon shrugged. "I don't hang with other vampires very often, except my boys. Maybe they worried meeting at a bar would prompt Jaret to disappear to go fuck some old guy in a truck."

Charon and Brady again laughed at their repartee.

Jaret ignored them by taking in the palace.

After the meeting in Florida, the Council instructed Jaret to meet them here, along with Brady and Charon, if possible, to discuss the next steps. The tan building ahead perked a historian's awe in Jaret. Opulent. Grand. Speaking of another era oozing with stories and history. The castle and grounds told the tale about how the Duke of Marlborough had won a decisive battle against the French. In reward, the queen bequeathed to him and his descendants the land and money to build the enormous estate. Generations later, Winston Churchill was born here on what was his grandparents' estate.

Jaret marveled at the statues high atop the building of the British lion eating the French cuckhold. Paintings, tapestries, and other artifacts throughout the palace and grounds commemorated the battle. The three arrived early enough to take a tour for themselves and had found the wine set out by the staff for the vampires to enjoy. They settled into the formal dining room to drink, where Charon and Brady began their sexual chats, when mercifully the

Vampire Council arrived to silence them.

They strode into the building together, neither morose nor carefree, seeming in command and ready for a serious conversation yet taking the time to admire their surroundings.

"I think Anthony would be pleased with our meeting here," Xavier exclaimed. He sat opposite Jaret and smiled, none of their previous tension lighting the air.

As Xavier said Anthony's name, Jaret's senses buzzed, as if Anthony had entered the room. Jaret glanced over to an unopen door, sensing he felt his lover's presence.

"Anthony told me he'd bring me here," Jaret answered. "Said he loved the place and wanted to share the Blenheim's history with me." Brady reached over and held Jaret's hand as Jaret worked hard to repress his grief at the mention of Anthony.

The vampires' usual behavior would allow for chatting about their location and other matters before getting to business, but the urgency of the issue and the solemn remembrance of Anthony kept them quiet as they took in their surroundings and drank wine. Jaret sensed a difference in the atmosphere. There was an absence of the anger and bickering of the last few meetings but a crackle of tension remained.

Jaret glanced around. He noticed how serious Harriet was, how Xavier appeared concerned, and how Thomas fidgeted. Catherine surveyed the paintings and tapestries in a nonchalant manner. Brady was wide-eyed with awe, while Charon winked at Jaret from across the room.

"Shall we get this party started?" Catherine took charge, one of her roles. "We agree we need to get on the same page. I think we can unite if no one resorts to bitchiness."

"Before we go any further," Charon said, "I feel at a disadvantage. I haven't met any of you." Charon played the part of a respectful vampire, not his typical hedonistic self, yet his innocuous announcement carried the reminder of his outsider status and dislike for the Council.

"But you know all about us from Jaret, I assume." Thomas smiled and tilted his head, calling Charon's bluff. "And we know plenty about you. You don't want us to get to know you, anyway."

Charon laughed. "I'm trying to play nice."

"Much appreciated." Catherine tapped her fingers on the table. "No one claimed this wouldn't be awkward. Let's stick to the issue at hand."

Jaret rolled his eyes and then squinted at the assembled vampires before speaking. "We haven't agreed on an approach to the war since the very beginning. Why frame anything as if we arrived at consensus tonight? I hope you're not planning on my jumping on board to wait another ten years to move."

Catherine frowned. "Our perspectives changed because Anthony died. His death escalated the inevitable conflict with Styx faster than we predicted."

"Faster than *you* predicted," Jaret corrected by pointing a finger at each member of the Council.

"And so," Catherine continued as if Jaret never spoke, "we may disagree on certain aspects about how to proceed with the war, but we do agree on two things. First, unity is essential. Those in this room possess power beyond the average vampire. Styx could slaughter everyone else, so we must keep other vampires out of the fray. But we can fight. We have much upon which we disagree, but collectively we're magical and fierce. Together we can defeat him. Any dissent?" Catherine stared at each person one by one, daring them to disagree, which no one attempted, though Charon looked as if he watched a boring tennis match.

"Good." Catherine nodded. "Two. The Council came to the same conclusion as you, Jaret. Based on Anthony's research and design, we know a location with mystical power can aid our combat. We can decide where we want to go later, but your experience with a vortex underscores what Anthony had determined about where to fight Styx. So we also agree on place as essential."

The others nodded, except for Charon, who still seemed distracted.

"So you agree with me?" Jaret asked in disbelief.

"We do," Xavier answered. He raised his hands in the air to indicate their surroundings. "Call this the Duke of Marlborough Truce."

"Seems more accurate to describe the moment as 'the enemy

of my enemy is my friend.'" Thomas grinned, causing Jaret to smile.

Jaret almost asked them to talk about tactics and decide the place, but Charon raised his hand. "I'm not sure. Sorry. I'm new to the party and everything. May I have a private word with you?" Charon turned to Jaret as he asked the question.

"Okay?" Jaret gave Charon a skeptical expression.

Charon stood and grabbed Jaret's hand, pulling him through the palace, outside and down a marble staircase and into the chapel.

"Always one for a holy setting." Jaret took in the opulent tomb of the palace's founder while he waited for Charon to speak.

Charon took several minutes to walk around the chapel himself. He peered at the architecture before ambling back to Jaret and standing face-to-face with him. "I have an idea. I think intimacy scares you. Our being one-on-one makes the connection personal and passionate. Too emotional. If you tried a three-way with me, we could call it sex and nothing more."

Jaret suppressed a laugh. "What are you talking about?"

"You, Brady, me."

"Are you serious? You took me away from them to propose sex?"

Charon stared hard at Jaret in return.

"No." Jaret shook his head. "Not going to happen. Brady and I are friends. Way too close to fuck up our relationship with sex. And my resistance to your debauched charm is a lot more complex than you understand."

Jaret turned to leave and walked a few steps before Charon wrapped his arms around Jaret's chest from behind and pressed his body into Jaret's back. "Wait. Stop. I brought you here for something else." Charon's fingers played with Jaret's nipples.

Jaret relaxed into the hold, once again mesmerized by Charon's carnal presence and strong arms. "Then, what?"

Charon's lips brushed Jaret's ear. "You like this, don't you?"

Jaret pushed himself forward, but Charon held tight. "I thought you said you had something else," Jaret prompted him.

"You'll cave, one day." Charon kissed Jaret's neck and let him go.

Jaret turned and adjusted his crotch.

"You're blushing."

Jaret closed his eyes and took a deep breath. He opened them to stare hard at Charon. "Why are we down here? Did you really think we'd have a quick fuck in the middle of the meeting?" Jaret pointed in the direction of the others.

Charon grinned. "No. I wanted to talk to you in private because I don't trust them. At all. I'm not sure I want to join this merry band of warriors. Maybe I will. You've made a compelling argument a number of times about joining your side in the war. I hear you. I know my involvement may be inevitable. But defeating Styx and then having to succumb to Council authority? Uh, no thanks."

"But—" Jaret stopped himself. Charon already knew every word about to come out of Jaret's mouth. No use going over the same territory. Jaret stepped forward and pressed his chest against Charon's, looking up into his gorgeous eyes. "Got it." He ran a hand down Charon's chest. "You do you." His fingers traced Charon's hardening cock. "Until we solve the problem, though, nothing else can happen."

Jaret spun around and hurried at vampiric speed back up the stairs into the palace before Charon could catch him. As he sat, the others peered at him in anticipation of hearing what had happened. But he waited in silence until Charon meandered back into the room and took a seat. Both looked at the assembled vampires as if nothing had occurred except a quick bathroom break.

Only Brady creased his forehead at Jaret, a twinkle in his eye indicating he knew his friend had experienced something odd.

"Are we back to business?" Harriet asked.

"Yeah. Unity. Magic place." Jaret gave a thumbs up.

Thomas began to speak when a flash of blinding yellow light lit up the room and sent all the vampires blasting out of their chairs and against the walls. Jaret last remembered watching Brady fly across the room like a rag doll before the world went dark.

Part Four

Chaos

CHAPTER ELEVEN

CARNAGE IN ITALY

1 MARCH 2019
Naples, Italy

First, a sense of being in his body returned to Jaret. Then, an ability to move his fingers followed by his hands, arms, and legs. He hesitated to open his eyes but blinked and looked around after he figured out he was intact. He expected to see the blown-out carnage of a bomb blast with all of Blenheim Palace in tatters and parts of his friends spread throughout the rubble.

Instead, nothing in the room looked any different, save for the fact each vampire and their chair had blasted across the room and smashed them into a wall. As Jaret regained consciousness, so did the others. They each stared at one another in wonder. They blinked and took in their surroundings. Jaret was relieved to see each vampire was also unharmed.

Except when he turned to account for Charon, who had been sitting next to him. An obliterated chair and the imprint of someone slamming into the wall remained a few feet from Jaret but no vampire. No Charon. Gone.

"Fuck." Brady uttered. "What happened? How long were we out?"

Harriet stared out a window before turning around. "Several hours. The sun approaches." She walked over and helped Catherine to her feet. Soon, everyone stood around the table while Xavier called forth Council magic to explain the situation.

An image of last night's scene popped before them, as if a surveillance camera had recorded what happened in 3-D. They sat having their meeting when a Council alert popped up before them, which Jaret had not seen because only Council members had the ability to view them. One second the four Council members turned their heads toward the message and then the yellow orb exploded like a bomb. The image launched forward, presumably to moments ago, when Charon first woke.

The vision showed Charon leap to his feet in alarm, glance

around, and then sprint out of the room. Mere seconds later the others woke. The scene vanished when it caught up to real time.

"So what did your little communication say before your own orb tried to murder us all?" Jaret asked.

"An alert about a vampire death." Thomas frowned. "I didn't see anything else, did you?" He looked at the others for an answer, but they shook their heads.

Catherine muttered a spell and waved her hands in the air, calling forth her Council magic to get the orb to reappear. Across from Jaret, Brady flinched in anticipation of another bomb going off. His reaction caused Jaret and then Brady to laugh despite the moment.

The Council members stared in terror at the message within the orb, still unviewable to Jaret or Brady.

"What?" Jaret asked.

"Annihilation." Xavier whispered.

Thomas took a deep breath. "Something slaughtered all vampires living in Italy. Ten of them. Dead in a flash. Our orb exploded because the magic couldn't handle power within the message. We need to go. Now."

They moved toward the exits in a hurry, except for Harriet who first cast a spell to repair the walls and chairs of the old palace. They hurried across Europe with vampiric speed, arriving in Naples as the sun prepared to appear over the horizon. Catherine and Harriet owned an estate nearby, complete with a hidden cellar with luxurious beds for the vampires. She and Harriet retired to one nook and bed, Thomas and Xavier to another.

"I don't want to hang alone." Brady glanced at Jaret with concern as he spoke.

Jaret grabbed his friend's hand and pulled him into a niche, where they fell asleep on top of the sheets, still holding hands.

Upon waking the next evening, the historian in Jaret wanted to explore the nearby excavations of Pompeii, where he had never been but about which he had read a great deal. Strange, the power of the mind to seek the routine and normal amid chaos and uncertainty. Gone were sorrows about Anthony, anger about the placid Council, or fears about the impending war. He sought to become a nighttime tourist.

Jaret meandered through the ruins, marveling at how he stepped upon stone streets created during the Roman Empire. He gawked at various sites where intricate tile floors remained intact. He paused to commemorate the dead while viewing casts made of their dying bodies after they were frozen in ash for centuries. Their bodies had decayed, leaving an imprint in the hardened stone. Archeologists had filled the spaces with plaster to get a rendering of what happened when the volcano lava engulfed the city.

His mind felt refreshed and ready to tackle Council business after time alone with Darth and history. When Thomas arrived and ushered Jaret to follow, they did so in silence until seated in the dining room above their nighttime chambers, where again their little conclave gathered.

"Everyone, report." Catherine then turned her attention to Jaret and Brady. "We forced ourselves to wake very early, except for Xavier of course, to investigate what happened."

Harriet nodded. "As we saw from yesterday's alert, I found three vampires in Rome, their heads appearing to have exploded from within and their bodies intact. I destroyed them and left after finding nothing helpful by way of evidence."

Thomas and Catherine confirmed the same from their reconnaissance. Both told of ten dead vampires and no clue except on the body of one. "Unlike the others," Catherine explained, "he'd been moved into the baptistry across from the Leaning Tower of Pisa. Styx had lain him out as an offering and signed his name in blood upon his stomach."

"And everyone concealed the deed?" Xavier asked, which the Council members confirmed.

"You're still fucking around with hiding from humans first? Seriously?" Jaret asked.

Xavier rolled his eyes before speaking. "Out of touch Council, with our rules and whatnot. Why would we worry about sending humans into a tizzy? Adding hysterical people afraid and searching for us—nothing sounds more brilliant. We should film everything and post a link online for all the world to see. Maybe everyone else can find Styx and let us off the hook."

Jaret ignored the sarcasm, at least happy Xavier was engaged in the seriousness of the matter at long last. "So what does this mean? We need to go."

"Go where?" Xavier asked in return. "Styx is pushing for the end game, and we need to move fast. But we don't know anything else."

"Can I go explore? See if I learn anything from Montgomery?" Jaret waited for their typical refusal but instead they assented.

Finding a good portal to channel the magical energy proved easy in Italy. The death and destruction in Pompeii wrought by Mount Vesuvius centuries ago continued to capture the magic of pain and terror within the ruins. This location provided enough energy to combine with Jaret's sorcery to send his spirit high into the atmosphere, flying across the ocean and moments later slamming him into the sanctuary in Montgomery. Styx and his people had disappeared. There was nothing for him to learn in Alabama.

Cleared out. Gone. Nothing remained of Styx or of an indication he ever lurked in the location. Jaret shot into the air, swirling around in an attempt to locate other information but came up empty. Jaret screamed in rage as he forced his spirit to whip back into his body, where he came to his senses, still shrieking and surrounded by the other vampires. He was incensed that the evil vampire got away again.

"He's gone. Fuck." Jaret leapt to his feet. "Let's go."

"Where?" Catherine asked.

Jaret waved his arms in the air. "You four possess so much

fucking Council magic and monitoring bullshit, but when we need tangible plans, nothing comes to you? Are you fucking kidding me?"

Harriet took a deep breath and started to answer when the yellow orb of a Council alert materialized before them, for some reason allowing Jaret and Brady to see its presence but still without the ability to read the message. Brady and Jaret ducked, expecting the thing to blow up but nothing happened.

The Council members stared at each other in alarm. Thomas shook his head, Xavier stared in horror, and Harriet and Catherine grabbed each other's hands.

"It isn't working," Catherine whispered.

"What's not working?" Jaret asked.

The Council looked back and forth at one another, no one saying a word.

"What?" Jaret shouted. "Jesus fucking Christ."

Thomas began to say something but before Jaret could hear, another message appeared before everyone, in a form Brady and Jaret could read. A note, signed by Charon:

Well, your war packs a big wallop. Come to Savannah and see how well your precious Council has protected us. I'll be waiting.

Brady pointed to where the Council orb had floated a moment ago. "You already know what Charon means?"

Xavier nodded. "Come."

Despite their magic and vampire ability, and regardless of the emergency, even the Vampire Council and Jaret's magic could only move them so fast from Italy back to the United States. They arrived in Savannah with little time to spare before the sun rose to force them to shelter.

As they settled into a crypt because no one owned property here and because they had no time to make their customary advance arrangements, Jaret questioned the Council again.

"Shouldn't we go to Charon first?" Jaret asked, staring hard at Thomas because he was the most sympathetic to Jaret's point of view.

"And let the sun incinerate us?" Xavier responded.

Jaret wanted to retort with something smart-ass of his own, but Xavier was right. They needed to wait until the following evening.

But Jaret felt guilty so sent a magical missive to Charon: *We're here. See you tomorrow.*

They're fools if they think they can win. Charon responded.

We don't have any other choice.

I do.

Jaret left Charon alone for the night and drifted to sleep, feeling like a dirty, sinister vampire straight out of Bram Stoker's *Dracula* as he lay on the grimy stone floor, surrounded by other vampires and nasty bones. "Fuck me! Shit!" He swore as a rat raced across his leg right before he drifted to sleep.

Jaret woke and gagged from the stench of the crypt. Jaret launched himself off the floor and brushed himself off. "Jesus fucking Christ!" he screamed. "I can't take it. Are you serious? A fucking crypt?" He pointed his finger at each Council member one by one. "You killed people. Inaction. Stupidity. Vampires are dying, and now we live like fucking Bela Legosi. No, wrong. His castle was nicer."

Jaret stormed out before anyone was able to respond and walked at a swift pace around the cemetery to gain control before he lost his mind. Darth circled him, jumped at him with her front paws, and gave him a few licks on the face. She was the one steady influence on him, always able to calm his nerves and ground him. She raced forward and disappeared, returning seconds later with a stick. They played fetch for a minute before Brady meandered up, stepping with caution toward Jaret.

"You okay?" Brady asked.

"Do I seem okay?"

Brady nodded. "I hear you. Dumb question. Anyway, the Council went to meet with Charon. I thought you should know."

Brady turned to leave, so Jaret followed, whistling for Darth to join them. Before the three caught up to the Vampire Fuckers, Jaret's new name for the Council. Jaret motioned for them to slow down and remain a half block behind the Council members. They walked in silence. Jaret guessed their destination before they got there. They headed to the house Charon had rented for his party, the spot where Styx murdered the basketball player.

Charon stood on the front porch, leaning against the railing and staring down hard as the vampires assembled on the street below. He pointed to Jaret. "I need to speak to him before any of you get closer."

The brave-in-charge-Council-Fuckers said nothing as they waited for Jaret to comply. Jaret climbed the stairs and walked inside, knowing Charon would follow.

Charon touched Jaret on the back and guided him into a side parlor, where he closed the door and stepped in front of Jaret. Charon reached over and brushed a strand of Jaret's long hair out of his face. "I don't know what to do," Charon stammered.

"Why are we here?" Jaret asked. "What happened?"

"I'll show you. I'll show the Council. I needed to see you first. I suppose we need those four assholes, but I hate them. They're fools."

"You won't get any argument from me." Jaret resisted an impulse to fall into Charon's arms for comfort. "I'm lost too. The Council acts like they have a plan, but vampires are dying and they still plod along. Is that what happened? Did more of your boys die?"

Charon took a deep breath. "One of mine. More dead ones are with his body—vampires I don't know."

"We better go."

Charon grabbed Jaret by the arm to stop him as he headed toward the door. "I needed to see you first, though. I—" Charon stopped himself. "I don't think we can let the Council lead anymore."

"Agreed." Jaret nodded.

"And—" Charon stared at the ceiling for an answer. "You and I are friends? Right?"

Jaret tilted his head and looked at Charon.

"I don't do shit like get deep feelings for a friend. People either like me or not. Fuck them. I thought, maybe, though, we had a bond."

Jaret understood. "Our lives are torn apart by a war with an unknowable outcome. Anyway, yeah. I consider you a friend. A maddening one. I'm not sure I trust you without reservation." Charon smiled at Jaret's comment. "Yet we're friends."

Charon nodded and reached over to take Jaret's hand. He gripped him as they walked through the nineteenth-century house, up the stairs and into a large back bedroom.

The scene in the room froze Jaret in terror. In a gruesome scene worthy of a serial-killer movie, five vampires were laid side by side on a king-sized bed. All were dressed, postmortem Jaret guessed, in black-tie attire, with no sign of injury except their lifeless eyes staring back.

"I don't know any of them except him." Charon reached out to touch the foot of one dead vampire. "Alex. He left the other day. Said he needed to get away. I don't know why." Charon shrugged. "When I first captured my boys, they agreed to remain confined in my castle. But after I turned them to vampires they enjoyed getting out. They remained obedient but had freedom to go outside my palace. I could have called Alex back, forced him to stay under my protection, but—" Charon stopped and choked back a sob. "I didn't."

"Pretty clear—" Jaret stopped himself from finishing the thought. He realized the words would sound like a jab and offer nothing to the conversation.

But Charon had read his mind. "Yeah. I know. My staying neutral in the war or complying with Styx's demands won't work. But I'm not on the Council's side either."

"They're blind fuckers. Me, either. Think of them as a necessary evil."

"Agreed."

Charon and Jaret left and went to a front bedroom where they opened a window and motioned for the vampires to join them. The four Council Fuckers went up the porch stairs and stepped inside. Brady remained in the street and asked Jaret to stay in the window. When the Council arrived on the second floor, Charon led them to the crime scene while Jaret leaned over the sill toward Brady.

"You cool if I stay here?" Brady asked.

"Of course."

"I don't want, you know, to see whatever." Brady jerked his head upward to indicate the second floor.

"You don't need to. Keep Darth company."

Brady nodded and turned to see Darth sitting next to him,

wagging her tail.

Jaret walked down the hall and sensed a vampire, but not a threat. A comforting presence surrounded him, as when Anthony came to him. Jaret shook his head to clear away the feeling.

Jaret joined the assembled fuckers and Charon in the bedroom. One of them had torn open a dead vampire's shirt to reveal the cause of death. One by one they undressed the other seven corpses to find their hearts ripped out, with scorch marks to indicate they were killed by incineration.

"Styx escalated faster than anticipated." Harriet looked at her fellow Council members with alarm as she spoke. "First the killing in Savannah, next Italy. Now this." She motioned toward the bed. "Is our magic working?"

"Styx is worse than expected but we need to stick with our strategy." Xavier spoke with a quivering voice.

Jaret tried to stop himself but lost control. "What the fuck is wrong with you people?" he shouted. "Stick with your strategy? If you really have a plan, which I seriously doubt, it's not working." He pounded the end of the bed for emphasis. "Dead, dead, dead. All dead. Murdered by Styx. Hey! Newsflash! You're losing the fucking war. And I am done. *Done*! I am done sitting on the sideline while your ineptitude murders vampires. Done."

Jaret stormed out of the room with Charon following him. They got to the first floor when he heard Thomas shout right behind them. "Stop!"

Jaret whipped around and glared at Thomas and Xavier standing before him.

"Jaret, you have to believe we hear you. I agree with you!" Thomas exclaimed. "But there's more going on. Styx is powerful. The danger is real. We'd never sacrifice vampires if we thought anything else would do."

"He killed them. He's slaughtering us!" Jaret shook his head at them as the blood tears streamed down his face. "He murdered Anthony. This is more than a little sacrifice here and there. You're getting annihilated, and I'm done."

Catherine moved down the stairs toward them with a stern expression. Her commanding presence silenced Jaret. "Harriet will take care of the dead vampires and the scene at this house. All of you, listen to me." One by one, she looked at each of them to get their attention. "I'm not going to ask you two to trust us," Catherine said to Jaret and Charon, "but you don't know a damn thing. We've kept information back and will continue to do so out of necessity. I know how the situation looks, but you aren't right. And you don't grasp the full danger."

"No! Not at all! Dead vampires seem right in line with a great plan of attack." Charon lashed out.

Jaret nodded assent.

"And what if I told you he could have killed us all in one fell swoop without our efforts? We need to plot this out, lure him into a defeat, or he could win in seconds. Do you think we're so stupid as to sit around while he picks us off, one by one? You two are not so superior and mighty. And we're not stupid. Now shut the fuck up and listen."

Jaret understood more than he had ever before how Catherine had commanded a financial empire in France amid the French Revolution. He felt stymied and contrite.

Charon threw his arms in the air. "What?"

"We're studying location," Catherine stated. "The Council has narrowed the plan. We'll move soon. You're right. We can't wait any longer. Before you two fools go off, do you really know what to do? Do you have any clue?"

Jaret shrugged. "Fight. All-out war. Who gives a fuck? Gloves are off. We're losing. Time to launch the nukes."

Catherine shook her head at them and continued. "Naïve. Petulant. Your power has protected you thus far, but Styx can win if we play this wrong."

Harriet joined them and stepped forward. Jaret respected her always stern yet calm demeanor. She reached out with her hands and wrapped her fingers around a forearm on both Jaret and Charon. "So much anger." She glanced around the room. "He wants us divided, shouting, and screaming at each other. Come. Five minutes won't change a thing."

They shuffled into the front room and took seats, except for Harriet who stood before them in preparation for a lecture.

"I know how angry you are," Harriet said. "I know our secrecy maddens you. I accept your frustration. But Catherine is right. There is more going on than meets the eye. You going off angry will not win this war. Here's the painful, bitter truth. More will die. We coped with the death so far as inevitable, because preventing the murders would have revealed our true power. We didn't want to send Styx back into hiding so he could reemerge in another five centuries. He is winning battles, not the war."

Harriet glanced out the window at the dark night, addressing the room but with her mind somewhere else, in another time. "I wandered fields for years. Helping where I could. But I suffered as I watched the vile white men slaughter my people. Rape them. Kill them. Torture and separate families." She turned back to stare at Jaret and Charon. "Don't think I don't understand. You know nothing of my pain. I obeyed the Council because if they killed me, even more slaves would have perished. I disagreed with the passive stance, like you, but trusted the process. Know what? Maybe Anthony was right to control me. Because if vampires annihilated the South, then what? Vampire rule? When vampires played the situation out and secretly funded abolitionist organizations, they helped lead to the South's defeat. In a painful, slow process making me want to pull out my hair, humans chose progress. I somehow survived watching Jim Crow and the KKK the same way. Civil Rights Movement. We live in the shadows. We help where we can but let humanity seek progress so no vampire dictatorship takes hold. Or worse, what if they discovered our presence and hunted us down?"

Harriet shook her head. "You might continue to disagree and dismiss me. Fine. But anything you do may set us back instead of move us forward." Again she turned her attention to Jaret and Charon. "I know what you're thinking, so go do your deed and we'll see where you lead us."

Without another word the assembly dispersed, with the Council going who knows where and Charon and Jaret remaining together.

CHAPTER TWELVE

KILLING SPREE

3 MARCH 2019
Montgomery, AL

"You'd think as a vampire I'd go anywhere without worrying about the social climate," Jaret said to Charon as he joined him on the veranda of a vacant lake home they'd occupied the previous night for their lodging. Darth sprinted into the nearby woods.

"What are you talking about?" Charon asked from his seat on a lounge chair facing into the trees.

"The rural South." Jaret pointed to the landscape before them. "Conservative Republican country. Evangelicals. They hate us."

"Vampires?" Charon asked with a smile.

Jaret laughed. "No. Fags."

"Ah, so you mean you still harbor those fears from being human and gay." Charon shrugged. "I always figured I could beat the shit out of anyone or get away fast so I never worried too much."

"You never worry about anything, do you?"

Charon squinted at Jaret. "Not very often. Sometimes a situation calls for worry, though."

"Now?"

Again, the slight shrug. "For sure," Charon said. "I thought I made my concern clear last night."

"Are you backing out of our plan?"

The previous evening, they had searched for Styx and discovered a new army of humans under his thrall. Styx had lured them by pretending to be an evangelical pastor wanting to help parents whose kids claimed to be gay or lesbian. He promised to turn them straight. Charon and Jaret decided to annihilate these followers of Styx. After they arrived in Montgomery and before the sun sent them to bed, the two plotted their move. They felt Harriet had offered them a blank check to do whatever they wanted.

Charon shook his head with sharp jerks. "No choice but to act. Still, we have a lot to concern ourselves with. I told you, Styx is nuts. I've never experienced someone crazier."

Jaret nodded. "Plus, we're operating with limited information. We know Styx gets discombobulated when faced with too much emotion. We *did* figure out how to lure him to a spot. But the Council kept something from us. They agreed with our theories, even though they pretended to try to stop us. Still. Why not tell us their whole plan?"

"You don't know?" Charon looked at Jaret with surprise.

"Know what?"

"Styx is using me as a pawn. And he thinks he can do the same with you. But the Council is doing the same thing in return."

"They're being used by Styx?"

"No." Charon came over to stand next to Jaret on the edge of the porch. He turned Jaret to face him. "Using us as pawns."

The idea stung Jaret. He never considered they would manipulate him. He believed they honored him as a friend but kept secrets because of an ancient Council code. But Charon's opinion made too much sense—the Council agreed with so much of what Jaret said but kept him at arm's length; they monitored him but allowed him to test their rules. He sensed they kept a secret whenever they met with him, but he never came close to learning the truth.

"So what should we do?" Jaret asked.

"Business as usual."

"Really?" Jaret frowned. "Serve as their puppets?"

"Harriet's story—she led us along like donkeys after a carrot."

Jaret giggled. "There's an ancient reference for you. They always reprimand me for doing my own thing. I'm supposed to trust them. They scold me if I defy even the slightest direction from them. Then last night they change course. We signaled plans to fight their archenemy against their wishes, and all they did was tell us a story and send us on our merry way."

Charon grabbed Jaret's hand and pulled them onto a path in the forest. They followed Darth, who trotted back to them, waited for Jaret to pat her on the head, then sprinted away.

"Think of the situation this way," Charon said. "We still believe we have to act." Charon leaned into Jaret. "If the Council intends to fight this war and defeat Styx, then either we have to lure them into our plan or they're manipulating us into their strategy. Either way, we want to kill Styx."

Jaret smiled. "When did you become the rational one? I've been trying to convince you to listen to reason, but here you pull me along. What changed your mind?"

Charon stopped them in a quiet clearing and leaned against a tree. "I always listened to you," he answered, "even when you thought I dismissed the gravity of the war. But it's never been my style to join the crowd or participate in the ole group think. You reminded me of when Styx forced me to play the game of becoming a vampire or dying. I won. Yet the memory had me recalling how fucking weird he was. He controlled me, and until I stole his knowledge of magic, I felt imprisoned. Until that moment, I never realized how captured he had made me feel."

"You think he allowed you to steal the magic?"

Charon shook his head. "No. I think I got one over on him there. Which explains why he keeps me at arm's length. He wanted me in this war on his side but thought he'd hold supreme power over me. When I snatched the knowledge of sorcery, I gained more advantage than he had intended. You know in *Batman* how Joker gets the upper hand because he doesn't give a shit? Lives for chaos? Doesn't even care if he ends up in prison or dead, so long as he pisses off Batman? That's Styx."

Jaret grinned. "I always thought that was you."

"You think me a total fiend? I'm more complicated. Closer to maybe Penguin or Riddler." Charon giggled at his comparisons.

"Or Catwoman."

Charon punched Jaret in the arm. "I'm not a girl."

"Nice sexism. You *do* use sexuality to your advantage and live a complicated life of crime without being a total ass. You started the analogy."

"Speaking of which, the Joker and Styx are not complicated. Death and destruction for their own amusement."

"But we still go ahead?"

Charon nodded. "Yep. At least our brand of chaos will off a bunch of fucking homophobes."

Jaret tossed his head back and laughed.

Charon grinned and cupped the back of Jaret's head in his

hand. "You have the most beautiful laugh."

Jaret blushed and stepped back, though Charon held tight to keep him a step away. With his free hand, Charon reached over and with his index finger traced the outline of Jaret's lips.

"I thought we had a job to do." Jaret protested and went rigid. His mind told him to pull away; his body fought to stay put.

Charon stepped toward Jaret, releasing his head but intoxicating Jaret with the proximity. "Stop resisting."

Thank the sex gods, Charon always moved too fast for Jaret, which snapped Jaret's mind back to reality. He laughed and moved toward the path.

"What's so funny?" Charon asked when he caught up to Jaret.

"Smooth operator. Luring me in. So innocent and completely hot. But you always go to a hard push, pun intended, and—*boom*! I remember what a fiend you are."

"I'm not playing some game with you."

"I know. You've never concealed your agenda or who you are. But you also can't accept me. I don't do one-night stands. I don't have the emotion to survive them. I fall in instalove at every turn. Steve and I, back in high school when I met him, went from not knowing each other to planning our retirement in about, oh, one night. Every time I went on a first date, I decided to marry the guy. I'm sure I freaked guys out with how fast I fell."

Jaret glanced at Charon to see him grinning.

"So you've fallen for me?" Charon asked.

"No. Stop. Don't go there." Jaret laughed, unsure if he was talking to himself or Charon. "I've never hidden my lust. You have a sex-on-wheels allure. But you'd break my heart. I could never bang you and walk away, and you don't want to commit."

Charon halted and yanked Jaret's arms so they faced each other. "Are you saying if I *did* commit, you'd be with me?"

Jaret froze. Trapped. Unsure of his own response. As he stared at Charon, a sensation swept over him, the feeling of protection and love he had felt with Anthony.

Ah, talk about instalove. The tall, blond vampire with long hair who swooped in to save him from a horde of football players. Jaret's heart tore open, wanting Anthony by his side to protect him, guide the way, and yell at him for defying the Council.

"Whew," Jaret wiped at a tear. "You almost had me. Almost. Good thing I remembered Anthony. I miss him. I think I succumb to your wiles because of the hole he left." Jaret reached up and patted Charon on the cheek. "You could fulfill the sex need, but what then?"

"With me, that's all you need." Charon grinned, his charming, smart-ass, I'm-so-cute grin. Jaret slapped him harder.

"Come on. We agreed to an act of war, not sex."

As they hurried down the path and then broke into a vampire run toward the city and Styx's church, Jaret again felt Anthony following him. Perhaps Anthony's spirit protected him even in death. Jaret was comforted because his lover had pulled him from the abyss of carnal pleasure with Charon. Concentrating on the war would distract Jaret from sex for the evening.

They arrived at the church to find the sanctuary full of people. A group of Styx's human minions were assembled, mesmerized into a cult, singing and worshipping with vacant stares. Jaret scanned his senses for another vampire, especially Styx, but found nothing.

"I don't feel him," Charon said.

"Me neither." Jaret thought the scene absurd. "You think Styx left these people unprotected?"

"If Styx is warring against the Council, why not? They're pawns. The Council would protect innocent humans. Besides, what purpose do they serve? They worship him as some angel sent from God and are probably under a spell, but Styx could gather fools like this around him without any effort, anytime and anywhere. Maybe he enjoyed their company for a while. Perhaps he was testing his ability to take over the world by controlling humans. He figured out how to accomplish the task and left these fools for dead. In his world, everyone is expendable."

"Yeah, no matter what, I say we go ahead. We get a two for one. Fuck Styx and fuck the Council by killing humans."

"Then fuck each other!" Charon exclaimed. He clapped his hands with enthusiasm.

Again, Jaret found himself laughing at the nonsense. "You go to the other side of the church and signal when ready."

Charon walked away, leaving Jaret to wonder about their

intentions. Had Jaret ever killed without discrimination before? No. He obeyed the Council. Then again, these deranged and duped fuckwads signaled their homophobic hatred. Fuck them. And they appeared to advocate for a Styx dictatorship, a stance worthy of death in Jaret's opinion.

At Charon's whistle, Jaret closed his eyes and enchanted the spell. He pulled forth the energy from underneath the church's foundation and guided the force upward. He felt the same magical power coming from the rafters at Charon's manipulation. With the flick of a wrist, he released the power and opened his eyes to watch the church explode.

He stood numb to the scene, watching the conflagration when Charon sauntered to his side.

"You're a fucking murderer. That was kind of a Joker move." Charon pointed toward the burning remnants of a church. "I doubt we abided by Council laws here."

"Let's go, Catwoman." Jaret turned and hurried back to the forest path, where he slowed to a human walk and patted Darth on the head when she greeted his return.

Charon joined their hike. "Are you sad?"

Jaret scrunched his brow. "No."

"Then what? You should be happy! Dead homophobes. Dead Styx underlings. The war escalated. But you seem morose."

"I feel weird defying the Council. But justified. Listen, I don't miss those assholes we torched. But they were humans. Good riddance but I can't gloat like you."

Charon giggled. "So you don't want to become my accomplice in the Christmas Eve murders?"

"Are you still planning to continue your weird ritual?" Jaret shook his head.

Every year on Christmas Eve, Charon selected a pastor and murdered him. He displayed the body in the sanctuary. The serial killings had become a sensation around the nation, with fruitless manhunts every year for the killer.

"Not weird." Charon shook his head. "Pure artwork."

They returned to their borrowed house and went into a basement bedroom, where they could better hide and perhaps protect each other if someone came along. Jaret preferred separate bedrooms, but with humans wandering around during the day, Styx pissed at their exploits, and the Council monitoring them, being together was a better idea.

Jaret remained clothed and lifted Darth into a trunk for their sleeping quarters. He jumped in next to her but peered over at Charon before closing the lid. Charon stood naked in front of his own crate, erect and flicking his dick at Jaret.

Jaret rolled his eyes but smiled.

"You want some. You know you do." Charon masturbated.

Jaret watched for a few seconds as if mesmerized by a hot solo porn video but reached up to slam his lid shut as Charon's body began to shudder and the first shot of semen launched out his penis.

Jaret woke with Darth by his side and got up. He rolled his eyes at the first thing he saw: Charon's dried come splattered on the floor. He banged on Charon's lid to wake him.

The cover to Charon's makeshift coffin opened to reveal him lying there, still naked and smiling. Before he said a word, Jaret tossed him a pair of pants and pointed to the floor.

"I'll be outside waiting. Clean up your mess."

Jaret grabbed a notepad and headed to the porch, happy when Darth decided to curl up by his side instead of romping around in the woods. He jotted down notes about his plan, including the pluses and minuses. Like when he wrote a research paper or thought through big problems as a human, he weighed the options and redid the notes until he was ready to act.

Next, he sent a missive via magical courier to Brady.

Montgomery, Alabama, on a lake. I'll flare some magic to lead you here. Come now if you want to help. Or be a Council tool.

I'm no one's bitch, fucker. Be there soon.

"I need to feed." Jaret jumped when he heard Charon behind him. Charon laughed. "So lost in your thoughts you ignored your warning senses?"

"Maybe you don't send off a warning bell."

Charon leaned over and kissed Jaret on the top of his head. "Because you're infatuated with me."

Jaret swatted at Charon's arm. "Go eat. I'm creating our next steps. Brady will be here soon."

"Did you invite him so he can help you control against wanting to suck my dick? Or, you agree with having a three way!"

Jaret pointed toward the forest. "Go."

Jaret finished his notes and felt confident in his strategy. The sensation of Anthony being nearby swept over him. "Are you watching over me?" he asked the air. No response, except the sensation remained. "I hope so. I'd get a little comfort if I knew you at least felt guilty for leaving me behind and so watched over me. But your presence won't get me to obey the Council."

"I thought Styx was the loony tune?" Brady appeared next to Jaret and took a seat. "I arrive to find you chatting with the trees."

"I knew you were here. I was talking to Anthony. I have a history with ghosts, remember?"

"Is he here?" Brady's eyes grew wide.

Jaret shrugged. "Not sure. I feel like he watches over me."

Brady nodded and sat in a chair next to him. "I bet he does. What's the plan?"

"Charon should be back in a minute then we'll discuss."

As if cue, Charon stood before them and spoke. "I'll start because Jaret doesn't want me proposing this to you. My idea gets him all hot and bothered."

"Stop!" Jaret yelled and held up his hand but grinned at what was to come.

Charon smiled and winked at Brady. "We need focus and energy, and nothing gets the juices flowing like spilling the juices."

Charon knelt in front of Brady and grabbed both his knees. "You. Me. Him. Hot threesome, then we go about this business of a war."

Brady barked a laugh, pointing back and forth at himself and then Jaret. "The two of us? Sex? Absolutely not." He shook his head back and forth with urgency.

Charon scrunched his brow. "Are you as prudish as him?"

"Nah." Brady shook his head. "But we're mates. BFFs. Getting sex involved would be so weird. No, the worst idea *ever*!" Brady laughed along with Jaret.

Charon appeared confused as to why the two of them found the proposal to be about the funniest thing they had heard.

Charon traced a finger up Brady's thigh and circled his crotch. "Then I guess you and me alone, baby."

Brady cackled even harder. He reached down and cupped Charon's chin. "Oh my God, you're just like Jaret described! Incorrigible. Like a fiend but so fucking sexy. I trust him." He jerked his head toward Jaret. "He says you're not a good idea. So I think you're not a good idea. Sorry."

Charon, with a giant grin plastered on his face, stood to go over and lean against a post. "Wow. I mean, wow. Single vampire boys with the world at their feet, but with no ability to let loose. What has the world come to? Is this some influence by the Vampire Council? You know, they practice monogamy like evangelical Christians are supposed to. So you two want to conform to their puritanical world. Weird."

"No!" Jaret and Brady shouted at the same time.

Brady held up his hand as if sitting in a third-grade classroom so Charon acknowledged him. "Brady?"

"For the record," Brady announced, "I've banged a number of very hot gentlemen since becoming a vampire of the realm." He gave a crooked grin. "Yeah, Jaret's a prude. Always has been. Not me. I've engaged in nothing but one-night stands with no intention of seeing them again. But I'm not subjecting myself to you." He pointed at Charon.

"Too bad. You don't know what you're missing. We can't keep all this sexual tension pent up and fight a war. Too distracting."

"Speaking of the war—" Jaret found a moment to get them back on track. "—we should discuss." He waved his notes overhead.

"What you got there?" Charon asked. "A term paper?"

"My plan. Sit down and get serious." He motioned for Charon to sit. Surprising Jaret, Charon obeyed by plopping down and leaning his back against a porch post. He wrapped his arms around his knees. "To recap the obvious, we want to lure Styx to a vortex to heighten our power against him. We'll need our combined magic," Jaret pointed back and forth between himself and Charon, "plus Council magic to overcome him. This presents three rather major problems. Well, maybe just two. The first would be where to go, but I figured out a location. We're left with how the fuck do we get Styx there? And, how the fuck do we drag the Council into our war plan?"

"I'm getting bored at this rerun," Charon said. He rolled his eyes, causing Brady to bark out a laugh.

"Don't encourage him." Jaret gave a mock frown to Brady. "I researched and visited a number of places. Nothing compares with mystical power and magical energy to Notre Dame Cathedral in Paris. I can't explain why with great certainty, but the cathedral is a religious shrine, has seen horrible acts of cruelty and wonderful blessings. It's old as fuck. Revered. Yet has darkness because of the way some people have been mistreated by the Catholic Church. And there's the whole conflict during the French Revolution when they defaced statues and went hard after the church. So much energy is captured at the spot. Perfect for us."

Charon nodded. "I agree. Go on."

"I also think luring him there will be easier than we first thought. Charon, he needs you. Wants you. And he thinks he already has you on his side. He believes you continue to fear him."

"I *never* feared him," Charon cut in with a sharp rebuke.

"I know. So you set up a meeting with him, maybe playing on his erroneous belief. Figure out a reason to do so in Paris, and he'll come."

Charon weighed Jaret's idea for a minute before he responded. "Let's say I can summon some reason to pull him halfway across the world without his being suspicious. What if he detects my treachery? What if he knows it's a ruse?"

"He's powerful," Jaret answered, "but is he *omnipotent*? I

think we've seen weaknesses. There are gaps in his ability and knowledge. He exudes a dominance he doesn't really possess. I doubt he can read your intent. You'll need to sell him on you. You already won him over once to become a vampire. Try again."

"And the Council?" Brady asked. "Say Charon's charm brings Styx to Paris. The Council won't abide by the plan. If we tell them in advance, you already know their answer: *Trust us. We know better. Wait for our signal; then we'll act.*" Brady spoke in a mocking tone. "I wouldn't put past their MO to blow Notre Dame up to stop your plan beforehand."

Charon laughed. "Yeah, they'd nuke the church to make their point."

"Come on, guys. Be serious." Jaret took a deep breath. "They piss me off too. But have we ever seen them blow shit up? Xavier reveres Notre Dame. Besides, you do ask a good question about the Council. Here's how we get their compliance. We don't tell them. We never utter a word about our intentions. No advance notice. They can't know Styx will be there to meet Charon until the meeting takes place."

Charon nodded. "Makes sense. We have some details to work out. But you got yourself a plan. I know I have to participate. We all do. I don't think we'll come up with a better strategy, and we're losing time to get anything done."

Charon's swift agreement surprised Jaret, given his previous reluctance and distaste for obedience to anyone. Jaret squinted at him.

"So easy, huh?" Jaret asked. "What gives? No more fighting me?"

Charon giggled and got to his feet. He walked over and rustled the top of Jaret's head. "I'm not always an asshole. You're smart. I agree with you, so accept the compliment."

"Okay." Jaret spoke but with a hesitant voice.

Charon laughed louder and knelt between Brady and Jaret. He reached out an arm to each one, cupping their heads with his hand and pulling them toward his own between them. He stopped guiding them in when Jaret resisted, a foot away from all three smashing their heads together.

Brady grinned. "What are you doing?"

Jaret shot his friend a look. "Wipe the grin off your face. You encourage him again."

Charon took advantage and yanked their faces together, causing Jaret to jump partway out of his chair as his cheek pressed against Brady's and Charon licked them both across the face. Charon let go and jumped away, laughing as Brady and Jaret tumbled out of their chairs in a heap.

"Can't you jack off and get these fantasies out of your system?" Jaret asked Charon as he and Brady got to their feet.

"Why fantasize when the real thing stands before you?"

"Because we said no," Brady answered.

"I heard you. You can't blame a guy for trying."

Jaret pointed at Charon. "You live up to every stereotype of a gay guy. Like all guys, you think first, second, and third with your penis. Then because you're gay and can shun all convention, you fuck, suck, and come with every man you encounter."

"Guilty as charged. And proud of myself." Charon laughed again.

Brady stared at Jaret with a huge grin. "You told me he thinks of nothing but sex. I figured you exaggerated since you're a prude. But you told me the truth. I mean, we plotted a war that very well could kill us. And he bookends the discussion with sex before and after."

Charon shrugged. "Right. Because I want to win the war to make sure I continue to enjoy constant sex. Not hard to figure out. Pun intended."

The banter continued a few minutes longer when their senses buzzed about an approaching vampire, coming at a frantic speed through the woods. The three vampires spun around in a defensive posture as Jordan, Charon's number two, sped through the trees and halted mere steps before them.

"Boss man!" He stared hard at Charon. "Come. Now." His eyes lit with terror as he spoke.

After Jordan turned and raced away with Charon in tow, Jaret realized blood was dripping from the young vampire's hands.

PART FIVE

COUNCIL TREACHERY

CHAPTER THIRTEEN

MOUNTAIN ATTACK

4 MARCH 2019
Nederland, CO

Rushing through the frigid Rocky Mountains reminded Jaret of the first time he watched *The Shining*. He and his friends had snuck to watch the movie during a sleepover, which scared the crap out of them, much to their delight. His pounding heart, the snow falling hard, and the desolate mountain landscape had Jaret worried Jack Nicholson's character would pop out from behind a tree with an axe to hack at him. He knew as a vampire he could kill him without any problem, but what if the batch of fucked-up ghosts from the movie appeared along with Nicholson? What if the gang of crazy spirits, once trapped at the hotel, were somehow released into the wild? Then what? Jaret had plenty of experience with ghosts fucking with him and loathed the idea.

Jaret shook his head, snapping back to a reality which was worse than his fantasy. As they approached a hidden tunnel leading deep inside James Peak to Charon's concealed castle, the blood trail running down the tunnel and into the palace entrance chilled Jaret to the bone. Much worse than a fictional story.

Jaret and Brady had stayed a respectful distance behind Jordan and Charon, sensing the need for them to be alone. At vampiric speed, the journey from Montgomery to Colorado took mere minutes but felt like hours because of Jaret's fear. Jaret could hear Jordan babbling incoherent words the entire way in a frantic, high-pitched voice. Charon tried to calm Jordan but failed so far.

The blood on Jordan's hands when he had arrived in Alabama haunted Jaret, and here in the tunnel the blood trail heightened Jaret's dread. They slowed to a human walk as they descended to the palace entrance, always glittering, opulent, and pristine, but today the gorgeous setting seemed out of touch with the blood smear running down the middle of the marble floor.

When Jaret entered with Brady right behind him, they found Charon standing in the middle of the room. Jordan circled Charon, gesticulating in a manic frenzy and uttering incomprehensible chatter. Charon reached out and grabbed Jordan by both arms, spinning him around to stare into his eyes. "Stop. Speak so I can hear you."

"Not with them." Jordan pointed to Jaret and Brady. "Can't trust. Bad. He came in. We tried. Boss man, we tried." Jordan took a deep breath and shook his head. "Show you. I'll show you. Only you." Jordan tugged free of Charon's arms and hurried down a hallway.

"Wait here," Charon instructed. His hand trembled as he pointed for Jaret and Brady to go into a side parlor. Charon then left to follow Jordan.

Brady sat on the edge of a chair and glanced around the room. Jaret walked in slow circles. After a few minutes of silence, Jaret chuckled.

"What could possibly be funny?" Brady asked but tilted his head and smiled.

"This is the first time I think anything drove the two of us to silence, yes?"

Brady laughed and nodded. "Yeah. I even got you talking again after Henrik offed your whole family, remember? When Xavier brought me to Fremont? Even then we talked. I guess I don't know what to say. I'm kinda scared."

Jaret walked over and touched Brady's shoulder. "Me too. But I'll protect you."

"I know." Brady reached up and patted Jaret's hand. "Let's talk. Way less awkward to say something. Besides, since you broke the ice, so to speak, I have to ask, What the fuck is this place?" Brady motioned around to indicate the room and palace beyond. "We're in the middle of a fucking mountain, but it looks like the Palace of Versailles on steroids."

Jaret laughed. "Yeah, right? This place is fucking nuts. When Charon became a vampire, he created this palace as his secret hiding place. Styx taught him vampire rules but also concealed Charon from the Council. So he never had to follow Council rules. Charon wanted to make sure to hide from Council authority and humans and shit. So he built his own secret fortress inside this mountain. Then he gathered his boys, as he calls them. At first, they were human and had to agree to come here and never leave. But as you can see, they had everything one could ever want. Except freedom. Then, when this war developed, Charon converted them into vampires. But with a catch—he hid them from the Council and maintained his control over them. They became vampires obedient to him."

"He has some fucking harem? Imprisoned against their will? That's fucked. Won't the Council go after him once the war ends?"

Jaret shrugged. "Don't know. And I get why you think they're slaves. But it's more complicated. I mean, they kinda are. They also like it. They chose to be with him and have one constant gay party inside the castle. Now as vampires they get to go outside. I don't know. They enjoy their life. Jordan is so loyal. Anything and every-thing Charon ever touches gets complicated beyond belief."

"Yeah, complicated." The sound of Charon's voice frightened Brady and Jaret. "And we have a fucked-up problem tonight. Come." Charon turned and marched into the foyer.

As they hurried through the castle with Charon in the lead, Jaret watched Charon for signs of what was to come. Charon's typical bravado escaped him as the vampire walked with hunched shoulders and, more surprising, with a slight tremble in both hands. Jaret felt as if they walked from one end of Colorado to another by the time they navigated a couple hallways, two flights of stairs, and then stood inside a sizable room filled with electronic games.

Charon entered first, followed by Jaret, and Jordan had disappeared. A second later, Brady inched into the room and gasped.

Styx had assassinated two more of Charon's vampires, displaying them on top of an air hockey game. The bodies lay next to one another holding hands. They appeared peaceful except for the gouge in each chest. As with Styx's other kills, he had removed their hearts. He left a note on the edge of the game.

Jaret walked over to read the message:

Dear Boy,

I wanted to make sure you remembered me after all our time together and my giving you the wonderful gift of eternal life. Your flirting with the nasty Council hurts my feelings. Such a crude betrayal. I understand your rapture with the long-haired twink. I do. His looks could turn me gay. Perhaps capture him for your realm once we finish this business. I might agree to spare him if you comply with me.

However, you best come around to compliance and soon. Did you forget my behavior? Has it been so long you fail to remember the chaos I bring? Why, we have not even touched the tip of the iceberg as to where we are headed. Think of these two lovelies as a warning, along with the other two from Savannah. How many more boys do you want to lose before you join me?

Charon, you disappoint me. You stole my magic—I will never underestimate you again. But you best return the favor. The victors write the history. Whose side would you like to be on? Dead with the ole oppressive Council? Or alive with me?

Best to you and your decision,

Styx

"He's fucked-up," Jaret observed.

Charon pointed to the bodies behind Jaret. "Phil and Travis. Two more." Charon bent and shook his head as he stared at the ground. "And he got inside here. No one gets inside without my permission. Not even one of my men can enter unless I allow them. The Council couldn't find me. So how did he get around my defenses?"

As if on cue, Jordan raced into the room almost breathless from his distress. "I know what happened."

"What?" Charon snapped.

Jordan drew a deep breath. "Kiki saw Phil and Travis come back with a hot guy. Thought they found someone for sex or something. He didn't get past palace defenses. They brought him in."

"I thought you said no one could enter without your permission?" Jaret asked Charon.

He nodded. "True. I failed to think of someone coming here by invitation. Phil and Travis disobeyed me and died because of it." Charon turned toward Jordan. "Make sure everyone hears what happens if you disobey my rules. The rest of you could end up dead too." He returned attention to Jaret. "If I give permission for one of the boys to leave, it allows them to return. Of course, Styx could slip in with them. Stupid of me. At least my magic held. We can secure everything again, and this time without a loophole."

Jaret jumped back a foot when Charon made two fists and slammed them against both sides of his own head. "Fucking stupid."

Jaret launched at Charon and grabbed both his arms before he could hit himself again. "You could kill yourself, you know.

Stop. It won't bring them back."

Jordan came over and grabbed Charon in a tight embrace around the waist as tears streamed down his face. "Stop, Boss man. We'll figure out how to win. We have to."

"Did you fix the problem? Did you recast the spell?" Jaret asked Charon.

Charon shook his head. He kissed the top of Jordan's head and pushed him away gently before walking a few yards away, closing his eyes, and muttering under his breath. "There. Fixed."

Charon walked over to the other three vampires, who had all turned to face away from the carnage. He hugged Jordan to him and addressed Jaret and Brady. "Could you two give us a moment to remove our friends? Two doors down on the left you'll find a dining room. I'll join you shortly.

Jaret and Brady obeyed his instructions, again finding themselves alone in an opulent room, a dining room complete with a crystal chandelier, marble fireplace, and table set for sixteen people, the finest China glistening under the light.

"For someone so cutting edge and defiant, his décor sure seems traditional," Brady observed as he paced the room. "I've landed in the court of Louis XIV."

Jaret slumped into one of the chairs at the head of the table. "The palace is eclectic, to say the least. I've seen a different dining room, which looked like a modern one with a glass table and faux view of the ocean. I think he lets the boys decorate different rooms to their liking. And I'd guess a vast majority of the creative expression comes while they're either high or drunk."

"Or both."

They fell into silence until Charon stormed into the room with a glare. His typical bravado had returned. "We act. Fuck the Council and its caution. Styx wants war, so he'll have war."

"So he didn't scare you into complacence? Or reduce you to fear?" Jaret asked.

Charon shook his head with fierce motion. "On the contrary. He showed the wrath with which he'll rule. The way he intends to keep me under his thumb. I'd never survive. And I won't obey him. Give us a couple days to mourn, then return and we'll send him my message of submission, but first a request to meet. We'll set him up to come into our trap." As Charon spoke, his face turned redder and redder.

When he finished speaking, Jaret stood and went to him, placing a hand on his shoulder and squeezing. "Good. We'll be back."

Jaret and Brady showed themselves out, remaining quiet until they stood in the frigid mountain air. The quiet night, with a soft breeze blowing through the evergreen trees below them belied the turmoil roiling the vampire community. They walked, neither indicating a purpose or destination, two midnight hikers enjoying the scenery but deep in thought. Lost in the solitude, both startled when an orange orb appeared before them.

Thomas's image spoke a magical communication: "You two

and me. Tomorrow night in Denver. I'll tell you where. No fucking games. Be there."

CHAPTER FOURTEEN

THOMAS'S IRE

5 MARCH 2019
Denver, Colorado

Thomas's message from the night before forced Jaret and Brady to change their plans. Neither had intended to remain in Colorado, but Thomas had summoned them to Denver, so they stayed in Estes Park. Jaret took Brady to his family home, which he kept as a sentimental remembrance of his human life. He never altered its appearance from the home in which he grew up, except to decorate every Christmas for the holidays. His sister, Jenn, often visited him in spirit form when he came home. Brady and he arrived with plenty of time to share a bottle of wine, play with Darth, and then settle into their respective rooms to sleep through the day.

Jaret woke the following evening and wandered through the house while he waited for Brady. To distract himself from the emotion threatening to spill out, he concentrated on the business at hand. Why did Thomas want to meet with them? Thomas seldom, if ever, scolded Jaret because he liked rebelliousness, having lived a life of defiance dating back to his human years and continuing to the present despite Thomas having a seat on the Vampire Council. Jaret could tell Xavier tamed him somewhat. But Thomas maintained a fierce distaste for rigid protocols. His summons felt like a warning shot.

Jaret and Brady hurried to Denver once Brady finished primping. They expected a quick subpoena from Thomas based on the tone of his missive but got into town without any more information. They sent magical questions to Thomas but got no answer so decided to hit a gay bar.

Beforehand, however, Jaret thought of an idea, so he stopped by a hardware store to purchase a security system. As they meandered toward the bar, he opened the box as Brady watched him with a smile.

Brady held up his hands. "I don't want to know."

"Good. Drink instead." Jaret motioned toward the bar and

followed Brady inside.

Settled onto bar stools in front of a TV showing music videos, they chatted and watched the people around them. Feeling a little nervous but with a nice buzz from his third coconut rum and coke, Jaret giggled and leaned against Brady. "Like old times, hanging at a gay bar and watching all the hot guys."

Brady patted Jaret on the head. "Always a good time. Helps ease the tension, all these boys enjoying life. I'm so geeked how we still get wasted as vampires."

"Wonder what Thomas wants." Jaret thought aloud. "Weird he hasn't asked for us yet."

"I think something's up with the Council. I don't know anything for sure. More Council secrets maybe."

Jaret started to agree when a guy thrust himself between their bar stools and grabbed both of them around the shoulders. Jaret glanced at a very handsome man between them, maybe in his thirties, smiling through glassy eyes. "Two pretty little numbers such as yourself, all morose and serious at the bar. You need something to liven things up."

Brady grinned. "We look morose to you?"

Dude mock frowned and nodded.

"What do you have in mind?" Jaret asked.

"Depends on what you're up for?"

Brady tilted his head and smiled when his ringing phone interrupted them. He held up a finger to the guy to indicate he had to take the call.

"Hello?" Brady asked. "Got it." He poked his phone off. "Gotta go. Sorry sweetheart." Brady smacked the guy with a full kiss on the lips and grabbed his ass as he also yanked at Jaret's arm to get him to follow. Outside and hurrying down the sidewalk, Brady explained. "Thomas ordered us to the Brown Palace Hotel. Again with these vampires and their old school fancy places."

"How did he sound?" Jaret asked.

"Normal, I guess." Brady squinted in thought. "Serious. But not pissed or anything."

Before entering the hotel, Jaret concealed part of his security apparatus nearby. "I guess we're about to find out more." Jaret opened the door and held it for Brady as the two walked into the ornate and old school hotel lobby.

Thomas leaned against a wall, watching for them and pushing away the second they entered. "Ah, my two favorite prodigal sons."

"What's with the biblical analogy? I thought Xavier was the priest," Jaret replied.

Thomas smiled and motioned toward them. "His religious references rub off on me. Come." He hurried toward a stairwell and bounded up several flights before leading them down a hallway and into a room. He was mysterious and quiet but not threatening or enraged.

Thomas closed the door behind them as they went into the little sitting room of the suite. Jaret sensed other vampires nearby, perhaps somewhere in the hotel itself, but not in the room with them. They each took a chair. Jaret watched Thomas but noticed nothing unusual in his demeanor.

Thomas smirked. "Stop studying me. If I want to be scrutinized, I'll go hang with my husband."

"I'm wondering why you called us here," Jaret explained. "And you and the others have been scrutinizing *me*."

"Touché. We'll cut to the chase." Thomas stared at Jaret. "You're up to something. What?"

Out of the corner of his eye, Jaret saw Brady squirm in his chair. His friend was not a good partner in crime with his body language giving away guilt.

"I thought the Council knew everything. Like the gods over all vampires."

Thomas nodded. "You know that's not true. You're stalling. I do admit, I'm not stupid and have put together some pretty good guesses. But life would be easier if you came clean without the drama."

Jaret grinned. "Pretend you're right. You know I won't or can't tell you my plan. On the other hand, maybe I'm running around with no plan. But I'm mad as fuck the Council twiddles its thumbs. Either way, you have no control over me. What's the point? You pretending to protect me?"

Unlike Xavier, who grew prickly when Jaret got snotty, Thomas barked a laugh and clapped his hands.

"I see my kind of defiance in you," Thomas said. "Perhaps I want to assist you. You could see my thinking as protective, but Jaret—you don't need me or anyone else to protect you. That's always been your curse. I didn't summon you to lure information out of you. If you come clean, I'll help you. Otherwise, I want to tell you something. Take my advice or throw it out the window. Your choice."

Thomas paused until Jaret acknowledged the statement. "Let me rephrase. I *know* you're up to something. You're not ambling around pissed off with no plan. Pissed off? Yes. No plan?" Thomas raised an eyebrow. "Not your MO. Before you go too far, listen to me. Do you really believe the Council has no clue about your activity? And with the decades—centuries—of collective experience on the Council, do you believe we have no clue what to do? That vampires die but we bumble along with no Council recourse? I'm trying to get you to listen, to *hear* what I can tell you and read between the lines at what I can't."

Jaret pressed his lips together. "You sound like Anthony." There, again, Jaret's skin prickled at the mention of his lover, as if he spied from above. "I expect more direct communication from you," Jaret continued. "And speaking of Anthony, all claims from the Council of being in control vanished the moment I saw him die."

Thomas got out of his chair and strolled over to Jaret, placing one hand on each arm of Jaret's chair and leaning over him, his long black hair almost falling into Jaret's lap. "These aren't stupid people you're playing with. You're not as clever as you think. And the Council's plan will go into effect with or without your cooperation, no matter what you think you plot. I know nothing I say will penetrate your thick skull, so let's move on. You want to inform the Council about the latest killings at Charon's Palace. But of course they already know. I'll go get them."

Thomas left the room, and the second the door closed, Brady spun in his chair to face Jaret. "Dude! You better come clean!" He slapped his hands on his knees. "They are so on to you. I get you want to do your thing. But I think you're on a dangerous path. Thomas is trying to tell you something."

Jaret tilted his head at Brady. "Since when did you become Mr. Compliant?"

"Since Thomas, whom we trust, tried to get through your *thick skull.*" Brady pointed toward the door Thomas had exited. "Didn't you hear him?"

"But if they know, or are monitoring, then the Council's failure to stop me means they want me to continue. Or maybe they need me to give them courage to fight instead of roll over. What if I know better than the Council how to fight Styx?"

He was grateful for the distraction when the door swung open and the entire Council entered the room, Catherine cackling. She raced over and pinched first Brady and then Jaret on the cheeks. "I love you! So sure of yourself, and sure of our stupidity."

The Council gathered around, some sitting and some standing. Jaret felt less sure of himself with them surrounding him in the small room.

"What do you want to tell us?" Harriet asked him.

Jaret shook his head. "You summoned me. Or Thomas did. Sounds like you already know the latest about Styx killing more of Charon's boys. What's the use of another little chat?"

Xavier shrugged. "To talk sense into you? As for Charon, he wants to live beyond the Council's grasp. He therefore lives beyond our protection."

"What protection?" Jaret spat. "Vampires outside his realm but in yours have died, too, with no protection from you."

"I understand your perception—" Xavier started to say more but Jaret held up his hand to stop him.

"Nope. No more of the 'I don't understand. Trust us.' Blah, blah, blah. Because I *don't* trust you and nothing you say will change my mind. Anthony's corpse speaks more loudly about your lack of abilities than the stupid words you spew." Jaret clenched his fists together. "Why are we doing this again?"

Harriet stepped forward and placed a hand on Jaret's shoulder. "Because we care about you."

Jaret felt his body relax at her touch. He nodded and then spoke. "Well, you must already know this too. Charon plans to meet with Styx. I think you should be there."

He glanced around the room to see if they detected his plot, but they looked back with stoic faces.

"We need to go." Catherine started to leave and the others followed. "Keep us informed about Charon's plan. Or *yours*." She shot him a knowing glance as they left without another word.

Brady and Jaret looked at each other in silence before they burst out laughing at the awkward tension.

"Let's go. This is so fucked." Brady got up to leave.

Jaret held up a hand to stop Brady. "One more thing. Wait here." Jaret ran to retrieve the device he had concealed before the meeting.

Jaret returned and, as he placed his doorbell camera in a concealed location, he spoke to Brady. "You suck at criminal behavior. Your body language so gave us away."

"Dude!" Brady pointed toward the door. "Those are fucking powerful vampires! They know shit. I do *not* want to end up in the coffin fire prison thing they told me about. Or have them smash my fucking head all over the room like a rotten pumpkin the day after Halloween! I'm with you. I told you so. But I think they know about your plan. You're playing into their hands, not the other way around."

"If they had such a firm grasp on everything," Jaret replied, "Styx wouldn't have been able to kill Anthony." Jaret choked back tears. "Each time I almost convince myself the same thing you said about them, I remember his death. They have a bit of a history of using smoke and mirrors to project authority and knowledge when they're really struggling to figure out what the fuck is going on." Jaret wiped his hands on his pants and stood. "Done."

"Speaking of going bonkers, what the fuck is this little home improvement project? Why is there a hidden doorbell in a hotel room? Because I am *not* on board if you decided to start a little side porn business of recording people in secret. I get the millions we could make from vampire porn, but it's not okay to spy on them."

Jaret laughed. "You're the perv, since your mind went to sex. Come on. I'll show you why."

Jaret led Brady through the hotel, up a set of stairs, and onto the roof. Jaret sat and leaned his back against a dormant air-conditioning unit and opened the computer on his lap. Brady joined him with a furrowed brow.

"They'll so know your little spy tactic." Brady frowned. "You know, right?"

"They'll sweep for magic, which will reveal we were there, but they already know that. I watch them everywhere they go. They never think old school or human."

"Um, yeah—they do," Brady said. "Check for spy shit each place when they arrive. Seriously, where have you been? They walk into a room and one of them points to every camera or source of security in two seconds. You never noticed?"

Jaret rolled his eyes. "Of course, I see how the Council checks for surveillance systems. But once they secure a space, they grow lax. They monitor for magic shit and other vampires but neglect old-school human stuff."

Brady sighed. "I'm so not convinced by you. In case they listen in as we speak, I want the record to show I think this one," he pointed to Jaret, "is a nutball and I'm here to keep him safe from himself."

Laughing, Jaret opened the internet and logged in to watch his newly installed security system, which showed an empty hotel suite.

Brady slapped him on the arm as he talked. "You're the worst PI ever. You might as well be hiding behind the curtain with your toes sticking out."

Jaret laughed despite the insult. "Do you ever take a break to breathe?"

Brady shook his head. "Let me ask you something else."

"What?"

"You ever wonder if Anthony's alive? Like, the Council brought him back from the dead? Or faked the killing?"

Jaret started to answer but paused. "What made you ask?"

Brady punched him in the arm. "Don't answer a question with a question."

Jaret wondered if he should tell Brady about feeling Anthony's presence. The most important thing, among many, keeping him from banging Charon was a sense of faithfulness to Anthony.

Brady leaned over and stared at Jaret. "Cat got your tongue?

Long time no words from you. You paused too long without answering, so there's my answer. You agree with me; he might be alive."

Jaret laughed. "You think too much. He's dead. Concentrate on the task here."

Brady squinted at Jaret. "Your mourning is off too. You sob and carry on for months when you lose someone. With Anthony, you walk around pissed off and nothing more."

"Why would they put me through his pretend death?" Jaret tilted his head. "No, I think he died. The cruelty of faking his murder for some Council ends would be harsher than their usual nasty behavior. And Anthony knows how pissed I'd be. I'd fuck Charon in the middle of a crowded bar if I thought he was fucking with me."

Brady laughed. "No, you wouldn't. You're all talk. You'd never hang your weewee out for public consumption."

"Shh," Jaret held up a hand. "Here they are."

The Vampire Council entered the room without speaking. As Jaret predicted, Harriet enchanted a spell to sweep the room for other magic before nodding to everyone and sitting down. From the camera he installed, Jaret saw Catherine and Harriet sitting on a couch next to each other, as well as what he thought was Thomas's leg in front of a chair next to the camera. Xavier remained out of the screenshot, but Jaret assumed he was there.

"So we're agreed?" Catherine asked the assembly. No one said anything but Harriet nodded, and Catherine scanned the room as if watching for the same assent from everyone else. "Good. Then we make the next move in this war. And, I doubt I need to remind you, Jaret and Charon can't know the details. They'll interfere. Especially Jaret. Or Styx will use them to discover our plans."

"Jaret's heart's in the right place," Jaret heard Xavier tell her.

"I need his head in the right place before we get him involved," Harriet retorted.

To Jaret's frustration, the meeting adjourned without anything else. They chatted about nonsense for a couple minutes, then got up and left.

"Fuck." Jaret slammed the lid of the laptop down in despair and embarrassment. "We didn't learn a fucking thing. Except they *are* doing something behind my back. We have to learn what."

Brady sat in another unusual silence but with his typical bemused look as he stared at Jaret.

"What?" Jaret asked him through clenched teeth.

"You still think they've got no clue?" Brady asked as he pointed to the laptop.

"What do you mean?"

Brady laughed. "Dude. Four super-close vampires. Someone is always talking or carrying on. *Always.* In a crisis. When having fun. No matter what, there is noise. But today they amble into the room all quiet and hush-hush, like they know the CIA lurks around the corner, and no one talks except Catherine. Thomas never uttered a peep. When does he ever hold his tongue? Catherine gives enough info to indicate they got a plan and then they leave. You figure nothing to worry about but their normal behavior? There's no reason for what we witnessed than they wanted you to see the meeting."

Jaret sighed. "You have a point." Blood tears formed in his eyes from his frustration.

"Oh!" Brady exclaimed. "Can I record you saying so? Admitting for the first time I was right and you were wrong?"

"I said you had a point, not that I was incorrect." Jaret frowned and wiped at the tears. "So what should we do?"

Brady tossed up his hands. "Don't ask me. I'm along for the ride. I told you, I believe you're right about needing to get this show on the road. The Council sounded like they agree. Maybe the only point of difference is about how much they want you involved."

A sense of embarrassment and defeat engulfed Jaret. His ideas, his careful plot to find out information, his wanting to urge the war to defeat Styx to a breaking point, sounded fucking crazy. Brady was right. The Council knew about Jaret's scheme and predicted his every move. Or they had a pretty good clue. They'd played him for a fool.

Brady reached over and tugged on Jaret's arm. "Relax. This doesn't have to be on your shoulders."

"But it is. They're wrong to exclude me. I know, I really do. My magic can defeat Styx. They need me. And the longer they wait, the more vampires will die."

"Then what do you suggest?" Brady asked.

"We continue to lure them to the *place*. Like good realtors, it's all about location, location, location. I think the Council underestimates the importance of *where* we fight. They focus on how to battle Styx and on manipulating Charon and me to obey them. But Styx is clever and powerful too."

"You don't think they figured out Styx's power? Anthony must have told them." Brady jumped to his feet and motioned for Jaret to follow. "Come on."

"Where are we going?"

"To clear your head. Sad Jaret is no good."

Jaret acquiesced when Brady held out his hands to get him on his feet. Then Jaret reached down and used his vampire strength to break the computer in half. Before they left the hotel, he also obliterated the other doorbell shit he had installed. The violence helped him release his anger and frustration.

They walked through Denver as if humans, slow and steady. Jaret had no will to talk while he contemplated how to react and to ponder his next move. Brady remained quiet except when he spotted some hot guy to point out.

They ended up on bar stools back in the place where they started the evening, each with a cocktail in hand and lots of happy people around them, laughing and talking and drinking.

"I think I figured out my strategy."

Brady held his hands in the air. "It's alive!"

Despite his mood, Jaret laughed. "I wanted a grand strategy. To prove how I knew what to do no matter what the Council thought. I aimed too high. I have to focus on getting rid of Styx. And I'm sure the Council needs me. I mean, if they really wanted me out of the war, then they'd go about doing their thing without bothering me. They could isolate me easy enough. Think about this point: if they knew I was spying on them in the hotel room, then they wanted me to hear what they said. Otherwise, they would never have gone back into the room or they would have destroyed the camera before talking. Something is going on with me and them. And I know what."

Brady raised an eyebrow. "Back to all-knowing, are we?"

Jaret nodded. "Location. I taught them the idea. My ability converges with location and will empower us at the moment of the fight. I have a duty to lead them to the correct place."

Brady held up his glass to toast. "To the master plan back on track."

"You're an asshole." But Jaret held up his glass and clinked them together in a toast before they slammed them back and ordered another round.

The rest of the night flew by in a blur, as the two friends acted as if they were back in college in Chicago, dancing and having fun on a night without a care in the world. They laughed and drank a lot. Flirted with guys around the bar. And partied until last call and the bouncers ushered everyone outside.

"Did you sense something?" Jaret asked Brady as he spied into the trees.

"No." Brady shook his head. "What?"

"A vampire."

"Styx? Something bad? I don't feel anything!" Brady spoke with alarm.

Jaret shook his head. "No. A presence." *Anthony.* He swore Anthony's spirit watched over him. Jaret walked down the sidewalk and motioned for Brady to follow. "Must be my drunken imagination."

Out of view from humans, Jaret and Brady raced back to Estes Park to sleep in Jaret's family home. Darth greeted them with high jumps and her spinning tail.

"Were you hunting elk tonight?" Jaret asked her as he patted her head.

"You should not let a vampire dog roam free," Brady scolded Jaret.

"Nothing will happen to her."

"I'm not worried about her. I'm worried about what she hunts."

CHAPTER FIFTEEN

SEX AND WAR

7 MARCH 2019
Nederland, CO

Jaret's mind spun with a whirl of emotion. He was pissed off at the Council, afraid of the war, determined to help defeat Styx, and laser focused on location. He was also bewildered. His feelings for Anthony, however, were even stronger. Jaret had come to accept Anthony's death despite sensing Anthony's presence.

Jaret shook his head as he and Darth walked fast through the

Rocky Mountains toward tonight's meeting. If Anthony were alive, Jaret would sense another vampire nearby. Instead, he sensed the essence of Anthony but not a physical presence. What was Anthony's ghost playing at?

Jaret looked at Darth as she peered up at him, probably wondering where they were headed. "I gotta get a grip," he told her. She wagged her tail in agreement.

"You can *grip* this." Charon appeared in front of Jaret, holding his crotch through a pair of joggers, so tight they left little to the imagination.

Jaret grinned. "I sensed you, you know. I let you follow me because you like watching my ass."

"You have no idea." Charon bounded over, reached around Jaret, and grabbed his butt cheeks.

Jaret swatted Charon's hand off and pushed the vampire away. "You're wearing a tank top and thin sweats in the middle of the winter in Colorado. Not very discreet for a vampire."

"Yes, sir, Mr. Obedient Vampire. I wouldn't want a passing moose to figure me out. Or heaven forbid a meandering wolf."

Jaret rolled his eyes. "This close to Boulder, we could happen upon tripping hippies lost as fuck."

"I'd feed off them and be done." Charon shrugged.

They reached the secret tunnel to Charon's underground castle and went down. Jaret followed Charon through the labyrinth and passed some of his boys until they arrived at one of the myriad rooms in the palace, a new one for Jaret.

"I've seen this place before." Jaret scanned his mind to place the location.

Charon laughed. "Yeah, you have! My favorite bar in Fort Lauderdale. I recreated the main bar here for old times' sake. I came here because we needed a room appropriate for a dog." Charon pointed to Darth.

"You always worry about her. She won't poop inside. A little fur won't hurt anything. One of your minions can lick it up while you watch. Seriously, all the come and body fluids you let fly around here, but Darth's wandering around gets your panties in a bunch? Can we get down to business?"

Jaret went around the back of the bar and grabbed a bottle of bourbon, making them a couple of old-fashioneds. "I figured some things out about the war but need to ponder other aspects." Jaret handed Charon his drink. He wanted to get down to business but not tell Charon about the turmoil roiling through him.

Charon sat on a stool across from Jaret and stared at him. "Do you ever chill?"

"All the time." Jaret rolled his eyes. "Except being in the middle of a war that threatens to annihilate us seems like a bad time to relax."

"Or!" Charon held up a finger of revelation. "Such a moment presents the perfect time! In the off chance we're about to die anyway, have some fun before the end. Go out with a bang. A literal bang."

Jaret suppressed a laugh, but a smile spread across his face despite himself. "Are you seriously propositioning me again? Last time I was here, you lost boys. They were murdered. You were a mess, rightfully so, and pledged to fight. But tonight, you already return to thinking with your dick."

Charon grimaced, then swayed his head back and forth in thought. "I didn't forget. I'm pissed. But moping around won't bring them back. And I await your command about what to do. So, in the meantime, we might as well fuck." Charon motioned for Jaret to move closer.

"We can talk from here." Jaret stayed his ground. "I've made myself clear, I believe, about needing to avoid sex with you."

Charon stood on the rungs of his stool with his legs leaning against the bar, his waist close to Jaret's eye level. His thin pants strained from the erection threatening to pop out. "Do you see what you do to me?" Charon asked.

Jaret reached over and flicked Charon's dick, causing Charon to lurch back and almost fall off the stool.

Jaret giggled. "Aren't you excited I touched you?"

"I am." Charon nodded. "I can get into violence with you. Please." He held his hands up in prayer. "I'll talk serious about the war for hours and hours to your heart's content, but first we have to come. I can't concentrate until I have you. Please."

Jaret downed his drink and made another one, while pouring

Charon straight-up bourbon. "You have tons of hot guys here, and all want to fuck you anytime, anywhere. Or you could walk into any dance party and pick up about any guy in two seconds. Have a fuck in an alley. In a stall. Take a twink for a trip to Europe. Have you ever suffered from rejection? So why the infatuation with me?"

"You reject me every time I see you."

"The allure of the forbidden fruit, eh?"

"Here you go again with the Chatty Cathy routine. I won't discuss your precious war, so you want a deep psychological dive into what motivates me. I can answer the latter pretty fast. Come. Coming. Fucking. Hot man-on-man sex. Bubble butts. Sumptuous lips wrapped around my cock. Orgies. I could continue."

"I acknowledged your sex motivation. You're dodging the part about your obsession with me."

Charon narrowed his eyes. "I don't know the answer for why." He shrugged. "Not worried about pondering why. You know you're hot. Your hair alone gives me a boner. Maybe you're right. You entice with the forbidden fruit. So, give me your ass, and we can move forward because I'll have tasted the banned hole and no longer will suffer from this longing."

Jaret threw his head back in laughter. "Always with the charm. At least you leave little to the imagination."

"You could never imagine with enough accuracy the complete and utter euphoria of what my tongue would feel like in your ass."

Jaret reached across the counter and patted Charon on the

cheek. "You know we're not having sex. Can we please talk about the war? We're threatened and you know it, no matter how flippantly you try to pretend. I need you. We can help the Council, whether they want our assistance or not. You and I possess a different kind of magic from Council magic. And you have a more intimate knowledge of Styx."

"I agreed to participate. I'm all in. So, what about this agreement: Can we have sex when this is over? In celebration?"

"I'm in mourning and fragile. We can discuss sex after the war, and I'll be able to better concentrate."

Charon frowned. "Not a very promising answer."

Charon lowered his head as if defeated. But from the side Jaret could see the wrinkle near his eyes betraying a smile. Charon spun around and called for Jaret to follow with the motion of his hand. They ended up in a corner of the recreated bar, where a set of loveseats and a coffee table offered a secluded parlor feel amid the chaos of what would be a thriving bar scene.

Jaret worried Charon would attempt to sit on the same sofa to persist with his seduction, but he allowed them to sit opposite each other. Before Jaret could relax and switch to the business at hand, Charon leaned back, spread his legs wide, and sighed. His hand drifted down his chest and landed on his erection, rubbing as he licked his lips and winked at Jaret.

"I thought we moved on from your horniness." Jaret crossed his legs to conceal his own growing excitement.

Charon shook his head. "I can't relax with you in the room today. You always get me. I forgot to jack off when I woke up and the pent-up energy might consume me."

"You forgot?" Jaret laughed. "I imagine you rub one out at least every hour."

"I like to build up the tension sometimes."

"You're incorrigible." Jaret shook his head. "We're at war. This is serious."

Charon stared across the table at Jaret, ignoring his last comments and continuing to feel himself through his pants. He blew Jaret a kiss and tilted his head in seduction. Charon grabbed the tip of his penis through the cloth and squeezed and manipulated until his legs tightened, his muscles became taut, and come streamed out to soak his clothes and press through the fabric and onto his fingers. Charon let out a long breath and rested his head against the loveseat cushion.

Jaret barked out a laugh as he adjusted his pants from his own erection. "I just can't with you."

Charon lifted his head and smiled. "You liked my show, didn't you? Want some?" Charon stretched out the come between his fingers.

Jaret smiled from ear to ear but shook his head.

"Come on, just a little taste." Charon pinched the come between his fingers.

"No. Now stop."

"But I'm a complete mess!"

"And who might we blame for your messy situation, I wonder?" Jaret rolled his eyes.

"At least I think I can concentrate on your serious shit now. Oh, but maybe you better finish yourself off first. So you're not distracted too."

"I'm fine."

"Doesn't look like you're fine." Charon pointed to Jaret's crotch.

"Stop." Jaret placed his hand over his junk. "I'm not big enough to show through my jeans. Leave me alone."

Charon giggled and adjusted his legs. "I feel a bit uncomfortable with the sticky goo in my pants. Please come over and clean up for me."

"Suffer. Can we please talk? This *is* serious."

Charon nodded and the smile fell from his face. "I know. You and I already agree. I signed on board with whatever we need to do. I told you after Styx invaded my castle and killed more of my boys. I quarantined them here, cast my security spells, and no one can get in or out of here until we finish the war. Also, I looked over your plans." Charon shrugged. "Easy. I trust your instinct and know from my own experience we'll need all the magic and vampire power in the world to beat Styx. So you do your thing and cue me in when I'm needed. I'll be ready to get him to your chosen spot."

Jaret frowned across the room. "I didn't expect such easy

compliance."

Charon leapt off the loveseat and surprised Jaret by landing right next to him on his sofa. Charon leaned toward Jaret and smiled. "Easy?" He smirked. "You've been recruiting me for a few years. Since we first met. Vampires died and I resisted. I'd say it was your persistence finally coming through to bring us to this point. So, to war! I feel like we should be singing songs from *Les Mis*!"

Jaret grinned. "Only you could get me to smile about heading off on a suicide mission. I'm glad my persistence has paid off because you are crucial to my plan." But he refused to turn his head and stare into those beautiful eyes, mere inches from his own face. The faint smell of come on Charon distracted him enough.

"We rewarded your persistence," Charon whispered. "What about mine? *Quid pro quo?*"

"I said—"

But Jaret choked on his words. He was overcome with sexual energy when Charon leaned over the remaining distance to kiss Jaret's ear. Charon then plunged his tongue in as he also reached around to feel Jaret's still erect dick.

Part Six

War Begins

CHAPTER SIXTEEN

SEDUCTION

7 MARCH 2019
James Peak, Colorado

Even amid the erupting vampire war, another and very different war raged in Jaret's head as he sat on a sofa in Charon's castle. Charon persisted with his seduction despite having come in his own pants. He sat with his tongue probing Jaret's ear and his hand placed on top of Jaret's crotch. Jaret wanted to rip off his clothes and have sex.

Jaret imagined turning his head to kiss Charon, to jab his tongue into one of the hottest vampires he'd ever seen and taste him. He envisioned allowing Charon to take control. He knew, if

Jaret gave the signal, Charon would lead them in whatever direction satisfied his longing. And Jaret loved an in-command top asserting his sexual will. He fantasized about Charon penetrating his ass and coming, about fucking over and over until, even as vampires, they spent all their available energy and collapsed into each other's arms.

Every sensation in Jaret's body wanted to give in to the pleasure with the god sitting next to him. Charon's muscular body and pleas for sex were pulling Jaret into Charon's orbit. Having no sex since Anthony died made the situation worse.

There Anthony appeared again, intruding into Jaret's mind with reminders of their love and eternal commitment. No matter where he went or what he confronted, Anthony lingered. Jaret felt the persistent pain of losing Anthony along with the nagging sense of fealty to him. As if, even in death, Jaret would betray their love if he had sex with someone else.

Being frozen in these ponderings helped nothing because as Jaret sat in turmoil Charon continued his foreplay. Jaret fought against the urge to come, the friction of Charon's hand against his jeans enough to release the pent-up energy. Charon pushed his own rock-hard cock against Jaret's side. Jaret almost hit himself in the head in reprimand when a sigh of satisfaction escaped his own lips.

"See. You want my cock so bad," Charon whispered into his ear.

Charon's words snapped Jaret out of the moment. He pushed Charon off, leapt to his feet, and laughed as he adjusted himself and straightened his clothes. "I'm glad you always open your mouth to bring me back to reality." Jaret took a deep breath and turned to compose himself. He closed his eyes and focused on the impending war and images of severed body parts until his hard-on went away. Jaret turned back to face Charon.

Charon flopped back on the sofa and spread his arms out wide. "I almost had you!" he shouted. "Dammit."

"Almost." Jaret slapped himself on the cheek and was happy to feel the excitement leave his body. "You are one sex god." He pointed at Charon. "Another year, another context, I'd go with the flow. In my naïve youth I'd have signed up to be one of your sex-slave boys and not realize my mistake until too late. I'd envision turning into your spouse and being the perfect couple, while you cheated on me and fucked anything moving, breaking my heart every time."

Charon grinned a wicked smile. "You'd follow me around like a puppy begging me every minute for more. You'd love living here!" Charon raised his arms in the air to indicate the castle. "You admitted you want to be my wife!"

Jaret grimaced. "Wife? What? No. And I was speaking in theory, as if you happened upon my naïve eighteen-year-old self. Present me knows the truth about you. Prison is not my style. I know the difference between lust and something permanent."

"You know what? I'm going to agree with you. You're too fucking independent. I'd have to lock you in a room and turn you into a captive sex slave. Which I'd enjoy. You would too, except you're so anal retentive you'd never give yourself over to the circumstances."

"Which means I *wouldn't* enjoy myself or your proposal," Jaret barked back.

Charon nodded. "Yikes. You're correct. It was not okay for me to insinuate rape. Sorry. I'll remind you for about the one hundredth time how my boys came here of free will. We were talking theoretically about capturing you, not actual circumstances here at my palace."

"Yeah, and what happens when one of them wants to leave?"

Charon shook his head. "You're trying to distract from how much you want me. I can't help myself. Dude, you do something to me. I can't stand not having you."

"You're going to have to stand without me because this," Jaret waved his hand back and forth between the two vampires, "is not going to happen."

Jaret's words contradicted how his dick tingled with the mere thought of sex with Charon.

They both started to say something else when Jordan stormed into the room, out of breath and babbling so fast and furious Jaret could not understand a word.

"What are you talking about?" Charon hurried over and grabbed Jordan. "You're not making sense. I don't understand."

Jordan took a deep breath and closed his eyes. Charon's grip seemed to focus his energy. He spoke with urgency but with better control. "We're being attacked. I don't know what to do. You gotta come. Now, Boss man, now!" Jordan shouted the last sentence, lurched out of Charon's hands, and raced back toward the door. "You gotta come." Jordan motioned for them to follow and hurried down the hall.

Charon ran after him. Jaret followed. At vampiric speed, even with the size of the underground palace, they neared the grand entrance in seconds, but Jordan had lurched to a stop and blocked their path with his arm. Some of Charon's other vampires huddled in a group in a corner, wide-eyed and alarmed.

"Give me more details," Charon commanded.

"They tried to invade. Pounded on the rock so I went to check who was there. They had moved the stone to our tunnel and attempted to storm into the castle but your magic held them back. When one stepped a foot inside, a force threw them out. They screamed and yelled but couldn't get in. They even threw shit at the entrance, but all of the crap flew back at them. They tried like five million times to enter, until something penetrated their brains, so they stopped. Now they're hovering outside, pissed as hell and screaming they want to talk to you."

"Who wants to talk to me?" Charon asked.

"I never saw the guy, but they said Styx."

Charon clenched his teeth. "And are these vampires with him? People? Who's out there?"

Jordan tilted his head. "I think vamps. Cray cray though. Because they kinda act more like zombies. Possessed. They're people but with fangs, like vampires, but they all stare vacantly and grunt. He controls them in a more sinister way than how you manage us. I think he'd sacrifice everyone of 'em if he could get in here."

Charon placed his hands on each of Jordan's shoulders. "Listen to me. Gather everyone and get them into the panic room"—he pointed toward the boys huddled in the corner—"and find the others in the castle. No more questions. Fast. Go."

Jordan sped off when Charon spun him around by the shoulders and pushed him forward. He raced to the group and instructed them to follow. Everyone ran away, leaving Jaret and Charon alone.

"Panic room?" Jaret arched a brow. "Vampire castles include panic rooms? Rather human of you."

"Is this the time for questioning me?" Charon asked. "You're all business until a real emergency, then you want to chat?"

"I've never heard of a vampire panic room!"

"Well, you don't exist outside Vampire Council control, do you? I have from the beginning and needed additional protection. And no, I won't tell you anything else about the room because I may need to hide from you or your little friends someday. So yeah, panic room. Now, we need to go address the fuck face out there threatening my castle."

Charon stormed toward the tunnel entrance but Jaret grabbed his arm to stop him. Charon turned around and frowned. "What?"

"Take a minute." Jaret rubbed him on the chest to calm him. "They can't get in, so we should plan. Yeah, this sounds dangerous, but it could also be our opportunity."

"Opportunity?" Charon spat.

"Lure Styx in. Make him think you want to cooperate."

Charon paused before nodding agreement. "I hear you. So what's your plan? What should I do? He's straight so I can't seduce him like I do you."

"I thought you told me he was at least bi, even if he never admitted he liked dick? You told me you kind of had sex with him."

Charon rolled his eyes. "Not sex. Foreplay. He transformed me by having me drink from his thigh while his hard cock slapped my face. But he refused my offer of a blow job. And there you go again, being Chatty Cathy while we face a crisis! Can you give me some help here?"

Jaret giggled. "You panic often for someone so calm, cool, and collected." Jaret thought for a second. "You can't act all buddy-buddy. Anything too obvious would alert him. You gotta start pissed off and angry. Then listen to his crazy ranting and pretend to consider his offer."

"Sounds plausible. But how do we explain you?"

Jaret shook his head. "We don't. We can't."

"Won't he sense you?"

"I doubt Styx can feel me. He already knows vampires live here. I'm probably on his radar as another vampire but no one special. My magic conceals my specific identity. You can wing the situation if he mentions me."

"Wing it?" Charon sputtered with exasperation.

"Yeah. Be in charge. What the fuck? Why am I Mr. In-Charge when you're supposed to be I-Command Charon? Top Boy never taking orders from anyone! Get back to yourself and take care of the situation."

"And where will you be?" Charon asked.

"Waiting." Jaret pointed toward the room where he had hung with Brady before.

Jaret watched as Charon started up the tunnel at a cautious pace, as if collecting himself.

Jaret felt a nervous combination of fear and excitement. The war had reached a stage of surging forward instead of plodding along.

Sitting in one of the ornate parlors in Charon's castle made Jaret impatient. He knew they had to hide Jaret's presence from Styx. But Jaret was not one to hang out and wait for information.

At first, he resisted the use of magic for fear Styx would sense his unique magical imprint. Jaret reasoned, however, that Styx and Charon possessed enough sorcery between them to account for any magic in the air. Despite the risk, Jaret had to know what was going on outside the tunnel in case he needed to intervene.

Jaret cast a spell and a large sphere of magic appeared before him, giving him an aerial view of the scene unfolding outside the tunnel. He felt like the Wicked Witch of the West peering at Dorothy and friends as they linked arms and sang their way to danger, especially when Darth trotted into the room and sat next to him like a Flying Monkey. Where the heck had she been? Jaret would laugh so hard if Darth pooped in Charon's bedroom. He patted her on the head.

Jaret looked into his magical image to see Charon standing rigid at the entrance to block entry, with four of the vampire minions facing him a dozen feet away. Jordan had described the situation well. The invaders had been transformed into vampires but swayed and stared with vacant expressions. They were vampire zombies, no doubt controlled by Styx and expendable to him.

At least Charon had regained his bravado. He rolled his eyes at the throng. "I'm not interested in talking to you zombies. I know you're watching, Styx. You wanted to talk with me, so talk. But be a man and get over here. Where are you? In some tree?"

"You want trick master. But he trick you," one zombie vampire announced. All of them raised a hand and pointed at Charon.

Charon laughed. "Me Tarzan. You Jane. What the fuck is going on, Styx? You can't even get them to speak in complete sentences? Get over here."

To Jaret's surprise, the four creatures stepped back and created a space so Styx could walk forward. Styx stood ten feet from Charon, dressed in a pair of jeans and a designer hoodie. He smiled but appeared more like a cartoon villain than someone happy to see Charon.

"Were you trying to come kill more of my boys?" Charon asked. "I don't make the same mistakes twice." Charon stepped toward Styx. "Your zombie fuckers aren't going to cut muster in coming after me. Besides, you've made your point. I hear you. I thought you were smarter than to pile up dead bodies like a stupid serial killer."

Styx's smile spread into a broad, genuine grin. "There's the Charon I selected to become a vampire. Brash. In control. Never afraid. I've rattled you, haven't I? But remember, I selected you to pester the Council, not join their cause. We can work together."

"You always had delusions of grandeur about yourself. What's the offer?"

Styx shrugged. "I thought I had made myself clear. Join me or die."

"Such a negotiator. Almost as good as a car salesman."

"You don't have a choice, Charon. I'm trying to explain to you. I *will* defeat the Council. They're nothing without Anthony. You think I took centuries to plot for the war and then allowed for gaps in the plan? No. Please. I targeted him and designed my trap. His lack of fight surprised me, but then I utilized an intricate magic, and he underestimated me. With him out of the picture, the rest of those fools will fall with ease. Come help me. Besides, as long as you worship me, I'll leave you alone to do as you please."

A second before he shot into view, Jaret's vampiric alarm

sounded about the approach of another vampire, not in a threatening way but sure to complicate the situation. One of Charon's minions lurched to a stop several feet from the two men with a questioning look. The slight lad, beautiful in an innocent college way, stared at Charon with absolute alarm.

"I thought I ordered you to stay here," Charon hissed through clenched teeth.

"I, uh—" the youngster stammered.

"Ah," Styx blurted, "bait has arrived." Before Charon or the boy could react, Styx sped over and clutched the young man in his grip, intoning a spell and then hurrying away. The four zombie things followed Styx but stumbled as they went.

Charon raced after them and out of the view of Jaret's magic.

Jaret snapped his fingers and his magical sphere vanished. He ran up the tunnel. "Darth, come!" But she had hurried past him and out the tunnel already. Jaret followed the vampire footsteps in the snow. Despite running at vampiric speed, Jaret felt as if time stood still with each passing second.

Going too fast, Jaret slammed into the back of Charon who had come to a stop. In front of them, the four zombie vamps blocked their path. Thinking Charon ridiculous for worrying about them, Jaret shot forward but got slammed in the chest by a zombie fucker. He attempted to dart around that one but was flung back by another one.

Enraged, he returned to Charon.

"Styx controls them," Charon said. "He left a magical shield behind."

"I figured as much. What the fuck?"

Charon looked unamused. "This move will piss him off, but he left me no other choice. I studied their makeup and they have no control over themselves. Use fire magic, and we'll blow their heads off."

"He won't counter us?" Jaret asked in disbelief. "How do you know?"

Charon took a deep breath of annoyance. "Because Styx wants us to kill the zombies and then follow him. Follow my lead."

Charon closed his eyes and muttered a spell, creating an energy field around them. Jaret cast his own fire magic so they could concentrate the energy into little balls of fire and spin four of them at the vamp zombies. As Charon predicted, and with relative ease, the four former humans turned weird-ass tools of Styx exploded.

Jaret grimaced at the disgusting scene: body parts and blood everywhere.

"You'd make a horrible soldier if you got sick every time someone died." Charon walked toward the bodies but continued through them instead of stopping. "How do you stomach killing as a vampire?"

"First," Jaret yelled after him, "I never fancied myself a soldier. And I don't mind killing assholes. These people are innocent." He hurried forward but stopped at the bodies. "Shouldn't we clean up?"

"Always with the Council rules and you," Charon shouted as he sauntered away. "Here." He snapped his fingers, and all the body parts burst into flames.

Jaret scurried to catch up. "Shouldn't we hurry? He might kill the kid he kidnapped."

"He's not going to kill Todd. Styx wants us there, and he needs Todd alive to get me to come."

"Us? He wants us?"

Charon smirked. "Pretty sure you were wrong about being concealed from him."

They walked through the mountains. At first they followed the path in the snow but then a little purple fairy appeared, motioning for them to follow and cut across a mountain.

"Dude, is that Tinkerbell?" Jaret asked Charon as they trailed the little fairy.

"Something like her." Charon sighed. "I doubt happy little Peter Pan is waiting at the other end. I told you Styx is fucking twisted. He told me about farting butterflies once when he worked on the magic to conceal vampires from the Council. I still don't know if the butterflies from the ass happened, if he made the story up to amuse himself, or if he hallucinated the scene. Styx is bonkers. His insanity explains the centuries-long war against the Council. And thus, we follow a little purple fairy through the mountains at a serious moment. Fucking crazy."

"Yet he's powerful."

"A lot of crazy fuckers become pretty powerful. We better be cautious."

The purple fairy flew over the last mountain and Jaret saw Estes Park spread out in the valley below. Having grown up here after his family moved to Colorado from Nebraska, he recognized the place and wondered why on earth Styx had brought them here.

They meandered down a slope, near one of Estes's icons, a huge cross on the side of the mountain they lit up at night. The structure glowed before them.

"Why is this here?" Charon spat as they passed by. "I should knock the fucker over."

"Feeling hostile? How does a cross harm anyone?"

"You know as well as I how many of those totally religious fuckers hate us."

"Vampires?" Jaret asked with a smile.

"Stop." Charon shot Jaret a look of exasperation. "Fags. Christians hate fags."

"Not all Christians do. Where is he taking us?" Jaret asked.

They arrived at the path around Lake Estes, devoid of people at this time of night in the winter cold. The fairy turned east, went up the large hill, then headed down below the dam, came around the putt-putt golf course, and then went back up a hill on the other side of the dam. They wound back toward the lake, crossed the river next to a golf course, and then headed toward the downtown.

"We went in a huge fucking circle," Jaret pointed out.

Charon laughed. "Styx thinks he's being funny."

They crossed the highway leading into downtown and climbed another pretty steep hill, passed the grocery store, and walked around the back toward a small residential community. Jaret lurched to a stop as Tinkerbell disappeared.

"Oh, fuck," Jaret muttered. "Not good."

Charon halted a few feet in front of Jaret and turned around. "What? Something new?"

"No. Something old." Jaret pointed behind Charon at the large structure looming over them.

"You think he went to get a hotel room?" Charon returned to Jaret's side, where they stared at the large white wooden hotel with the maroon roof looming ahead.

"Not any hotel," Jaret answered. "The Stanley Hotel. Haunted as fuck. Not good."

"Oh! The place where Stephen King set *The Shining*, right?"

"Yeah, but the Stanley is haunted by actual ghosts, not made-up shit. Talk about a nasty vortex."

"He has Todd, so we have no choice." Charon headed forward, no longer moseying but jogging.

"Wait!" Jaret screamed. "No!" But he shot into motion behind Charon with Darth next to him. "Styx picked a magical location. He knows about vortexes! We can't charge in there!"

But Charon never heard him. An unseen force halted Charon

in his tracks. Alarmed, Jaret stopped but too late realized he'd already stepped onto Stanley Hotel land. The magic buzzed around him, spirits flew toward him, and his entire body seized up. He attempted to cast a spell, but nothing happened, even when he concentrated on the power of his jewels in his pocket. Nothing freed him. The family heirloom gems burned against his side but otherwise proved useless and then went cold.

Against his will, Jaret's body moved toward the hotel, entered the visitor tour entrance at the lowest level, and followed Charon's also-compliant form into a basement storage room where ghost energy sizzled. Styx stood in the center of the room, smiling and laughing, with Todd nearby and also incapacitated.

"*Tsk, tsk, tsk*," Styx shook his head. "You youngsters thought you could outwit me, did you? I knew you were in the palace." He stared at Jaret. "And you"—he pointed at Charon—"naughty boy, thought to hide him from me. Your little game failed, I'm afraid. Shall we reconsider whether you want to help me?"

CHAPTER SEVENTEEN

STANLEY HOTEL HAUNTINGS

7 MARCH 2019
Estes Park, CO

With no ability to move or counteract Styx's spell, Jaret closed his eyes and centered his concentration to avoid panic and to seek any solution to their captivity. He felt stupid at being manipulated because he had underestimated Styx's power and never grasped his intent in the first place.

Styx had bided his time until they got to the Stanley Hotel, then he threw magic as powerful as the Vampire Council's at Jaret and Charon, somehow hooking his forces onto the ghosts and evil energy of the famous hotel and capturing the two witch vampires before they could protect themselves.

Jaret felt the ghosts looping around him, sending tendrils of energy into his body, linking with Styx's enchantment and rendering Jaret's gems ineffective. Jaret opened his eyes and scanned the room, noticing how Charon stood immobile too. He saw Styx pace about in a casual manner and spotted Todd off to the side staring with vacant zombie eyes.

"Well, boys." Jaret flinched at the sound of Styx's voice. "A penny for your thoughts? I know magic. Of course, I do. And the hotel adds to my ability, as you know," he lowered his eyebrows. "A vortex can enhance a spell. And then together, my spirit friends and I turned your magic against you. This hotel contains some creepy ghosts."

Styx circled them, eyeing them up and down and smiling. "Here, let's be civil," Styx said. He released their bodies to move at their own discretion, yet a spell held them captive in the room and prohibited Jaret from reaching any of his magic. The gems were dead in his pocket.

"Let him go, at least." Charon motioned his head toward Todd. "You got what you wanted. We're here and under your control. He's not part of this."

Styx wandered over to Todd and patted him on the head.

"Another nice specimen you chose. All your boys are so pretty. Again, Charon, you almost make me want a man." Styx kissed Todd on the cheek and then walked over to stand in front of Charon. "Remember when you begged to suck my cock and I refused?"

Despite the predicament, Charon spoke with the same nonchalance as Styx.

"Unbelievable," Charon said and grinned. "I recall offering you as much, yeah. You have a nice cock. But I never begged, and you know I never would. I've never begged for a dick in my life. As for you, you can pretend you're straight as an arrow, but you sure love kissing guys and dreaming about having sex with them. Let Todd go and the three of us can discuss a hot, gooey threesome."

Styx roared a laugh, thrust his hand toward Todd, and released the young vampire from the spell. Todd stumbled, peered around the room in bewilderment, then concentrated on Charon. "Where are we? Who is this?"

"Listen to me," Charon spoke to Todd. "Leave. Go home. Find Jordan. Don't worry about us. Return to the castle as fast as possible and find Jordan."

Todd stared incredulously at his master but after a pause nodded and walked out of the room.

"So what do you want?" Charon sneered at Styx. "Remember how unstable you were during the game to create me? How you can't concentrate and go off the rails because you're a little loony tune? Actually, a lot loony tune. Well, you're getting even crazier this time."

Jaret stifled a groan, questioning if Charon's antagonism made sense. He was supposed to deceive Styx by pretending to come to his side. He remained silent since he had nothing to counter Charon's strategy.

"You want to bait me into a fight," Styx said and waved a finger at Charon. "To distract me. Always with the games and you."

Charon shrugged. "Or truth telling. Anyway, you want me to join you. But, to get me to cooperate, you murder my boys, piss me off, and kidnap me. Does your plan make sense when you think about it? Really?"

"You doubted me during the game too" Styx replied. "But I led you into becoming a vampire."

"Except I stole your witchcraft when you pretended to commit suicide. Seems like a draw there because I thought you had offed yourself, but you never anticipated my stealing your shizzle."

"Perhaps I *wanted* you to control magic." Styx tilted his head toward Charon.

"Right." Charon nodded. "And perhaps I'd like a good orgy with five women."

Styx grinned. "Your intellect both attracts and exacerbates me to no end!" Styx leapt across the room and planted a huge kiss on Charon's cheek. "We'll work so well together! 'Join me, and we can rule the galaxy.'" Styx performed a horrid impersonation of James

Earl Jones as Darth Vader. Jaret thought about the butterflies out of the butt story and confirmed Charon's assessment of a crazed villain.

"*If* I decide to join you." Charon pushed Styx away.

"When. *When* you join me." Styx clapped.

Jaret was amazed at Charon's move. Instead of pissing Styx off he somehow turned him into thinking Charon would comply with his demands.

Jaret was startled when his pocket buzzed a split second after Styx last spoke. He jammed his hand inside to find his gems abuzz, their magic returned and power coursing through his hand and into his head. He glanced up to see Charon scanning the room, something alerting him to a change, followed by Styx's eyes going wide and then a frown spreading across his face.

"You—" Styx pointed at Jaret and started toward him. "What did you—"

But the door to the storage room blasted inward and slammed against the other wall, followed by purple smoke and three figures storming into the room.

Pointing toward the intruders, Styx shot a bolt of lightning through his fingers. The flash slammed into them but had no effect. To protect himself, Jaret took out his gems and created a magical shield, so when Styx's electricity bounced off the intended victims and raced toward him, his force field held and the power ricocheted to the ceiling, cracking the plaster and creating a cloud of debris.

Charon moved behind Styx to grab him in a bear hug, but Styx sent the energy in his hands at Charon's face. Charon's head snapped back, his body collapsing to the floor.

Before Jaret could move to protect Charon, he found himself being yanked into the air against his will and carried out by an unseen entity. The force thrust him onto the lawn outside the hotel. He sensed Anthony nearby, but instead of wondering whether or not his dead lover had been responsible for removing him, he jumped up and started to run back inside. When he got to the basement door, he recalled Darth being with him when they got to Estes, but he couldn't sense her nearby.

"Darth!" he screamed and looked around for her. She was nowhere in sight.

Nothing was more important than Darth. He began a frantic search of Estes Park. With her vampire ability and hearing, she always obeyed him, no matter how far she ventured. Had something happened to her when they arrived at the hotel? Did Styx kill her? Who were the unknown intruders?

"Darth!" he screamed again, cracking a nearby car windshield with the force of his sound.

"She's busy." The familiar voice behind him calmed Jaret immediately.

Jaret cringed as he turned around and saw the expected glare.

"We need to stop meeting like this," Xavier said, kneeling on one leg as he petted Darth and kept her from running to Jaret.

"Are you kidnapping her?" Jaret asked.

Xavier laughed. "No. I well know her loyalty and have no desire to get bit. However, she's insurance."

"Insurance?" Jaret parroted.

Xavier nodded. "To keep you here."

"Am I going to vampire jail?"

"You should." Xavier stood and came to Jaret, releasing Darth who leapt in one bound to Jaret's feet and then jumped to lick him on the cheek. "But no, I'm not taking you to jail. I need your help. We can talk about your fate later."

"What do you need?"

"Those creatures Styx invented by kidnapping people. He unleashed a few more around Estes to distract us. We need to subdue them."

"Is this the war? Are we fighting him?"

Xavier made a dismissive facial expression. "This easily? We're here because two fools defied our orders and engaged Styx. If anything, you provided him with information.

"We have to go save Charon!" Jaret yelled, but Xavier grabbed his arm to stop him from going back to the hotel.

"He's fine. We'll discuss Charon and you later. Come on." Xavier tugged at Jaret's arm, then released him.

Xavier hurried away so Jaret followed. When they got to the entrance to Rocky Mountain National Park, a vampire zombie leapt at them from the trees. Jaret began to utter a spell to blow the fucker's head off, but Xavier held up a hand and stared daggers at Jaret. Instead, Xavier pointed his finger at the vampire, who fell to the ground.

"Pick him up and carry him with us," Xavier instructed.

"I'm not one of your minions." Jaret obeyed despite his proclamation. He was thankful Xavier ignored his snotty comment and continued into the park.

Jaret lugged the guy up the mountain until they arrived at a beautiful lake, where another zombie entity attacked before Xavier subdued him.

"Him too," Xavier pointed.

"Can't you carry one?"

Again, Xavier ignored him and resumed his tour of the park until they reached the Continental Divide. Outside the tourist center, Xavier subdued the last of the zombie vampires and pointed for Jaret to lay the other two next to him.

"You two out of control assholes killed innocent people when you imploded the four earlier." Xavier touched each body on the forehead and then stood back to wait.

"Styx controlled them."

Xavier nodded. "Yes. But you could have done something different."

"They were vampire zombies!" Jaret rolled his eyes.

"Zombie describes them well enough. Vampire, no. Styx half changed them without giving them full power. His spell can be reversed. These were innocent victims. Now, carry them back down the mountain."

Xavier spun around before Jaret could protest and walked away. He stayed several paces in front of Jaret until they got back into town. Jaret felt a bit silly, carrying three bodies down a mountain as if showing off his vampire strength. In a secluded park along the river, Xavier had Jaret line them up before staring hard at the inanimate bodies and motioning for Jaret to hide behind a boulder with him. Xavier shot a pink laser bolt at them, causing the three to spring to life. They shivered and looked around, human and befuddled. But they seemed to know one another, and Xavier yanked him away before Jaret could learn anything else.

"Come on. You're hosting the Council at your house."

"I am?" Jaret asked, still a rather compliant puppy.

"You are."

"Styx too?"

Xavier shook his head. "I imagine he escaped. No more questions. The Council would like a chat with you and Charon. Darth can come along, though she's the innocent in this mess."

Jaret and Xavier ambled along Fishcreek Road as Darth darted back and forth across the pavement, leaping over the creek and back again, hunting and playing without a care in the world. Even with vampire strength, she lived the typical life of a dog and provided Jaret endless distraction, love, and support.

Jaret assumed Xavier avoided talking because of his distaste for bickering. He no doubt disapproved of Jaret's actions so felt more comfortable with the quiet than with a confrontation. In the same regard, Jaret hated feuding with his vampire mentor and friend.

They rounded a bend in the road and his family home came into view. They plowed through a great deal of snow to reach the brown structure built on the side of a hill. They passed the garage door at the base of the house and climbed an outer staircase to the main level, where a wooden deck surrounded three sides of the home and offered beautiful views of the mountains. Jaret unlocked the front door and entered, brushing off the snow and commanding Darth to wipe her paws before she ran around the house to make sure no intruders had invaded.

Xavier went into the kitchen, while Jaret turned the lights on, straightened up a bit, and lit a fire in the great room fireplace for ambiance. He had anticipated a great deal of scolding from the Council but instinct told him to be a good host, regardless. Besides, creating a welcoming atmosphere gave Jaret the chance to release his nervous energy while he waited.

He went to Xavier, still in the kitchen, to find him preparing snacks from the frozen foods in the fridge. "Snacks for vampires?" Jaret asked.

"We enjoy acting human," Xavier answered as he popped a tray of appetizers in the oven.

"You're looking for something to do to avoid me."

Xavier let out a chuckle. "I could say the same."

"Yeah. I guess."

Xavier reached out to pull Jaret into a hug. "You infuriate me," he stated. "You *are* in trouble. But I love you. *We* love you. And someday you'll learn to trust us. We aren't the blundering fools of your imagination. Nor are you as clever as you surmise."

Jaret pulled away and wiped a tear from his eye. "I trust you. But this war is frightening and you—" Jaret stopped. "I love you too."

Before the interaction became any more awkward, the front door flung open and Charon stormed into the house. "You"—he pointed to Jaret—"and I are going to talk before the rest of the asshats arrive." Charon fled up the stairs, so Jaret followed, glancing at Xavier who gave him a bemused smile.

He found Charon sitting on his parents' bed, the room exactly as his mother and father had left it before being murdered by Henrik in Nebraska. He thought of movies and TV shows where a child dies and the parents keep the room as a shrine. He used to think those depictions were ridiculous; not everyone would refuse to change the room of a dead loved one. He had known one friend from high school whose younger sister died in an accident, and the family altered the room into a crafts room soon thereafter as a way to move forward. Yet here he was, with his home little changed from the one in which he had grown up.

Charon patted the bed for Jaret to sit next to him. Jaret obeyed but sat rigid a couple feel away.

Charon laughed. "Afraid of me?"

"This is my parents' room. I'd so not even flirt with you in here."

Again Charon giggled. "Makes it more exotic." He grabbed his crotch and winked.

Jaret reached over and grabbed Charon's wrist to stop him. "Seriously."

"Okay, okay. Besides, the shitheads will be here soon."

"What happened after I left?" Jaret asked.

"Catherine, Harriet, and Thomas used some mojo to take away Styx's ability to gather power from other forces. Styx seemed to control his own magic though, so there was some kind of stalemate. I was sitting on the floor after he blasted me, not sure what the fuck to do or whose side to be on. I almost attacked him again but remembered I was supposed to pretend to be on his side. Lame how I had to sit there like a slug. Before I could understand what had happened, Styx fled the room, and the others followed, so I went after them. But when Styx got to the outskirts of town and headed down Thompson Canyon, they stopped, headed back to me, and ordered me to come along."

"And you obeyed?" Jaret raised an eyebrow.

"Right? Weird, I know. But what else was I going to do? I needed to see you. I went back to the Stanley with the Council, where they covered our tracks and returned everything to normal.

We even had to erase the memories of humans who came down and saw what had happened. Then we headed here."

Jaret blew out a breath. "And?"

"And what?"

"Why did we need to talk?"

Charon shrugged. "Not sure. To confirm our strategy?"

"I think so. We need to hear their reprimand and shit. But we'll keep the same plan. This was a bump in the road, not good. But we learned a little more about Styx and can move on. Fuck them. We've got to continue to push. I thought you were moving in the right direction, even if it led us into a shitshow."

"I was! Styx is pretty easy to manipulate." Charon patted Jaret on the leg. "Let's get this over with."

They stood and headed for the door, but Charon grabbed Jaret by the arm and twirled him around, pulling him into a close embrace and taking his free hand to brush hair out of Jaret's face. "A quickie to release the tension?" Charon whispered.

Jaret giggled. "You never stop." Jaret removed himself from Charon's hold. "No. Once again, no. I could never get it up in my parents' room, anyway."

Jaret went downstairs into the great room, followed by Charon. There they found the Vampire Council assembled as if gathered for an evening social engagement, drinking wine and nibbling on appetizers and chatting as if they had not fought a battle against a crazy vampire. Jaret wondered when and where they bothered to grab food during the chaos.

They fell silent as Charon and Jaret joined them. Jaret plopped onto the couch next to Xavier while Charon poured himself a glass of wine. Charon twirled his finger in the air.

"Please," Charon said, "don't stop on our account. Proceed." He prepared a second glass of wine, brought it to Jaret, then sat between Jaret's legs on the floor. Charon leaned his head back and rubbed on Jaret's crotch until Jaret flicked his ear.

Sipping his wine, Jaret noticed the sensation of Anthony watching him. Jaret looked out the window into the dark night as if Anthony perched atop a tree and stared at him. Did his spirit hover outside to protect Jaret? The presentiment made Jaret self-conscious about Charon's deliberate intimacy in front of others.

"Can we get on with this?" Charon asked with his impatience.

"You killed innocent people." Harriet glared at them from a chair across the way, the same one Jaret's father had sat in for family meetings.

Charon guffawed. "I explained why. I thought they were dead creatures controlled by Styx. I thought it was mercy killing."

"Yeah," Jaret added. "We faced an emergency and had no time to contemplate the finer details of vampire zombie fuckers and their status." He and Charon snickered at themselves while the Council glared in return.

"Which, of course, proves our point." Catherine got out of her own chair next to Harriet and paced in front of them. "You two are not fit for this battle. You're too impulsive and ill-informed. And too powerful for your own good. Lucky for you, we had Thomas monitor from afar so knew when you got into trouble. You put Brady in danger."

"What happened to Brady?" Jaret asked.

"Nothing. I hid him from you." Xavier answered in a measured tone.

"You spied on us?" Charon asked. "Not okay."

"You're welcome for saving you." Catherine stood over Charon. "You got yourself into a mess with whatever grand scheme you've concocted. He could have killed one or both of you. Maybe we should have let him."

"We would've been fine without you barging in," Charon responded. "I had the situation under control."

"Why are you so quiet?" Catherine aimed her attention at Jaret.

"Me?" he asked.

She rolled her eyes. "Either you or the cushion behind you."

"I'm listening," Jaret answered. "Nothing I say will make a difference, and nothing has changed my assessment. You four plod along like you have all the time in the world, but Styx keeps pressing. He's murdering vampires and none of you give a shit. Charon keeps losing his boys. You may disapprove of how Charon was made and what he did to create his world, but his boys are vampires. They deserve better than to be executed by Styx while you ignore them." Jaret held up his hands to stave off their protests. "Unfair, I know. But until you act, until you fight this war, what else am I supposed to believe?"

"Speaking of the war," Thomas said. "We need to go. Finish up with them, Catherine."

As the other vampires cleaned up, Catherine remained in her authoritative stance in front of Jaret and Charon. "Stop interfering. We can't afford to keep Thomas as a spy on you two, so you're on your own. But stay out of the war. Stay away from Styx. I've argued on your behalf for the last time. I doubt I can keep getting a split vote not to punish you. If Anthony could vote from the grave, you'd both be in an iron box."

Jaret joined the silent vampires in cleaning up. But not Charon, who sat on the floor drinking his wine. When the Council left, Jaret joined Charon with a refilled glass and sat in his favorite rocking chair.

"Their behavior tells me a lot." Jaret swirled his wine.

"Really? I got nothing."

"They're playing us, for sure. I know how they act. We defied them, and they scold us like little boys who got muddy and came inside. No way." Jaret shook his head. "They aren't concerned with what we did. They're playing some game. They're hiding something."

"What game are they playing?" Charon finished the last of his wine. "Nice bottle, by the way."

"Thanks. I let rich, old vampires stock the wine around here. I don't know shit about vintage and crap. And I don't know the Council's game. But I've been naive to doubt them. No way they meandered along while Styx controlled the situation. They're way too smart and calculated. Maybe they intended the sacrifices, maybe not. But they have a plan. I'm more convinced than ever, they're using us. Maybe they want us to push them forward. Otherwise, we'd be in jail."

Charon jumped to his feet. "I hate being used. Assholes."

"Yeah." Jaret nodded but stared out the window at the beautiful Colorado night. Jaret's agreement was half-hearted because maybe he needed to trust them, after all. Maybe Xavier labeled him correctly as a petulant child not listening to his superiors. The idea of Anthony imploring him to mind the Council hit him full force.

"So," Charon said, "what's next? Can we have sex? We can pick any room you want. Where'd you wank while you were growing up? We can fuck there."

Jaret finished his wine, grabbed Charon's glass, and took them to the kitchen. He cleaned the dishes as he answered Charon. "I need time alone. You better go see your harem. They were scared shitless and need their fearless leader. Fuck them and come as much as possible to get the longings out of your system. You can close your eyes and think of me every time you come. And continue your effort to woo Styx. We're going to lure him to the vortex, but I think maybe the Council knows already."

"You do?"

"Maybe. Anyway, seems like we have some time. I need to be alone." Jaret led Charon to the door. "See you soon." He almost stood on his tiptoes to kiss him goodbye but stopped himself. He instead tapped him on the nose and pushed him into the winter.

PART SEVEN

EMOTIONAL TURMOIL

CHAPTER EIGHTEEN

JENN'S ANNOYING VISIT

7 MARCH 2019
Central City, CO

Walking through the center of the old mining town turned gambling destination, Jaret remembered family outings to Central City. He and his sister had run around to the stores and pretended to live in the Wild West. The family enjoyed the history of the town. Jaret reflected on the old mountain village of his youth as he meandered the deserted streets.

Jaret looked into the candy store, wishing to transport himself back to the days when Lincoln, Jenn, and he stormed inside and picked what candy their parents would buy them. The memory signaled to Jaret why he got rid of Charon, why he felt such embarrassment about his own behavior toward the Council, and why his emotions whirled in chaos. Jaret's mind returned him to a youthful doubting of himself when he had wished he could disappear from everyone with nothing more than his dog at his side. As if on cue, Darth trotted up and nudged his leg.

Jaret kept moving down the street and stood outside the Central City Opera House, his favorite childhood destination here. He laughed, thinking only a gay boy would love the opera at a young age. Lincoln and his mom had despised going but liked the dinner beforehand so went along, but his dad, Jenn, and he had reveled in the atmosphere and music.

Jaret went around back and pulled out a sapphire ring, commanding the gem to unlock the door as he scanned for security devices and cast a spell to hide himself. He entered the old building, admiring the history and feeling of past generations as if they remained in the theater. The building and entire town reminded Jaret of his undergraduate and graduate career, where he majored in history and could transport himself into the past with nothing more than imagination. He'd never put the degrees to practical use, what with becoming a vampire in the middle of completing his doctorate. But the discipline grounded him, distracted him, and reminded him about an individual's obligation to participate in something bigger than only self-interest.

Jaret sat at the edge of the stage and dangled his legs. He called for Darth, who meandered to him and sat, leaning into his body. Her presence cracked the dam holding back his feelings. Jaret burst into a passionate fit of crying. Since Anthony had confronted him at Lake Estes about his friendship with Charon, Jaret had denied the turmoil within himself. He suppressed his own feelings, his doubt, his fear, and had lost himself in bravado as a way to escape his insecurity.

He felt lost, embarrassed, and stupid. And alone—hopelessly alone. So much of what he had said and most of the actions he had taken came from a profound sense of insecurity and loneliness, despite how they appeared to the outside world.

Jaret thought about the sexual temptation with Charon, his feelings and actions fitting the emotional turmoil to perfection. The physical attraction and Charon's persistence made Jaret feel wanted and alive. But Jaret knew giving in to the lust would last for the duration of the encounter and then leave him feeling more exposed once Charon moved to his next conquest and left Jaret in the dust. Oh, Jaret wanted to lose himself with Charon. He protected himself from the mistake by remembering how his emotion ruled too strongly. The aftermath of sex with Charon would be unbearable.

Jaret had also tried to act nonchalant like the Council

whenever they found murdered and maimed vampires. He hid behind an outward indignation toward the Council's cavalier attitude. In truth, the inanimate bodies of vampires he had never met were seared into his memory. They were innocent victims, nothing more than the war's collateral damage.

He desperately wanted to play the role of fierce warrior, unafraid and full of righteous anger. Instead, he cowered and mourned.

And what could Jaret do with his conflicted emotions about the Council? He thought the four members slow and ineffective, but the last month and especially the confrontation with Styx at the Stanley Hotel forced him to see a more rational truth: no way could Jaret Bachmann be duping the Council. Xavier, Thomas, Catherine, and Harriet protected the vampire world with their entire souls. Much as he disagreed with Council strategy, logic and a more removed analysis told him of his own folly. These new thoughts also left him feeling used and manipulated by the vampires he loved.

What if they all thought him a fool? What if the war and the disagreement severed their friendship, even if they allowed him to live? He cared for them with all his heart yet had acted like a spoiled brat. In his defense, however, they *had* pissed him off.

While these inner thoughts contradicted his brash attitude, they squared with his frustration at how the Council kept him in the dark. He and Anthony had never resolved keeping Jaret off the

Council. Or, if the Council wanted to preserve their odd number for voting, Jaret thought he should at least be privy to secret Council business. After all, Jaret was married to one of their own. But Anthony had fought Jaret's attempts to get information more than anyone else on the Council.

Jaret choked on the sob bursting from within. He wept with such brutal sorrow Darth shoved herself into his side and licked and kissed his face with manic attention. She imparted a dog's desperate attempt to will him to happiness with her love. Anthony, gone. Anthony, dead.

Memories of Anthony flooded his mind, threatening to overwhelm him with grief. He envisioned the tall, blond, long-haired god who had appeared on the path along Lake Michigan in Chicago to save him when a group of college football players threatened to beat the crap out of him; Anthony after he was exposed to Jaret as a vampire, comfortable with Jaret's being a witch. Then, there was the breakthrough when Anthony gave up his attempts to block Jaret's transformation and their relationship because of Jaret's witchcraft and had converted him—still the hottest, most passionate sex Jaret recalled in his short life. He recalled every moment as vampires when they planned their future together, decided on a movie to watch, or hung out like a normal couple, and the thrilling escapades, such as a wild tour of Alaska Anthony had orchestrated for Jaret's one year anniversary of becoming a vampire.

Of course, Jaret and Anthony had struggled with each other.

They disagreed about Anthony's initial reluctance to make Jaret a vampire. Anthony feared how Jaret's powerful sorcery, impatience, and insecurity would be too volatile a mix if added to vampirism. At times, the lovers had bickered about keeping Jaret from knowing Council business, a tension that escalated because of their disagreement about the war.

None of those conflicts mattered to Jaret anymore. They seemed trivial with Anthony forever lost. Jaret thought the tears would never end when he sensed Anthony's ghost watching him, protecting him.

Jaret had made his typical effort to ignore his emotion about Anthony's death, to smash the feelings into oblivion. With every such attempt for as long as Jaret could remember—going back to childhood, the more he repressed his feelings, the more they would eventually explode out of him.

He recalled the image of Anthony hanging limp in the throes of Styx's magic, glaring at Jaret and ordering him to leave. And then Anthony had died.

Jaret stopped crying after what felt like hours. He was left empty and alone, except for Darth, who he clutched to his side.

"That was very dramatic."

The familiar voice and smart-ass comment made Jaret smile. Maybe Jenn was the only person, or ghost, who could get such a reaction. The spirit of his sister plopped down next to him, her face smiling as she reached out a semitransparent hand and rubbed his shoulder.

"Not many people could make me laugh at the moment." Jaret wiped a tear and smiled at his sister. "I don't even know if you're real or some false vision I've conjured to help me through the drama."

"Good question. If I say I'm real, your mind will think you made up the comment to convince yourself. If I say I'm a figment of your imagination, you'll still think you're bonkers. Which you are, by the way." She smiled.

And Jaret laughed. "Why are you bugging me?"

"You looked like you needed someone to annoy you. Does a sister need an excuse to visit her brother?"

"A dead sister coming back through the ether does. You don't follow me around all the time. I've seen all of you on the other side, happy and hanging out. Something or someone brought you back."

"I won't give away my secrets. How about you accept my help without the questions? No need to worry about my realness. Is re-alness even a word?" she asked. "Could be Darth asked. Or your emotion shook the entire universe and the gods ordered me to get you under control before the entire universe exploded. Maybe some*one* sent me." Jenn shrugged. "Who knows? Who cares? I'm here so let's deal with you."

"What about me?"

Jenn laughed. "Even as a vampire you like to ask a stupid

question to stall for time?"

"Fuck off."

"Better," Jenn said. "Closer to the truth."

"And aren't you sophisticated and smart in your ideas? I guess dying as a teen didn't freeze your intellect at that age."

"I was *very* mature for my age if you'll recall. And no—I'm not frozen. I've learned so much in death."

"Figures you'd even handle being a ghost all mature and shit."

Jenn's ghost leaned against him. She reached over and itched Darth behind the ears, to which Darth wagged her stub of a tail. "See. She knows I'm real. But you got one thing right: I like the other side. So let's get on with our business so I can leave and you can go back to pretending you don't have emotions."

Jaret chuckled. "I thought being a vampire would end how I repress my feelings. I hid myself while growing up because of my seeing ghosts, witchcraft, and being gay. But I came out and admitted those issues and still lean toward concealing myself."

Jenn nodded. "Yep. You are who you are. You're working on being better, though. You've had a lot to deal with."

"You came all this way to play Captain Obvious?"

Jenn threw her head back with laughter. "Yeah. You want blunt? You're lost. You're searching for yourself. You've got to find who you are before you can deal with the war and other shit. Well, none of the problems will disappear, but if you don't look for yourself amid them, you'll flounder and make more dumbass decisions."

"Like thinking I fooled the Council? Or can fight the war on my own? What?"

"All of the above. And more. Like thinking with your cock."

Jaret held up his hands to stop Jenn. "I'm not talking to my sister about my sex life. And I don't know what to do." Jaret started to speak but choked on the words, having to control himself before he continued. "I'm not even sure who I am."

Jenn pulled Jaret into a hug. "Yes, you do. You need to accept the truth and the feelings. I need to go but I'll say this: Hold onto what you feel. *Believe* what you *sense.* There's more going on than meets the eye. I'm going to give you a hint. Your idea about using Notre Dame as a vortex is correct."

Jenn vanished before his eyes.

"What the fuck?" Jaret asked Darth. "Always cryptic. The supernatural world is fucked up."

Darth wagged her tail as if in agreement.

After Jenn's spirit visited him in Central City, Jaret took the next day to clear his head and get centered.

Jaret had lost himself amid his vampire transformation and relationship with Anthony. Those events were followed too soon by an impending vampire war and Anthony's death. Though powerful beyond belief with his vampire body and senses, not to mention his magic, Jaret had to remember his age in human years. He was a young adult, still developing his own identity. Becoming a vampire did not grant the wisdom that comes with age. He was too sensitive to what other people thought of him or how they judged him.

Jaret's being lost had led him to act like a wounded child when he felt left out by the Council or treated like a little kid by Anthony. The war compounded the problem by sprinkling in a serious dose of terror. The major benefit of becoming a vampire, even better than its strength, power, and wealth, was eternal life. Styx presented the very real possibility of dying.

Frightened, Jaret had attempted to control a situation beyond his authority. He had tried to force the Council and Charon to fight the war on his terms as a way to calm his own panic. In retrospect, Jaret felt ridiculous. But, to move beyond his childish behavior, Jaret had to face his feelings and stop berating himself.

The Council *had* made him feel insecure and alone. From his earliest memories, Jaret was inclined toward mistrust and thoughts of isolation. These sentiments grew worse for him when he lost his entire family. Thus, when the Council had left him out of their deliberations, especially when Anthony did it, Jaret was devastated. Throw in Anthony's death, and who the fuck *could* hold everything together?

Sitting in the cold air on his parent's deck, Jaret forgave himself.

Powerful feelings had always surged through him and guided him for better and for worse. Recognizing this truth calmed Jaret. He vowed to move forward with more caution and logic, but also by facing his emotions and not running from them.

Jaret also determined to listen to his own senses moving forward. He had already decided to push for the war to occur at Notre Dame before Jenn confirmed the location. He was certain the cathedral was the place for them to defeat Styx.

Before Jaret could conclude anything else, his guest arrived.

"You sounded better in your message." Xavier sat next to him, though clothed in nothing but a long sleeve T-shirt and jeans.

"Should we go inside, in case anyone sees?" Jaret asked.

"Look at you, enforcing Council rules. You and Thomas act all defiant and then become Council police." Xavier smiled. "You're right."

They settled into the great room, sitting together on the couch while Xavier waited in silence.

"So," Jaret began, "I've been an ass, but sometimes the Council makes me into one. I know I sound like I'm giving a half-assed apology. Because, I mean, I *am* saying sorry for being a shithead. But I'm not apologizing for disagreeing with you or being hurt by how you treat me. Those are real emotions."

Xavier grinned. "You packed a ton into a couple sentences. I accept your apology and offer my own in return. I recognize how the Council behaves in keeping its secrets. I can't account for how Anthony handled you. He twisted himself into knots when dealing with Council business and you. But I didn't have to go along. Nor do I need to continue with how we've treated you. I can't tell you everything, but I can be more forward in explaining and less high and mighty."

Jaret nodded. "Sounds good. Because I hated fighting with you guys. I was a mess and, well, I don't know if I can explain but, anyway, I'm happy we're chatting and feel normal."

"Me too." Xavier smiled.

"I gotta ask another question. Did you send Jenn to me?"

"She may be dead," Xavier answered, "but Jenn makes her own decisions."

"Someone with the ability to commune with the dead could always reach out to ask her for a favor."

"Does the reason for her appearance matter?"

"You're doing the Council thing: *hidden agenda, I won't tell you.*"

Xavier laughed. "Right. I see how the Council can bother the shit out of you. Let me try again. I don't want to comment on why Jenn came. You needed her, and she appeared. Nothing else matters. You heal yourself."

Jaret chuckled. "I'd rather have a direct answer, but I like the lack of bullshit. I prefer you not telling me than when you used to give me fucking riddles."

"So what did you learn from Jenn?"

"I gotta find myself. I mean, I kinda came to the same conclusion before she got there because I had a mega cray-cray breakdown crying fit. But Jenn helped me confirm the problems. I have a lot of emotions about the past, the present, and the future. They were too much to handle. And I *hate* dealing with my own emotion. So I hid from everything until I exploded. Here's how I'm feeling: I'm going to fight in this war, and I still disagree with the Council. But I also want to stop being a shithead all the time."

Xavier laughed aloud. "I appreciate the returned candor. The Council knows what we're doing, even if you disagree."

"What *is* the Council's plan? Tell me."

Xavier began to say something but stopped. "I was almost going to be cryptic like old times." Xavier rubbed his face in thought. "I can't tell you. Styx is powerful and we're keeping Council plans concealed to protect everyone. Including you. You'll be a part of this war. I assure you. But until the correct moment, you're better off in the dark."

The words stung but not as much as before today. "How many more vampires are you four going to let die before we fight?" There, Jaret could also use words as a weapon.

"Touché." Xavier grimaced. "We don't want anyone to die, but Styx is hell-bent on death and destruction. We're going to win. I promise. But we have to be deliberate."

"Sounds a little evasive."

Xavier nodded. "Yes, because I won't tell you the specifics."

Silence fell between them. The stark honesty felt so much better. More adult.

"How about the same from you?" Xavier broke through the

quiet. "You gonna keep up with the plan you hatched with Charon despite how Styx thwarted your efforts?"

"I believe in what I think needs to happen. And if I can save vampires, I will. Since I don't know the plan, I want to forge ahead with my own. I'm not undermining you. I feel right about my actions and guided by my magic and even by Anthony."

Xavier jerked his head with surprise to stare at Jaret.

"What?" Jaret asked.

Xavier shook his head. "Nothing. Well, I mean. Actually, I mean good. Keep your feelings about Anthony front and center. The loss of Anthony could be a good opportunity for you to find your *true* self."

"Yeah. I think you're right. In some twisted way, the pain and chaos gives me a window into myself. I was thinking the same thing because I'm pretty young, you know?"

One side of Xavier's mouth inched into a grin. "I do know. You'd do well to remember as much. In a number of ways."

"I'm working on balancing being myself without being immaturely impulsive."

"Speaking of which," Xavier said, "in a roundabout way, I have one other thing to discuss."

"Okay." Jaret drew out the word, wondering what was coming.

Xavier fidgeted with the cross underneath his T-shirt, a sign whenever he got nervous. "This business with Charon. You need to be careful."

"I don't think you understand him. And I'm not being naïve. I know he lives for himself. But he means well. The situation with his having the men under his control is more complicated than what you see. He sides with us against Styx. In fact, he knows Styx better than any of us. Charon learned a great deal during the time he spent with Styx before he became a vampire. And his magic can help with the war. Charon wants to defeat Styx."

"I wasn't referring to the war." Xavier grinned.

"What?" Jaret furrowed his brow before the answer smacked him in the face. "Oh. Well, no. Nothing sexual ever happened. Won't happen."

"He's a very dangerous rebound."

Jaret smirked. "Yeah. Listen, um, I get your concern. Of all the things to worry about, Charon and me is *not* one of them. Okay, so I feel way awkward here. Listen, I find him incredibly hot. Mesmerizing. Dominant. Commanding. Too cute for words. I also know him pretty well, and I know myself. He sees me as something to conquer, and I'd never be able to do a one-night stand. Trust me on this one, if nothing else. I've had numerous opportunities in about every place you can imagine, and we never did anything. Well, he came in his pants once—"

"Wait! What? I thought you said you never did anything!" Xavier shouted.

"We didn't! I was refusing his offers, sitting across a coffee table from him, and he was being seductive but ended up creaming his pants."

Xavier shook his head. "Sounds close to *some*thing, not nothing."

"I know. But we've never had sex. Lots of flirting but nothing else. I swear."

"Good." Xavier scrunched his face.

"What?"

"I want to make sure you don't do something with him you'll regret later. Let's leave the matter there."

"Weird. Okay. I'll resist Charon with all my might. Though you should know it's not easy to go without sex. I know my grief is strong, but so is my sex drive."

"Jack off," Brady proclaimed as he walked into the room. "I assume you two knew I was here."

Xavier and Jaret laughed. "Yeah," they answered in unison.

"Good. I agree with Xavier, by the way. Charon has you wrapped around his finger. Or maybe I should say his dick. You're lubed up and ready to go. You need to watch yourself."

"I am!"

Xavier stood to leave. "I brought Brady because I thought you two could use a night of movie watching."

After hugs goodbye, Jaret turned to Brady. "The Council keeps you like a little pet. They hide you away until they decide to take you for a walk."

Brady laughed. "Nah. They're protective, which I appreciate.

I could use a night without talking about the impending war though."

"Me too." Jaret led them into the kitchen to make drinks and then to decide on a movie.

CHAPTER NINETEEN

THOMAS STIRS THE POT

10 MARCH 2019
Estes Park, CO

Jaret felt more centered than he had in months, perhaps years, after first Jenn and then Xavier had assisted his latest journey of self-discovery. Time with Brady helped too, with nothing more exciting than getting drunk and watching movies. He and Brady had acted like two twentysomething friends gathered for an evening of entertainment, as if nothing in the world plagued them. Even as the universe felt on edge and a vampire war threatened their lives, Jaret found a renewed commitment to finding himself within the chaos.

Yet a tension ran through Jaret. Yes, he felt more at peace with the Council. But Jaret also intended to keep working against their plodding strategy in the war. Jaret sensed the essential role he must play in the final battle.

Whether the Council admitted his importance or dismissed him, his magic called for him to further solidify going to the vortex because his side needed more power than ever before to defeat Styx. Jaret's capacities with witchcraft would become essential.

Thomas, Xavier, and Brady planned another visit so Jaret prepared some wine and cleaned the great room but finished and had an hour to himself before they arrived. He and Darth went to the lowest level of the house that contained one small bedroom, a tiny hallway, a one car garage. Off the back of those two rooms was one of the weirdest rooms Jaret had ever encountered. The house was built into the side of the mountain, with half this level containing the bedroom, hallway, and garage, and the other half a strange storage room. His family had always called it the "rock room." At the door into this space, one stepped onto a small cement pad that had a normal room's head clearance, but the rest of the room had an enormous boulder for a floor that sloped gradually upward until only a couple feet separated the rock from the next floor's beams. His family used the unheated space for storage because it had no other practical use.

Jaret sighed as he surveyed the crap crammed into the room. He had meant to clean out the shit but cringed because no task in the world appealed to him less. He'd rather fight a war against Styx. To his family, the immense storage area had meant keeping anything and everything, piling one box on top of another and, at other times, throwing an object into the room without worrying where it landed. And no one ever used anything once it arrived in this gem of a spot. He wondered what creatures or mold or other substances might lurk underneath.

Jaret walked the boulder's incline toward the center of the room, dodging stuff as he went along and hunching over to avoid hitting his head when he got to the middle. He cleared a space on the rock and sat with his legs crossed. Darth came up next to him and stood with an annoyed expression as she stared at him. She let out a grunt, turned in a circle, and tripped over several objects. Her vampire agility allowed her to jump sideways and backward several feet, where she landed on Jaret's lap and growled in frustration.

Jaret hugged her and leaned over to kiss her on the head as he stifled a laugh. Seeming to know his amusement and not sharing the merriment, Darth folded her ears back.

"You're fine, you maniac. Here." Jaret grabbed an old dog bed of hers from nearby and situated it next to him. He lifted her onto the cushion and held her there when she started to move around. "You don't have space to spin around. Chill."

Darth glared at him but curled into a ball to rest, no doubt quite intentional in placing her back to him.

Once he stopped snickering, Jaret closed his eyes and relaxed his body to feel the energy around him. Though without the same magic as the Bachmann Mansion in Fremont or other locations such as the Stanley Hotel, Jaret noticed the tingling around him. Jaret reached inside his pocket and removed the gems, holding them in the air and feeling them hover before his closed eyes.

Streaks of color shot past his eyelids, the atmosphere became lighter, and Jaret's essence lifted out of the room, straight through the house, and high into the atmosphere above the Colorado Rockies. He drifted away, not paying attention to his surroundings before he came to float over Notre Dame Cathedral in Paris. The cathedral was a place of majesty, exploitation, and wonder. It symbolized France's rich history, as well as how religion could be used for good and evil.

Jaret's spirit peered down at the structure's iron roof and saw the energy encircling the entire structure, an orange-red glow of passion and emotion, of evil and triumph. He swore the gargoyles peered up to him at the same time and squinted, not in anger or approval but as if apprising the reason for his presence.

Jaret returned his soul to his body and opened his eyes.

Darth, next to him, had twisted her head around to stare at him with a lingering look of disapproval plastered on her face. Jaret laughed again.

"Okay! Okay! We'll go. I saw what I needed. It'll be the

perfect place. Maybe you can go along and meet the gargoyles." Darth sprang up and leapt from the dog bed to the door, nudging the doorknob. Jaret caught up to her and released her from captivity. "At least you didn't bust through the door this time."

Once upstairs, Jaret waited a couple minutes before his senses alerted to approaching vampires and soon thereafter he heard the front door open and felt his three friends enter his house without knocking.

Before he could see Jaret standing in the great room, Brady shouted, "If you're not done jacking off put yourself back in your pants because we're coming in! No one here wants to see the family jewels!"

If not for his prudish nature, Jaret would have whipped out his dick to stroke away as they entered. Instead, he poured each of them a glass of wine.

Brady entered first with a smirk. "I so hoped to catch you in action." He mimed jerking off before grabbing a glass of wine and sitting. "I'm here for you after they chat you up. I think I'm here to babysit you. The Council needs to talk, first, of course. Blah, blah, blah with them. Lots of talk. I've never known a group of people to have more meetings. And I've only known them a few years. Can't imagine centuries of these discussions!"

"You're not helping our cause," Xavier announced as he entered and pointed at Brady. He sat on a couch and waited until Thomas got two glasses and handed him one before sitting next to

Xavier.

"How many more of these little rendezvous must we endure?" Jaret asked but smiled. "I know I sound snarky, but Brady has a point. You meet and discuss shit without any action. You four are worse than Congress. Sorry. But really, does being a vampire mean century after century of long-ass conversations about every detail of life?"

Thomas laughed. "The Council loves these chats. You have no idea." He rolled his eyes. "We came to protect you. I know you disagree, but we *do* have your best interests in mind. So Xavier mentioned how you two stopped bickering. I'm even better at being direct, so we need to know—what are you planning?"

Jaret tilted his head and grinned. He took a chair opposite them and swirled his wine to seem like he knew what he was doing, when in reality he had no idea why. Anthony mentioned oxygenating the wine or something one time. The delay gave him time to frame his answer. "We agreed no bullshit. Not necessarily to divulge our secrets. Unless the Council had a change of heart and decided to tell me everything?"

"Nice try." Xavier smiled. "We control the vampire world, not you. Please Jaret. For your own good, explain this plot you hatched with Charon. We already know bits and pieces."

"How?"

"Surveillance." Thomas stared hard at Jaret. "You think the Council let this continue without watching you? Before you freak out, we were protecting you. You distracted us from preparing against Styx, but we'd do anything to keep you and the others safe."

"Tell that to the dead vampires." Jaret took a deep breath to stop himself from uttering the litany of invectives racing through his mind. After a moment he spoke in a measured tone. "If you spied on me, you already know everything."

"I wish we did." Xavier shook his head. "We know you transport your spirit to distant locations. We learned you're planning something with Charon against Styx. Tell us the details."

Jaret frowned. "No. Listen, we agreed to be honest and less bitchy. You won't tell me everything, and I need to keep things from you."

"Like how much you want to bang Charon?" Thomas asked.

"Fuck you." Jaret jumped out of his seat, paced the room a few times, then sat again. "I've never done anything with him. Why are you two so concerned with Charon and me? I can fuck whomever I want. Not my fault he likes my tight ass. I'll put whatever, and whoever, I want into it."

Thomas roared a laugh and nodded, then reversed himself and shook his head before shrugging and laughing more. "Maybe."

"Please, listen," Xavier pleaded. He shot a look of reprimand at Thomas. "Yes, we watched you. We can watch all vampires when we want. We learned a little. Your plan, whatever it is, risks your safety. We're worried about you." Xavier's soothing voice calmed Jaret.

"Yeah, I know." Jaret nodded. "I understand. But I need to do my thing."

Thomas got up and pulled Xavier to his feet but looked hard at Jaret. "Your thing. Well, do *your thing* with Brady tonight, okay? Nice and quiet here in Colorado. We gotta go."

"So fast?" Jaret squinted at Brady. "They asked you to get the goods on me, didn't they? Otherwise, they wouldn't be all casual, time to go, nothing to worry about here."

Xavier, Thomas, and Brady laughed.

"Something along those lines," Thomas said and escorted Xavier out of the house.

After Thomas and Xavier departed, Brady and Jaret obeyed their edict and enjoyed another night of staying inside, watching movies, dancing to Mika songs after they got plastered, and dreaming about what Hollywood crush they wanted to turn into a vampire and live with for eternity. Jaret loosened up so much with the alcohol he enjoyed their game without feeling like he cheated on Anthony. By the end, Jaret laughed because he mimicked Charon with the creation of a make-believe harem of Hollywood hotties for himself. He and Brady avoided talk about the war.

They woke the following evening and intended to hang out at home after they cracked open a bottle of Colorado distilled whiskey.

Jaret threw a shot back and poured another. "Before we chill, tell me what the Council wanted you to do. Spy? Double agent?"

Brady took a drink, snorted, then had whiskey shoot out his nose when he laughed. "Dude! My nose burns!" Brady wiped at his face with his sleeve and hollered about the pain through his smile. "Not funny!"

"Then why are you laughing?" Jaret held his side.

"Masochism. Fuck. I thought vampires healed and shit but damn shit going from your throat to your nose hurts like a human."

Jaret nodded. "Yeah. We heal but can hurt like a motherfucker in the process. We have tolerance for pain, or at least most do. Not you."

"Nope. Not me. Dealing with pain was never a strong suit. Anyway, about your question." Brady shook his head as if knocking away the rest of the pain.

"Yeah. What was so funny?"

Brady's face lit up with shock. "Don't be Mr. Innocent! About me being a double agent or some shit? Speaking of things outside my wheelhouse, spying and secret agent crap are not strengths either. I have some good attributes, you know. But of late everything relates to my weaknesses. War. Conniving. Spying. Secret agent. I love movies about those topics. I couldn't live them in reality. Maybe with time my vampire powers will change my attitude and ability."

"Doubtful," Jaret responded. "As a vampire, I feel the same as when I was human. The Council members have lived centuries. I think they act like they always did when human. They changed a little over time with all they learned and experienced, but their essential personalities seem intact, at least from what they say. Tell me about this spy agenda of yours before you shoot more whiskey out your schnoz."

"You make my role sound so sexy, or duplicitous. I wish I could tell you a thrilling story like a Dan Brown novel to keep you on the edge of your seat. Reality will bore the shit out of you. You already know the gist." Brady shrugged. "The Council knows you have a plan to intervene in the war. For whatever reason, they can't figure out the details even though their magic seems omnipotent. I've seen one of those orange orbs pop up, and two seconds later they know a vampire was naughty. With you they get blocked, I guess. Cock-blocking the Council!"

Jaret giggled. "My magic. Like Charon. Some spells cloud their ability. What does all this have to do with you?"

"Simple. Xavier wants to know what you're doing, so asked me to find out. Dude, I never said a word about what I know. I dodged and shit and they never pressed. But they keep sending me to you. At least they didn't start pulling out my fingernails to get information. Maybe they have a spell on me and can see through my eyes." Brady rubbed his eyes and glanced around the room with alarm.

Jaret laughed at him. "If they could, they'd do so without telling you and would already know everything."

Brady nodded. "Right. Okay. So, pretty much I've told you

the scoop. They want me to dig around and report. I know you disagree with the Council, but I think they honestly want to protect you. Anyway, I hope you know my loyalty resides with you. I'd never betray you, of all people. I'm the fucking little pawn in the whole mess. I told you before I agree they act too passive and shit with the war and will help you if I can. End of story."

Jaret teared up. "You're going to make blood shoot out my eyes. Stop. I know your loyalty. I'll always do the same for you. Never get yourself in trouble with them on my behalf, okay?"

"Yeah. Okay."

"What else?" Jaret asked. "You got something on your mind."

Brady drank the last of his whiskey. "I'm making something fruitylicious before we dive into your question." Brady left and Jaret heard him in the kitchen for a few minutes before he returned with thirty-two-ounce glasses of some punch concoction full of alcohol. Brady handed Jaret one and held his in the air. "Cheers!"

Jaret took a long drink. "Whoa! Not a lot of fruit juice in here. Is this straight liquor?"

Brady nodded with a huge grin. "Almost. Good, huh? But your liquor is getting a little low." He sat beside Jaret. "This kinda gnawed at me for a while. Like going back to the shit at the end of college. Steve stalks you and dies. Henrik offs your family." Brady stopped and lowered his head. "Sorry I sound flippant."

"You're fine." Jaret touched Brady on the shoulder. "Sounds like this gets heavy, so I hope you'll keep the conversation light when you can."

Brady took a long drink before he spoke. "You've experienced heavy shit in a short amount of time."

Jaret chuckled. "Jenn's ghost visited me and we enjoyed the same fun reminiscences. I'd rather not make the list again."

"Right. I'm not saying this because of the Council, by the way. My point is that I don't think you ever found yourself. I agree with Jenn. I feel like you hold yourself back a lot. Grief. Fear. Uncertainty. Your experiences grabbed you by the nuts. Flash forward to a vampire war brewing. You know about the situation but are kept out of the loop. You want to act, but they block you. Then Anthony dies. Who could survive? You. But at a cost. And I think your reaction to the Council and the problems gets worse because they continue to remind you of all the shit."

"I agree."

Brady turned his head to squint at Jaret. "That's all? Our work is done here?"

"No! I mean, I agree. I figured out the same thing myself. I existed in a perpetual state of survival mode. If you want to take the story back even farther, I hid myself earlier, when I was in grade school and saw ghosts for the first time. I was sent to psychologists and heard loud and clear how everyone thought I was nuts. So I began repressing my feelings and never stopped. If you want to go to another layer, this explains a rage within me. I hide my feelings until a violent anger explodes out of me."

"What can I do to help?"

Jaret looked into his half-empty cup for an answer. "What you already do. Be here for me. Besides, I doubt I can find the solution in the midst of the war."

"Maybe. Or...maybe the chaos is the perfect time."

Jaret took his turn to peer at his friend with a frown. "How could chaos possibly help?"

"By making you confront your feelings. Instead of hiding your emotion, take time to feel. You can still fight and plot and do whatever. But get some insight into yourself along the way."

"I'll try."

"Hey!" Brady exclaimed. "I can help you! I'm not as powerful as the Council or a vampire witch so I tag along like a lost puppy everywhere. But if you let me help you, then I have a purpose too!"

Jaret grinned with a tear of happiness forming in his eye. "Yeah. I'd like for you to help." Then he giggled. "You sound like the song from *Avenue Q*. About finding your purpose."

"Hot puppet sex. Nice."

They imbibed the remainder of their drinks in silence. Jaret thought about what Brady told him, glad for his friend's assistance.

Jaret got up and took Brady's glass. He made them a much simpler drink of coconut rum and Dr. Pepper before returning to slide onto the couch next to Brady.

"Any advice?" Jaret asked. "I think I know myself pretty well. I'm loving but mistrustful. Hopeful but, at the same time, pretty cynical. Longing for acceptance and then bitter angry if I get rejected. Wanting the best for people but expecting the worst from the assholes of the world."

"Sounds about right. You're also shy but devoted to those with whom you connect. You gotta find yourself so you can balance doing what others want with your needs. You could then help yourself not to be a complete dick when you do defy people."

Jaret took his turn to shoot his drink out his nose but swallowed before disaster hit. "You think I'm a dick?"

"No. Well, seldom. But when you bottle up shit and then decide you can't take the crap anymore, you lash out like a motherfucker. Never toward me. But to the Council all the time. And I am *not* defending them. I get your reaction. Except your anger never helps. You act kinda like a little kid with a temper tantrum."

At first Brady's words stung, but Jaret heard the love. "You're right. I'll work on my responses. You can help me."

"How?"

"Point out when I act like a douche."

"Okay. But maybe not right in the moment. Because I don't want the douche aimed at me."

Jaret laughed. "Deal."

"This got heavy." Brady jumped to his feet. "I know they wanted us to stay inside, but we got a couple hours before the bars close. Let's at least go watch people."

"Where? In Estes?"

Brady nodded. "Sure. Downtown. The little bar with the patio overlooking the river."

"Not our typical scene."

"Snob." Brady yanked Jaret to his feet. "Come on. Let's go. We can drink more, maybe flirt if a few cute straight guys are there, then feed on the way home afterward."

"Charming. Straight guys and drunken blood drinking."

Brady laughed hard. "I always have great ideas. We finally hit on one of my strengths!"

Part Eight

Finding Himself

CHAPTER TWENTY

ONE-NIGHT STANDS

13 MARCH 2019
Boulder, CO

Jaret thought he had figured out a resolution to his problems and overwrought emotions without much trouble until he found himself alone. With Jenn, Thomas, Xavier, and especially Brady, he identified how lost he had become—if he ever even knew for sure who he was in the first place. He realized the need to connect with his feelings. Tuning into his emotion with someone else's assistance or on a limited basis proved much easier than a daily dose of pondering the million-dollar question: Who *was* Jaret?

In his head he imagined a game show where people took turns quizzing him about his true self. Contestants could craft a fake event and ask for his response or drum up a past experience and force him to articulate his moods. All sorts of torturous ways came to mind for Jaret to dive deep into his feelings.

Not to mention how what he felt inside was easier to think than to live out, especially if his desires flew in the face of the Council or prompted confrontations. Jaret despised confrontation. And some of the emotions were so painful Jaret thought he *should* avoid them.

He spent a few days alone then determined to take a break from self-reflection. He needed to get away from the humans or vampires he knew, hang alone with Darth and no one else, and try to get a reprieve from the drama. No psychoanalysis. No vampire war.

He considered a vacation, but the impending war forced him to decide to stay close to home. The bars in Boulder? No serenity there! And he had gone to many of them while in college or even when he and Anthony visited Colorado. Yes! Just what he needed.

No matter the time of year, the Boulder night scene hopped with college kids and other partiers. Jaret liked a couple large night-clubs in particular, where a mixed gay/straight crowd congregated to dance and drink. He journeyed down the mountain from Estes Park and arrived at a bar. People lined up to show their IDs, pay the cover, and enter.

He felt self-conscious standing alone, waiting to get in, when everyone else seemed to be with friends or a partner. He peered around to watch people and almost engaged in chatter with the guy behind him. He was too shy, however, so jammed his hands into his pockets and stared at the ground until he reached the front of the line. A big burly guy sat on a stool and smiled.

"ID?" he asked in a higher pitched voice than Jaret expected from the hottie with a chiseled body. He looked at Jaret's driver's license, took his money, and then winked. "Have a good time, sweetie."

Jaret grinned, the closest he could muster to flirting back. "Thanks."

Jaret felt no less awkward about being alone inside the club than in line. However, his vampire acute hearing and keen eyesight in the darkened club helped him notice the number of glances and downright stares he received from both women and men. His muscles relaxed a little because of the notice and helped his brain engage, so he ambled to the bar and ordered two drinks.

Jaret took the straight shot of whiskey and downed the whole thing at once, then walked away pretending to sip his Jack Daniels and Coke. He pushed through the crowd to go to the other end of the bar and ordered three shots. Jaret paid and grabbed the alcohol. Heading back into the crowd, he gulped the shots down as he walked toward a staircase to a second level.

The feeling of a buzz hit fast, warming his senses and creating a giddy sensation. He was still too shy to talk. But he began an inner monologue about the people he saw as he made his way to the upstairs bar.

Two additional shots later and holding a drink, Jaret walked to the side of the room overlooking the first level dance floor. The pounding, ear-splitting music, raucous and happy crowd, and his inebriation had him swaying to the songs as he stood alone.

He almost dropped his drink with surprise when a beautiful man stepped up beside him. "Hey."

Jaret smiled. "Hey."

"My friend over there wants to buy you a drink. Okay?"

Jaret looked in the direction the guy pointed and saw several people. "Which one? Why didn't he come over?"

"He's shy. He has his back to you in the blue shirt. I'll get the drink."

What a weird approach. Jaret had nothing else to do so he waited until the man returned with two drinks. He handed Jaret one and clinked the glasses together. "Cheers!" He took a long pull, and Jaret followed.

"This is too weird." The guy rolled his eyes. "Let me go get him."

"Cool," Jaret said. A second later Jaret's buzz turned into something much more intense. He concentrated hard to remain standing as the room swirled around him.

While he wiggled his fingers and tapped his cheeks to regain consciousness, the blue shirt guy appeared in front of him. Hot body. But Jaret tried to focus on his face and never saw more than a smudge, a muscled dude with a head that looked like the videos when they blurred out the face to protect someone's identity. Or the creepy porn videos where someone replaced their face with a weird smiley head.

Blue Shirt leaned over and whispered in his ear, "You're so hot." Then he rubbed his hand along Jaret's crotch, bringing him to excitement.

"Um, cool. Yeah." Jaret knew his words slurred because he had a hard time getting them to come out at all. "Who are you? What's your name?"

Blue Shirt laughed. "Such formality."

Jaret giggled, too, though he wasn't sure why and felt more uncomfortable than excited, his erection notwithstanding.

"Want to go somewhere?" Blue Shirt asked, leaning into Jaret.

"Maybe I better wait a little. I don't feel so good."

"I'll take care of you. You drank too much. Come with me."

"You didn't even kiss me." Another weirdness, Jaret thought as he spoke. The kiss meant a great deal to Jaret, and its absence felt off tonight, as if the groping was forced and the seduction faked. Didn't people kiss first?

Jaret shook his head. Maybe whatever drugs were in him flooded his mind with dumbass contemplations about kissing. He had to get a grip.

Blue Shirt ran his hand down Jaret's back. "You're so gorgeous I want to take care of you. Please. We can even wait until you sober up to have sex. Come with me." His breath tickled Jaret's ear even though his lips never touched skin.

Jaret turned his head and leaned in to lock lips. Before their lips could touch, Blue Shirt stepped away.

Feeling disoriented, Jaret grew alarmed that something was wrong with him. Not drunkenness. Something much worse. He tested to see if he could engage vampiric speed to race away but nothing happened. Instead, he fell into Blue Shirt and blacked out, not coming to until he found himself being dragged along by Blue Shirt and the guy who initially approached him with the drink.

Jaret glanced around and saw a bouncer nearby, watching them. "This one had a little too much to drink. We gotta get him home," Blue Shirt said.

"Are you sure he's okay?" The bouncer stepped toward them.

A false laugh. "Yeah. Not the first time with him."

Unable to move or talk, Jaret attempted to plead for help from the bouncer with his eyes but moments later was dragged outside and around the corner of the bar into a dark parking lot. Near the back, Jaret realized Blue Shirt remained alone with him, carrying Jaret in his arms and moving much too fast and lifting him with too little effort for a human. A vampire. Shit.

Jaret panicked but no muscles obeyed his commands, and his

attempt to call forth the power of the jewels in his pocket went un-answered. He could think and open his eyes but otherwise could do nothing more than flop along in the guy's arms. He again tried to see his captor but the face remained a blur. And he doubted his attempts to scream into the ether reached anywhere beyond the rumblings in his own mind. He cursed himself for getting so lost in alcohol at the bar he had ignored the warnings about an approaching vampire.

They had moved outside the city limits into the foothills, away from roads, houses, or other signs of civilization. Jaret decided he wanted to give himself a stroke and die before getting to whatever awful scene awaited him at the other end of the journey.

He figured he had stroked out when a brilliant flash of white blasted before his eyes, Blue Shirt dropped him to the ground, and Jaret saw nothing but dancing orbs of speckled light high in the sky above him.

First his vision cleared and then his eyesight. Like a rag doll, he listened to the chatter above, noticing the arrival of someone else. Unfortunately, he had lived, notwithstanding his desire for a stroke.

"Give him to me. You want an alliance, so remember he's mine. Or else we end all other agreements."

Blue Shirt snickered. "You're in love, aren't you?"

"He's my friend. I'm not playing your games. You want to win the war, and you need me on your side. I don't know what you're up to with him but you either release him to me or I join the Council."

The fog lifted a little in Jaret's mind, enough to figure out Blue Shirt worked for Styx. Shit. No. He *was* Styx. Which seemed more than obvious. Jaret looked up at Styx, his kidnapper. Jaret could not move his head to see the other person though the voice told Jaret everything.

"So cute," Styx said. "Saving your little boy toy. Has he even given up his ass to you yet? Anyway, I never intended him harm. I was sending a message to you, Charon, to remind you of my power. I'll assume you understand and will work with me now."

Charon never answered, but a moment later, Jaret felt someone else lifting him off the ground as Styx stood motionless without intervention.

"You owe me, then. He's yours."

Styx ran away as Charon cupped Jaret's head in one hand while carrying him with the other arm. Charon leaned over and kissed Jaret on the forehead before starting into the mountains at a swift rate.

"He drugged you," Charon explained. "I'm taking you to the castle. Can you move?"

Jaret had no way to answer, though in his mind he shook his head.

"Blink once if you can move, twice if no." Charon chuckled. "I don't know why asking you to blink seems silly."

Jaret blinked twice, though found himself laughing inside at Charon.

"Same thing with speech, yeah? Once for you can talk. Twice for no."

Jaret blinked twice.

"I pretty much knew the answer before all the blinking. Rather obvious. I wanted you to flutter your eyes at me like a damsel in distress."

They arrived at Charon's castle, where Charon carried Jaret around the palace and commanded Jordan to prepare Charon's bed. From previous visits, Jaret recognized Charon's private quarters as he was laid on the soft mattress. Someone removed all his clothes except his underwear, then Charon stretched out next to him and held him in his arms by spooning him.

"You need to rest." Charon pressed his face into Jaret's long hair. "The sun will rise soon enough and help you drift to sleep, I hope. If not, I'll figure something out tomorrow."

Jaret's mind eased from the stress and soon he fell asleep, gripped tight by the vampire who had saved him.

Jaret woke the next evening in a panic as he recalled the previous night of being drugged, unable to move or speak, and then Charon saving him. He jolted his head upright to see his body on top of Charon's bed, then looked around to realize he lay alone in the room.

He wiggled his fingers, then his toes. He stretched his neck and one by one tested every muscle. Everything worked. "Fuck," he whispered, the last test to find his voice functioning too.

He felt like a vampire again, capable of moving and sensing with his preternatural ability. From his discarded pants on the floor beside him, he called forth magic. A ruby ring buzzed to life in Jaret's senses before emerging from hiding to float in front of him.

"Wow, I'm back." Jaret grabbed the gem from the air.

Charon appeared from a neighboring room with a gigantic grin. "Hey, gorgeous. You look better. I was hoping you needed mouth-to-mouth or an anal probe to heal." As Charon sauntered across the room, Jaret stared in awe at his friend's nakedness, his beautiful penis swaying back and forth.

His own dick perked to life, so Jaret shot his hand down to cover himself because he wore nothing but underwear. He moved to the edge of the bed to retrieve his clothes, but Charon raced over and sat between Jaret and his pants before he could grab them.

"I like you in your underwear." Charon smiled.

"I think I was drugged." Jaret wanted to figure out what had happened and to dodge the sexual tension with Charon.

"You *were* drugged. By Styx."

Jaret relaxed a little and moved to sit with his legs crossed on the bed but both hands covering his junk. "Not cool."

Charon nodded. "Not cool. But I saved you."

Jaret smiled. "Very chivalrous. I can't believe you didn't take advantage of me.'"

Charon's face fell, and he leaned over, taking Jaret's clothes and throwing them at him. "You can hide your boner better in these."

Jaret grabbed Charon's forearm as he started to get up. "I was kidding. I appreciate the rescue, more than you can imagine. And I calmed down and fell asleep last night because you held me. I felt safe."

Charon eased back onto the bed, the gleam in his eye returning. "You felt wonderful next to me. I mean, I had a raging boner when I pressed against your ass. Lucky for you I don't fuck sleeping men. That hurt, you know."

"A bad joke."

"Well, you're welcome for the save. He captured you to get my attention."

"How do you know?" Jaret asked.

"This." Charon waved his hands in front of himself and a magical image of Styx, about one foot tall, appeared before him and spoke. "I don't trust my agreement with you, Charon. I'm taking something precious from you as a warning. You'll see my power and agree to join me. If you can figure out what I'm stealing."

"How'd you figure out he took me? And where to find us?"

"My boys have remained at the castle where I can protect them. There's nothing out there I care about," Charon waved a hand in the air to indicate the rest of the world. "Outside these walls and the vampires within them, I really know only you. Styx has seen us together, so I assumed he targeted you."

Jaret grinned. "So I mean something to you?"

Charon smirked and squinted at Jaret. "I think we can presume a friendship."

"I like to think so. But this sounds more like you're enchanted with me."

Charon barked a laugh. "With your ass."

Charon's nude presence intoxicated Jaret. His sparkling eyes. His muscles. And the fact he had saved Jaret the previous night, then held him in bed without making a move. Jaret felt stupid, sitting on the comforter and smiling like a teenaged, star-crossed lover.

Charon reached around Jaret and grabbed the back of his head to smash their lips even tighter together as Jaret latched both his hands around Charon's huge biceps and scooted closer until his knees pressed against Charon's enormous thigh.

They kissed, as if sucking the very air out of the room to merge themselves together. Beside himself with passion, Jaret ran one hand down Charon's rock-hard chest, over his belly button, and then held his throbbing dick in his hand, swirling the precome around the tip with his thumb.

Jaret pinched the precome between his fingers and pulled away from the kiss so he could lick the sweet substance. At the same time, Charon reached over and ripped off Jaret's underwear, cupped Jaret's balls in one hand, and pushed his other hand between Jaret's ass and the mattress, while his finger probed Jaret's anus.

Jaret was arching his back in pleasure when Darth leapt onto the bed and wagged her tail at him. Jaret laughed and pushed himself toward the headboard and away from Charon. Though he did miss Charon's finger in his ass. "You saved Darth too!" Jaret exclaimed.

"Are you fucking kidding me!" Charon shouted. "Cockblocked by a dog! I should have left her in Estes instead of having Jordan go get her for you."

"She saved us from a *big* mistake."

"A mistake!" Charon pointed to his cock. "We can't leave him like this! I had you! You want me. You *know* it. And I want you. You overcame your shit so we could do the deed and release the tension between us! Please let's finish." Charon flopped onto his stomach and squirmed over to Jaret, licking along Jaret's thigh and fumbling to hold Jaret's continued erection.

Jaret laughed and pushed Charon's hands away. "No. Too close for comfort. For the love of God, there's a war going on. We can't spend our time fucking."

Charon sat up. "People fuck during war."

"Not a good idea."

"To take our minds off the problem. A little bliss and we'll be able to concentrate better. How can we plan anything when our mind thinks of nothing but coming?"

Jaret hurried off the bed and started dressing, feeling embarrassed when he leaned over to pull on his jeans. He had no underwear because they lay shredded on the floor. He could feel Charon drooling from behind him as he watched.

"Oh, sweet Jesus, I could come from just one look at your hole."

Jaret spun around, pulled his shirt over his head, then rushed to a dresser and yanked out shorts and a shirt for Charon. "Put these on and meet me somewhere else."

"Where?" Charon asked.

"Anywhere but your bedroom," Jaret answered as he whistled for Darth and exited the room. He wandered the hall for a minute.

Charon emerged from his room, grinning. "I took my time so my hard-on would go down."

Jaret laughed. "You jacked off."

"I jacked off!" Charon burst into laughter. "You're so fucking hot. Please promise to finish what we started sometime. Please. I'm not used to being denied."

"Denial is good for you. Besides, we have work to do."

"I agree." Charon's face fell. "Styx pushed me over the edge last night. We've got to figure out our next move. He's done playing around. But I have news of my own to add."

"What?" Jaret asked.

"Follow me." Charon led them through the castle. Jaret ignored any attempt to remember where they went, how many stairs they climbed or descended, or otherwise to learn the labyrinth of the underground dwelling. He tailed Charon like a good puppy while Darth stayed close to his side.

They entered an elaborate room, one of what felt like hundreds in the castle, again making Jaret feel as if he was transported to another realm altogether. "So you have a wine bar." Jaret admired the walls of wine refrigerators, every shelf full of bottles, and the tasteful décor of wine barrel stools, tables, and a center bar full of every type of wine glass imaginable.

"Yeah." Charon grinned. "Brian took charge of this room. He's my boy from Sonoma. I thought he was mostly a fried-out pothead when I converted him. Sweet as hell. But I didn't feel like he had much going on up here." Charon pointed to his head. "Turns out he was studying to become a sommelier and knows a shit ton about wine. I developed an affinity for the high-end stuff myself, so he created this little slice of nirvana."

Jaret took a seat at the bar. "I'm not very knowledgeable about wine."

Charon uncorked a bottle, searched around for specific glasses, and poured them each a generous share. "Everyone has to start somewhere. I can teach you."

"So you can get me shit-faced and take advantage of me?" Jaret tilted his head.

"Are you making another allegation?" Charon handed Jaret a glass and clinked them together in a toast, despite the edge to his question. He also smirked.

"No. But alcohol lowers my inhibitions. Makes me horny."

Charon narrowed his eyes. "More flirting to give me blue balls. My turn to distract you. I communicated with Styx this evening, before you woke. Told him I'd join him. I made him promise to let me be alone after we won and do my own thing. He agreed, even though I knew he was lying through his fucking teeth. I was working toward getting him to meet with me, hinting we should get together. But first he suggested he wanted to show me something."

Jaret swallowed a drink of wine. "Nice."

"The wine or my efforts?"

"Both. Good wine. And I appreciate your joining us against Styx. We have to get him to Notre Dame Cathedral in Paris. I studied a lot of places, many with potential. Notre Dame will be perfect. Its powerful and haunted, full of good and bad energy. Everything we need in the ancient dwelling. Can you get him there?"

Charon nodded. "He asked me to pick the place."

"Do you worry this is too easy? You think he's on to us?"

"Sometimes." Charon shrugged. "Styx, though, I think he trusts me. Yeah, we need to be ready for shenanigans, for sure. But I can sense when he's up to something. He believes he and I have a special connection."

"Great. Then arrange the meeting."

"What about the Council?"

"What about them?" Jaret asked.

"Don't we need them involved? I thought we agreed."

Jaret nodded. "Definitely. But they're on their own schedule and won't take orders. Who the fuck knows what they're doing?"

The two vampires sipped their wine in silence for a couple minutes. Jaret *did* enjoy good wine and thought maybe he would take Charon up on the offer of lessons. "You're right. I want you to teach me."

"Great!" Charon smiled. "Rip off your clothes, hop on the counter, and give me a doggy style pose. First lesson in enjoying sex is to let go."

Jaret shrieked a laugh. "No! Lessons about wine!"

Charon scrunched his face into a grimace. "I had to try."

"You always think you have to try. I'd better go before this charade starts again. Let me know when and where to meet Styx." Jaret got up and started for the door. "Oh, I need you to show me the way out of the castle."

As they walked through the halls, a magic sphere materialized in front of Charon.

"What is it?" Jaret asked.

"You better get your swim on. We gotta get to Paris to meet Styx outside the Louvre on St. Patrick's Day."

"Fast. Three nights away. He's not fucking around. You think St. Patrick's Day has significance?"

"He told me I could pick the location, but he was choosing the time. We better go with his day. And with him, nothing is ever as random as he wants you to believe. He'll at least want to drink green beer."

"Maybe we should go tomorrow. Run and swim to get there fast."

Charon nodded. "Okay. Do we need anything?"

Jaret shook his head. "If we go tomorrow, we'll have time to take what's on our backs and then buy or steal shit in Paris. Anthony has a flat we can use."

"Of course he does." Charon rolled his eyes.

"Well, he did. I don't know how inheritance works with vampires. Maybe I got everything, maybe it's gone." Jaret held back the gulp in his throat at the memory of Anthony.

He took two steps forward when Charon grabbed his arm and spun him around, pulling him into a hug. With Jaret's face pressed into his chest, Charon kissed the top of his head.

Jaret wiped at the blood tear in the corner of his eye after he pushed away. "Sweet and affectionate Charon confuses me."

Charon grinned and tapped Jaret on the nose. "Good."

CHAPTER TWENTY-ONE

ZOMBIES IN PARIS

17 MARCH 2019
Paris, France

Jaret and Charon had arrived in Paris a couple nights after the kidnapping. They traveled together along with Darth and Charon's entire harem. At first Jaret objected to Charon's boys coming along, but Charon worried about leaving them too far away and vulnerable. Besides, Charon argued, they could help in the war and then added the caveat that if Jaret could bring a dog, he could bring his people.

In Paris, they found Anthony's flat vacant of humans but otherwise prepared for a visit, complete with an underground crypt large enough to house everyone while they slept through the day. They spent their first night buying clothes and other provisions. On the second night, while Charon and the boys went out partying, Jaret remained in the house with Darth to read.

Though Styx had scheduled their next meeting for the seventeenth, the evening arrived with no communication or news from him. Jordan convinced Charon to take the gang on a tour of Paris while they waited. Jaret declined to join them and looked forward to more solitude while waiting for Styx's next move.

After watching one of his favorite movies, *V for Vendetta,* Jaret decided to take in a sitcom since it would be short. He was scrolling through a list of options on an online service when he heard commotion from the entryway on the floor below, followed by Charon screaming for him. "Jaret! Come down here this minute! I have news!"

Jaret patted Darth on the head. "I don't suppose they'll go away if we just ignore them?" She tilted her head.

"Jaret!" Charon bellowed.

Jaret got up, straightened his clothes, and sauntered downstairs. "We're all vampires. I could hear you coming from miles away. You don't need to scream."

"Would you have come if I asked in a casual way? I was

communicating urgency." Charon stood rigid in front of his army of gay vampires.

"And so I stand before you." Jaret bowed with great drama. "What news do you bring of the outside world?"

Charon's face lit into a slight grin. "I enjoy how you make even the most serious circumstances funny. I believe Styx decided to toy with me. I don't know if he's testing me, threatening me, or he could be playing some stupid game to amuse himself. Whatever the reason, he created an army of at least fifty of those zombie fuckers on the outskirts of Paris. Styx sent one to me with a request to follow the zombie. So we did, leaving a lovely little club I might add, and the zombie showed us the bizarre army camped out in a field. Styx's dead people sat around campfires like Napoleon's army awaiting their next orders. None moved or even looked in our direction. No one would talk. Nothing. Nada. Styx never appeared either. I didn't even sense the presence of a nonzombie vampire."

"Matches his general insanity," Jaret observed. "If *you* don't know what he's up to, I doubt I can add much."

Charon nodded. "But explaining to you what I saw helped me think. You and I know, as does the Council, the beasts he transforms have no capability to threaten us. We mowed them down with ease. Even at fifty strong, I could wipe them out alone. He's not creating an army for the war."

"Why then? Who's he testing?"

"The million-dollar question." Charon nodded. "We can

eliminate his sending a message to the Council. Those four could annihilate the army with the flick of a magical wrist without even coming to Paris."

"So he's not testing the Council, which leaves either you or me."

"Or both." Charon turned around to face his men. "I want you to stay here. I warded the place and will monitor your safety from afar. No going out. Hear me? Fuck each other tonight instead of finding strangers."

As the men disbanded, chattering about what to do, Charon stepped toward Jaret. "I got it. He wants to know if we're together."

"Why?" Jaret asked.

"To see if we're allies or if we have a secret affiliation with the Council. He had figured out you meant something to me, and my saving you exposed the truth. He wants more intelligence on us."

Jaret's heart fluttered at the thought of Charon saving him, that his action even brought Styx's attention to Charon's feelings for Jaret. "So what do we do?" Jaret asked.

"Styx knows you'll kill the zombies. If I participate, he'll know we're working together. I say we call his bluff. You go wipe out his latest soldiers and I'll show up after you finish. I can protect you if he attacks."

"Won't he realize we came to France together?"

Charon shrugged. "Maybe. He wants to see us and offered the bait."

"In most movies, the action heroes don't take the bait like fools without a plan." Jaret laughed.

"Most action heroes aren't as charming and adept on their feet as you and me."

Jaret roared. "I'm sure you nailed the perfect approach to him! We'll fly by the seat of our pants and pray to the vampire gods we figure out a solution in the middle of a cluster fuck!"

They laughed as they left the house.

They arrived in a field outside Paris full of dead humans transformed into Stormtrooper obedient vampire beings.

Charon backed away into a nearby cluster of trees as Jaret moved into action. With vampiric speed, he moved through the campfire clusters and murdered the zombies. Some he killed with physical force, some with magic, and tiring of the macabre scene he threw up his magical jewels and sent them ahead to blow up the campfires and alight the zombies to their death. In minutes, Jaret had annihilated them and walked out of the carnage. He enchanted a spell and watched his gems swirl into the night sky to create a rainbow of streaking light as every remnant of the dead souls disappeared from the field.

Having sensed Styx arrive at the edge of the field, Jaret ambled toward him and stood a few feet away. "Did you ever notice in *Star Wars* how easy it was for the rebels to mow down Stormtroopers?" Jaret asked Styx. "Those clones, or I guess in the latest movie, stolen babies, represented the Empire's extreme power. But

Stormtroopers fall like ants being stomped on by a three-year-old." Jaret tilted his head and smiled at Styx. "I'll give you a flare for being an evil genius. You forced me to execute innocent people. Otherwise, you seem like the Emperor with huge amounts of power but dumb ideas and an ineffective army."

Styx chuckled. "I'm so much hotter than the Emperor."

"Not if you peer inside your soul."

"Nice to see you too." Styx smiled. "I think you know I have more than simple carnage in mind. Oh Charon, you can come out of hiding behind the tree. As if I didn't spot you from the beginning. I anticipated you'd be here."

Charon wasted no time in coming to stand with them. "Can we not play games?" Charon asked Styx. "You forget I know how weird you get. Remember all the theatrics you created in the game to transform me? You attempt to distract with your crazy but your act gets stale. Like moldy bread."

"You always remind me why I picked you." Styx wiggled his finger at Charon. "I believe I figured out the situation, so my ploy worked. What else do you need to know?"

"What did you figure out?" Jaret leered at Styx.

"Tough guy, huh?" Styx grinned. "Or are you defensive because I know the truth?"

"I gotta agree with Jaret here." Charon jerked his head toward Jaret. "Get to the point."

"You two are no fun. Charon, you agreed to follow me. But

the presence of Jaret nagged at me. How could you join me and remain with him? Or why? Now I understand."

Charon lifted a brow. "Do tell."

"You're lovers."

Charon and Jaret laughed at the same time.

"He won't even jack off together," Charon retorted, "let alone allow me to fuck him. We are *not* lovers."

"Oh, maybe you deny yourselves the carnal pleasures—well, *Jaret* denies you those indulgences. You may even ignore the depth of your feelings for each other. But your attraction goes well beyond mere sexual desire."

Jaret started to protest but stopped himself, first because nothing he said would change Styx's mind and then because they could use Styx's supposition to their advantage. Styx had staged the zombie army to determine their relationship. He feared a threat from Charon and Jaret. If Styx had decided they were lovers then he had an explanation without alighting on the truth of their alliance against him.

Styx pointed at Jaret. "The truth bugs him. See his eyes? He's squirming."

"Am not." Jaret heard the unease in his voice.

"*Am not,*" Styx mimicked Jaret with a whiny voice. "Are too."

Jaret had no comeback and stood in silence. Styx had hit too close to home and thus Jaret experienced one of Styx's greatest weapons. Styx reveled in finding a person's weakness and exploiting it by toying with emotions. That was how he had killed Anthony. Styx winked at him.

Charon stepped between Styx and Jaret and spoke with an assertive voice. "We're friends. Yeah, with every inch of my cock I want to fuck his brains out. But he won't have sex. So we're friends. I like his style and the fact he has the same power as me. Sexy gay vampire witches gotta band together. Truth be told, he can help us. He's close to the Council."

Styx narrowed his eyes, and Charon then glanced behind him at Jaret. "He sides with them."

"Yep," Charon said and slapped Styx on the shoulder. "He does for now. But they piss him off, as you can well imagine. They never tell him a thing and keep him in the dark. Hell, you murdered his hubby and they sat around like you swatted a fly and nothing more. He's not on board with your whole evil grand master taking over the world plot. But I'll bring him over. We agreed: I join you, you leave my boys and this one to me." Charon pointed at Jaret.

"Why are you being so honest?" Styx asked.

"We're pals so I'm keeping it real with you."

Styx poked Charon in the chest. "We're not pals. We just need each other."

Charon held up his hands to show Styx had discovered a deep truth. "Good. Then we're back to our agreement and you can feel better because you know about Jaret and me. We symbolize pent-up lust and a conquest denied. But he's muddled since Anthony died, so I can bend him to our will."

"Guys, I'm right here." Jaret felt compelled to say something as they talked about him like he was miles away.

Charon reached behind and patted him on the butt. "We know." He turned his attention back to Styx. "We good?"

"I didn't think you'd be this honest." Styx reached out to shake Charon's hand. "We end this on April fifteenth. Agreed?"

"The final battle?" Charon asked and shook Styx's hand.

"Yes. The end. I pick the date. You select the place for me to conquer the Council."

Charon forced a laughed. "You want Jaret on our side? Let's do the deed at Notre Dame Cathedral. He likes historic places."

Styx grinned, nodded, and walked away.

"That was weird." Jaret spoke first as he and Charon returned to Paris.

"*Everything* is weird when Styx is involved. But we survived. And now we know the date and got to pick the rendezvous point. Seems like a win."

Jaret fidgeted with the gems he held in his hands. "I was uncomfortable."

Charon smiled. "His theory about us hit too close to home, huh?"

"A little."

"I thought keeping it close to the truth would help him believe us."

Jaret nodded. "Yeah. Good."

"What's the matter?"

"You make me feel funny. And telling someone else about us had me feeling even funnier."

"Because you're falling in love with me."

"I—" Jaret stopped himself from the obvious lie he almost told. "You and I together is a *very* bad idea. Nothing has changed my mind."

"Yeah, well, your penis keeps sending you—and me—a much different message."

CHAPTER TWENTY-TWO

THE COUNCIL IN PARIS

24 MARCH 2019
Paris, France

Jaret entered the living room unsure of himself. His emotions were a jumbled mess ever since the latest encounter with Styx. Having gained clarity about the time and place for the war, if not the precise circumstances surrounding the battle, Charon, his boys, and Jaret fell into the routine of being tourists. Except Jaret's feelings plagued him. Was he still finding himself? Mourning Anthony? Falling for

Charon, like a fool in a bad movie going for the wrong guy who will break his heart? All of the above?

At his weakest moments, Jaret almost hoped to lose the war and die. End the confusion. Maybe his ghost could hang with Anthony's.

He moved toward a vacant chair to join Charon and a few of the guys watching a movie but Charon grabbed Jaret around the waist as he passed him on the couch and pulled him onto his lap. Every muscle in Jaret's body tensed.

"Relax." Charon held him close.

"This isn't a good idea. We've got to stop." Jaret whispered as if the other vampires couldn't hear and felt embarrassed to know they could.

Charon tickled Jaret's neck by rubbing his nose back and forth on his skin. "No sex but you like our little games. At least humor me before we die in a grand vampire battle for the ages."

Jaret laughed. "You could be right, you know?"

"Yep. So why die denying yourself?"

Jaret fell back against Charon and went limp in his arms. His body language contradicted the words about to escape his mouth. "How many times do I need to explain I'm a one-guy kinda gay vampire? Once you get inside me, you'll toss me aside or try to add me to the harem. Not gonna happen."

"You like to make a lot of assumptions about me."

Jaret glanced out the corner of his eye and turned his head

slightly to see Charon. "You into monogamy all of a sudden?"

Charon grinned and shook his head once. "No."

"Settled. Now shut up so I can watch the movie."

Lying entwined in Charon's arms and watching a romantic comedy, Jaret groaned when he sensed approaching vampires and started to get off Charon, but Charon refused to let go.

"They're here," Jaret explained.

"I know. They should see us."

"And we do," Thomas said as he stepped into the room, followed by Xavier, Catherine, and Harriet. Thomas peered hard into Jaret's eyes to convey his reproval. "A cute conniving couple."

Charon's boys had leapt to their feet, alarmed by the Council. They glanced nervously between each other then looked to Charon for direction as they also backed away. Jaret pushed off Charon and stood while everyone waited for Charon to get up. Charon moved in a deliberate and slow manner, a way to convey his own authority and lack of fear.

"They won't do anything to you. I promise." Charon grinned at his boys before turning to the Council. "Will you?"

"No." Harriet shook her head.

"Good. Because we don't need a scene when we've decided to work together."

"We came to speak with Jaret." Xavier said and glared at Charon. "Maybe you and your gang can go have an orgy somewhere."

Charon walked over and stood in front of Xavier. "You'd think a gay vampire would reform over time and throw off the yolk of the Catholic Church, even if he had been a priest."

Xavier squinted back at Charon. "There's a difference between overcoming oppression and falling into hedonistic gluttony."

"Okay, time to go." Thomas stepped between the vampires and motioned for Charon and his men to leave.

Charon spun around, winking at Jaret, and headed toward the door. "Come on, guys. We'll leave them to their secret meeting."

Once they left, everyone took a seat. Jaret was the last one to find a chair, trying but failing not to laugh.

"What could possibly be funny?" Xavier asked.

"You four. I'm sorry. I know you're powerful and have the weight of the world on your vampire shoulders. But you hang around in meetings to talk shit to death more than any group I know. I think it's funny. Growing up, I remember mom complaining about the ladies at our church talking everything to death and driving her insane. You'd fit right in." Jaret shrugged. "I don't mean to be disrespectful. You can see a little of the humor, yeah?"

Jaret should have known Catherine would come to his rescue. She burst into laughter, leaned forward, and clapped her hands. "And you don't experience half our droll little meetings!" Her laughter prompted Thomas to join her, though Harriet and Xavier remained unamused.

"Our meetings serve a purpose." Harriet pressed her lips

together before she continued. "We're not pondering the next casserole to serve at a funeral."

Rather than calming the situation, Harriet's reference got Xavier to laugh with the rest of them.

Xavier wiped a blood tear from the corner of his eye. "Thank you, I needed to laugh." He stood and went to Harriet, bending over to hug her. His embrace even got Harriet to grin.

"I doubt you wanted to see me about a casserole," Jaret said. "What's up?"

"We're letting you in on part of the plan." Harriet returned to her businesslike tone. "There's something you deserve to know."

"Yeah? Why?" Jaret asked.

"Because we're being cruel." Xavier frowned. "And maybe you'll trust us more with what we don't tell you if we come clean on what we can."

Jaret bobbed his leg up and down as the meeting took an unexpected turn.

"Anthony died on purpose." Thomas spoke in a monotone as Jaret choked on a sob. Thomas took a deep breath to gather himself. "He plotted his own execution because we, the Council, had developed a powerful magic to combat Styx. We tried a million methods but knew someone had to die because defeating him requires more magical energy than we've ever produced before. Anthony, as you know, felt responsible for Styx being in the world. And he blamed himself for failing to reform Styx. We were in the middle of arguing about who should die when Anthony went off the grid and invoked his own spell without our knowledge. In allowing his own capture and pushing Styx to kill him, he came to possess a key part in our ability to win. He can manifest in ghost form, which is why you feel him. He hasn't been able to talk to us yet, but we know when he's there. I don't know if you held out hope he was alive. We kept this information from you because of the war, but I think it became too cruel. You deserved to know sooner about Anthony being dead."

Jaret had guessed a thousand announcements the Council could have brought to him but never what Thomas revealed. Jaret's hands shook and grief overtook him. He bent over in anguish as tears streamed down his face, and his stomach clutched into knots. Since he had seen Anthony die, he'd fought to accept the loss but had held out hope he had survived because of the times he sensed Anthony's spirit nearby.

Xavier leapt across the room and embraced Jaret.

"Why would he do this to me?" Jaret sputtered when he could at least catch a breath. "After everything else I lost, why wouldn't he stick around for me?"

"Ah, child. I know you hurt." Xavier petted his hair. "You'll never agree with him. In time you may see his reasoning. But he died for you. For all of us, but you in particular. To protect you. He insisted Styx would target you so long as Anthony lived. And he couldn't bear the thought of fighting and winning the war only to lose you."

Jaret cried even harder. He looked up at the vampires and shook his head. "Anthony always seized the moral high ground, didn't he? He sacrificed himself to save vampires, especially me, and so now I feel guilty because I'm so pissed off with him for leaving me."

Thomas smiled as he wiped tears from his own face. "He's exceled at that for years. A complete, self-righteous ass." He shouted the last sentence into the air, as if Anthony's ghost hovered nearby.

And, in fact, Jaret did sense his presence. "I didn't always care for how he acted like God," Jaret explained, his hands shaking. "I should have known he'd turn himself into Jesus at the end. Dying for our sins or some such shit. Fuck. Does this mean you'll tell me how we're going after Styx, at least?" Jaret wanted to move away from the Anthony talk, already uncomfortable with his emotional display. He was also suppressing his rage at the vampires in the room for their secrecy.

Xavier stared hard at Jaret. "We can't tell you everything because keeping information from you is part of the plan. A necessary aspect. It's not about the high and mighty Council knowing better than you or not trusting you."

Jaret grimaced yet nodded his understanding. "Thanks. That beats the bullshit of the past. What do you know about my own plans?"

"Everything." Harriet shrugged. "And since we didn't stop you, you best keep going. You can assume you're playing an essential and known role. Charon is too."

"My plan is part of your plan?"

The four Council members looked with blank faces at him. Jaret stood and shook his head. "Nothing has changed my mind about you being a bunch of assholes. I deserved to know before today. Anthony was my husband." He sputtered the last sentence and stopped before he blubbered more vitriol.

Jaret reached the door when Thomas called to him. "One more thing. Don't rebound with Charon."

"What the fuck do you care?" Jaret spat without turning around.

"We care about you." Xavier's gentle voice softened Jaret, or at least kept him from flipping them off.

Jaret nodded and left the room. In the street outside he sensed Anthony again and then felt a gust of wind whip through his hair. The smell of Anthony's cologne hit his nose.

Jaret glared into the empty air before him. "I love you. And you can fuck off. And don't fucking follow me."

Jaret stormed down the street in search of Charon and his boys.

PART NINE

A COMPLETE MESS

CHAPTER TWENTY-THREE

VAMPIRE DOGS

31 MARCH 2019
Amboise, France

Jaret stumbled as he stepped toward the window overlooking the picturesque village of Amboise. He gulped another drink of whiskey and leaned against the sill, the quiet evening and beautiful scenery doing little to quell his turmoil.

Darth stayed close to his side, staring hard at him with worry. He reached down to pat her on the head. "No worries, girl. I'm drunk. I won't do anything stupid." She continued her apprehensive look in his direction, and he could not blame her concern because even he was having a hard time believing his words.

He thought escaping the confines of Paris would free him from the dark cloud hanging over him. While he was right to get away from Charon, the time alone otherwise proved unsatisfying.

His emotions ran amuck at every waking moment. He regretted the failure of his first love with Steve followed close behind by the vision of Steve's lifeless body. Next, he cried at the memory of his entire family dying at Henrik's hands. He recalled joy with meeting Anthony, winning over his love, and then Jaret's conversion to vampirism. The happy feelings served as a temporary reprieve. A new horror arrived with a vampire war in which his lover, after promising forever together, committed suicide in order to save vampires and in particular, to protect Jaret.

Who could blame Jaret for losing himself in alcohol?

Jaret wiped at the blood tears. His mind sought hope for the future, but the Council had pissed him off. The war frightened him. And his lust for Charon made his head spin. He had never felt so rudderless, which said a lot, given some of the horror he had experienced.

Even the notion of reaching out to Xavier or Thomas offered little appeal with their lecturing and reminders of Anthony. He wanted to call on Brady, but the Council asked Jaret to protect

Brady by leaving him out of everything until later. As much as he needed Brady, he also would never do anything to put Brady in harm's way.

Jaret had toured the Loire River Valley to immerse himself in the castles and wineries, an effective diversion for a few nights until he again felt lonely and distraught.

"Darth, we better go for a walk before I get too sloppy drunk. We don't want another evil vampire to kidnap me. Maybe fresh air will help. I need to stop these dark thoughts."

Darth wagged her tail as Jaret dressed, anticipating their getting out of the rented house and going on an adventure.

They broke into the castle overlooking the town and explored the old structure before heading into the countryside. Without intention but unsurprisingly, they arrived at Jaret's very favorite castle in the entire world, Chenonceau. He sat under a tree to stare at the structure stretching over the river like a fairytale castle.

"Darth, we need to talk." Jaret had sobered a little but continued to buzz. "What options do you see before us?"

She glanced at some nearby ducks but obeyed his motion for her to sit next to him. She lay her head on his leg.

"You don't have any better ideas than I, do you?" Jaret asked his dog. "The past is the past. No going back to our years of youthful ignorance and hope. Blissful ignorance left us in the dust." He petted her when she twitched, wanting to give chase to a rabbit. "I doubt we can remain obedient servants of the Council either. They can be my friends but not the only game in town anymore. Oh, and I know. Everyone is correct by asking you and me to stay away from Charon." Jaret sighed. "Even if he is sex on wheels. So what's left?"

Darth peered up at him. He liked to pretend she was engaged in the discussion. More likely, she was bored and hoped he would move them into action.

"I mean, we could become *like* Charon. An all-powerful witch vampire and vampire dog living life by doing whatever we want, wherever we want, however we want. This assumes, of course, the Council wins the war, and Styx dies. If he wins, well, there we get into an even uglier possibility we do *not* want to contemplate."

Jaret jumped to his feet, to Darth's delight. They ambled along the river. "Or what if we lived without people or vampires? No community. I don't know. We're a mess, aren't we?"

Darth's stub of a tail whirled around in circles, and she raced ahead. She captured a goose and fed. Watching her joy and loyalty, Jaret hit upon the perfect idea to lift him out of the doldrums. The very notion risked Council wrath but maybe they would allow him one indiscretion. He wondered where to accomplish his new goal when he came across a small village and heard a commotion in a nearby home.

Jaret hurried to look inside and saw a large man lording over a woman while two children cowered in the corner. Jaret's stomach growled in hunger. In seconds he accomplished the deed, moving so fast the family never got a clear view of him as he rushed inside, drank from the man, and left his body dead on the floor in what would look like a heart attack.

The blood enlivened Jaret and sent him off on his newly inspired quest. Before he got outside the village he spied another person—this time a young man leaning against a shed and smoking. When Jaret came into view, the guy looked at him with alarm and tensed.

"Bonjour." Jaret held up his hands to show he meant no harm.

"Hey." They were speaking French. Jaret was thankful Anthony had helped him learn languages as a vampire. "You scared me."

"Sorry. I didn't mean to. My dog and I are out for a walk."

"At this time of night?"

Jaret shrugged. "You're out too."

"Because my mom won't let me smoke inside. Or outside if she knows." He rolled his eyes. "I work and contribute to the house. I stay here to help since Dad died, but she treats me like a child. I can't smoke, let alone have a guy over for fun." He stopped himself and glanced up for Jaret's reaction.

Jaret took the words as permission. He walked over, cupped the cute guy behind the head, and pulled him into a kiss. Jaret almost never took the lead in sex, but he needed a release. In moments, the men lay entwined on the ground, naked and stroking each other to completion. After the dude wiped up the come with his shirt, he stood up and grinned.

"I gotta go inside. Thanks." He jerked his head at Jaret and walked away.

Jaret dressed, surprised he had enjoyed the encounter and felt no remorse or sense of cheating. The moment of lust and bonding with a stranger satisfied something within him.

Once alone again with Darth, Jaret set out on a mission to create a new family. First, he went to a pet store and stole six dog collars and returned to his house to get the same number of gems to attach to them. With the necessary gear Jaret headed out on his mission.

With no experience in hunting for packs of dogs, Jaret relied on his gems to guide the way. They directed him to a remote forest area, where he heard a dog yipe nearby. Darth raced forward when they neared a clearing inside a dense forest and found what he had sought: a pack of dogs of varying sizes and breeds, some playing and others lying content nearby. Jaret had no idea if they were lost from homes or born in the wild. He watched for a while, thinking of several in particular tugging at his heart strings, before he decided to see if Darth would help in the selection.

"Listen," he whispered to her, "no feeding here." He knew she did not understand the verbal command but ensured her compliance with a spell. Jaret also insured her obedience by clasping an emerald bracelet around her collar before letting her romp into the clearing.

The entire pack leapt to its feet or spun around to confront her. A couple bared their teeth and inched forward, putting themselves between Darth and the others. Darth lowered her body in deference and wagged her tail as she trod forward. Jaret worried the spell he gave would fail to allow her to protect herself, but the ritual dog communication averted his fear because soon enough she ingratiated herself with the pack, her charm and exuberance winning the pack over.

As with Darth, Jaret walking into the clearing put the dogs on edge. They reacted differently to his being a human. Some canines fled into the woods while those remaining backed away from him. Darth raced across the tundra and leapt into his arms for kisses. Her exuberance toward him led a few of the wild dogs to approach him. A couple dogs who had run into the woods peered out of the dark brush and then returned to the clearing. One dog Jaret especially wanted to meet followed Darth's lead and hurried over to greet him. One by one, Jaret sought out the mutts he had chosen and greeted them. He secured a collar and Bachmann gem around their necks, and then commanded them to leave the woods and wait together nearby.

Jaret enchanted the six new dogs to play with Darth while he took them one by one to the side with him. Jaret's lifelong connection with dogs, starting when he was about three and his parents adopted Darth, helped him get the dogs to feel safe. Next, his spell allowed him to grasp their individual personalities and feel close to them within minutes. When Jaret returned to his new pack of seven dogs his heart lifted with joy.

He cast the final spell and commanded the Bachmann family gems to obey. One at a time his magic transformed each dog. Moments later, Jaret called for the seven vampire dogs to come sit before him. He kissed Darth on the head and greeted her first, before giving them names.

He named the little beagle mix Lily, after Lily Munster, because Jaret loved the show. She also had the most caring disposition of the dogs, much like Lily watching over the Munster family.

Jaret chose the name Dancin' Boy next. The little dog was a dead ringer for Benji, the blond long-haired mutt from the movie. Dancin' Boy loved to jump around and get attention from Jaret. Jaret named him after one of his favorite musicals, *Billy Elliot*, because Billy's best friend nicknamed him Dancin' Boy in the musical.

The short pup with the black-and-white markings of a border collie became Nosferatu. He already howled with delight whenever Jaret said his new name.

The black lab mix, the most affectionate of the dogs, leapt into Jaret's arms for attention after being christened Mika because Jaret had to name one of them after his favorite singer.

The golden medium-size dog, who loved giving kisses, he named Cher. Cher was pushy in how she demanded Jaret give her attention. Of course, he named her after a diva.

And the largest of them, all black except for a white chest and small patch of white on his chin became Chewbacca. He wanted a name from the light side of The Force to balance Darth's dark side representation.

Jaret had soothed his doldrums, the dogs taking his attention away from his travails. He again pondered spending all his time with his new pack and ignoring anything formerly or currently human.

CHAPTER TWENTY-FOUR

SOLITUDE

6 APRIL 2019
Amboise, France

Jaret woke in his large coffin in the cellar to find dogs snuggled next to him everywhere—except for Mika, who had crawled on top of Jaret and curled up on his chest to sleep. The puppy pile inside a coffin made Jaret giggle as he opened the lid and allowed them to scamper out. Some played, some watched Jaret, and Cher leapt up and down at his side a thousand times until he bent over to allow her to give him a million kisses.

As they had every evening since he created his pack, they headed for the countryside where he allowed them to feed and play. He tested his ability to control them and, like Darth, the conversion spell worked to perfection, creating obedience to him but otherwise letting their individual personalities shine.

In addition to having the dogs run around together, he spent a little time each night with them, solidifying his bond and causing him to wonder why he had waited so long to gather more dogs. He worried at first about Darth, not wanting her to feel abandoned or jealous. She settled into her new mates with surprising ease, however, and seemed to detect her position as top dog. In fact, Jaret had always known Darth liked a bit of alone time away from him. She appeared to be fine with the other pooches giving Jaret attention while she took a break from him.

Jaret found himself more and more enthralled with this part of France, its history, beautiful landscape, and slower pace of life than the larger cities offered, in particular, Paris. He even found he could divert his attention away from the impending war for a little while.

The few times someone contacted him he answered but never met with anyone. The Vampire Council, seeming to take turns, reached out to him. He replied he was fine and did not need to see them, nor did any of them push for a meeting. He rebuffed Charon too, including the most recent dispatch in the form of a magical 3-

D image of Charon standing in front of Jaret, naked and winking. Brady proved more persistent, no doubt because he knew Jaret better than anyone else, and because the Council had given him permission to visit Jaret. He promised Brady to talk soon and planned to follow through this evening.

After touring another old castle and drinking a bottle of Vouvray by himself along the Loire River, Jaret sauntered back to town as the dogs raced around him. A few times in the last couple days he had sensed Anthony's spirit nearby. Jaret never acknowledged the ghost. He smiled this time when the wind whipped through his hair and the scent of Anthony's cologne hit him.

"I know you're there," Jaret said to the wind.

Instead of agitating Jaret, Anthony's presence comforted him with a sense of being cared for. Jaret headed back to his house to relax. He settled into the living room with another bottle of wine and watched the dogs fall into various routines. Some of them chewed bones, Lily curled up at his feet for a nap, and Mika leapt onto the couch to lay as close to Jaret as possible.

Anthony lingered.

"You know I'll never forgive you," Jaret spoke to the invisible ghost. He knew his words contradicted how he had come to peace with Anthony's death. Jaret missed Anthony desperately and hated his lover's suicide. However, Jaret had to give Anthony space to be himself, the vampire who always wanted to save the world.

"But maybe we'd have learned a different way to defeat Styx,"

Jaret said aloud, as if Anthony had posed the last thought and not Jaret's own mind. "Or maybe you and I were headed for centuries of tension as we figured out our shit. I would've liked the chance for us to stay together but I understand who you are. I do. I hope you find peace."

A breeze swept by Jaret. Jaret peered at the coffee table to see writing in the dust. He recognized the old-time cursive scroll etched into the top, where moments before he saw nothing but an empty wooden surface.

Yes, we needed this. Don't lose yourself. I love you.

Jaret rolled his eyes. "Always with the riddles," he said. The Council mentioned Anthony was gathering strength for the battle and thus stayed hidden. Jaret chose to see the communication as an act of love even if, once again, Anthony's note annoyed him. "To lose myself I'd have to know who the fuck I am in the first place."

Jaret's recent self-reflection and spending time with his dogs, however, had brought him a new sense of calm. Anthony and he had loved each other with a deep passion and *would* have lasted forever. But their relationship came with a cost to Jaret. Anthony would always have remained much older and in charge, able to scold Jaret or dismiss him as too young. Jaret had loved Anthony's protection, but the dynamic infantilized him too much. His whole life, he had lived to please his parents or other authority figures until Anthony took on that role.

Jaret let out a sigh and headed back into the French

wilderness. He fed and allowed the dogs to do the same before commanding them back to the house. Then he sent his promised message to Brady.

Instead of chatting or some weird magic vampire shit, why don't you come to Amboise? I assume you're already in France because I know the Council is babysitting you. Come tomorrow.

Jaret grinned wider than he had in a long time the following night as he sat admiring Chenonceau, two unopened bottles of Sancerre sitting next to him. The dogs were playing in the woods when Brady strolled over and plopped down.

"You criticize the Council for babysitting me, but you do the same fucking thing. You knew I was already in France and were monitoring me. And they aren't babysitting. They're protecting me because of the shit going on."

Jaret laughed. "They totally babysit you. And I'm not spying. Pretty obvious they'd keep you close with war about to go down in Paris. I spotted them in France." Jaret opened both bottles of wine and handed one to Brady. "We'll look like winos, but I didn't want to fuck around with crystal in the middle of nowhere France."

Brady clinked his bottle against the bottom of Jaret's. "Cheers!"

They drank in silence until Jaret looked over at Brady. "To be serious before the alcohol takes over," Jaret said, "you doing okay? For real?"

Brady nodded. "Yeah. I mean, it's relative, right? No one in the know about the mess before us could claim to be all chill. There's too much shit going down. Given the circumstances, I go with the flow. I don't have authority with the Council. No witchery like you. Just me, newbie vamp and nothing more. I could hide in a corner scared shitless or deal." He shrugged. "So I deal. I ignore reality most of the time because I don't have anything else to do."

"Sounds reasonable. I'm glad you're doing okay. I hope you'd come to me if you ever need help or to talk."

"Of course." After another minute of quiet, Brady continued. "I'm scared. I didn't mean to sound too flippant."

Jaret took a swig of wine. "I'm scared too. Worried. But I agree with you about not fretting every minute because we can only do so much and then rely on the Council to fight and win."

"You sound different."

Jaret frowned. "Different?"

"Speaking of chilled. You seem more like you. I mean you from before everything."

"Everything?"

"*Everything!*" Brady laughed. "You from when we first met in college."

"Huh." Jaret pondered Brady's words. "I wouldn't say I'm totally back to normal because I miss Anthony and, as you pointed out, some big-ass fight with a crazy fucking vampire is coming. However!" Jaret held up a finger of revelation. "I had time to think. In fact, I came out here to be alone and figure myself out. Here's what

I decided. I need time alone. I don't mean without friends. I mean, no relationship. No family pressure. I need time to find myself, my own desires and shit. Anthony was the most amazing person I ever knew. Well, vampire or whatever the fuck you want to call him. We loved each other so much. I look back and see how he became a surrogate parent to me. But I also think he allowed me to fall into my pattern of pleasing others, of having an authority figure watch over and approve of me.

"I see his death as destiny for both of us," Jaret continued. "His sacrifice will save vampires, including me. And his death will release him from the grief he felt for centuries after losing his first lover. I believe that with my whole heart. And I'm pretty experienced and good at the grief thing myself. I can mourn him but grow and move forward."

Jaret stopped, overwhelmed by the truth of his words. A breeze blew across the field and again the hint of Anthony's scent hit Jaret's nose. A spirit of approval from his lover.

Brady leaned over and gave Jaret a big hug. "Good. And don't forget, I'm still here for you."

"Same here. Always."

They clinked their bottles together and drank the rest of the wine before Jaret jumped to his feet in excitement. "I gotta show you something!"

"Whoa! Big switch." Brady got up.

"We got too heavy. Plenty of time for deep contemplation

after the war. Or, in the event the war goes tits up and we die, why waste our remaining time with deep shit? Come on."

Jaret hurried back to Amboise with Brady close behind. They entered the living room, where seven bouncing and enthusiastic dogs greeted them as if they were the most exciting people to ever walk into a room. After getting kisses from Jaret, Darth leapt at Brady and greeted him with more exuberance than the others because she knew him.

When the pack settled down and allowed the two vampires to come into the room, Brady scrutinized them with more care, his eyes became wide, and he spun around to stare at Jaret. "Dude! What the fuck?"

"What?" Jaret played innocent.

"What? You're a fucking lunatic! These are vampire dogs!" He pointed to the happy dogs meandering around. "Are you out of your mind? What are you doing? Oh, I know. The Council left you alone and ignored your shit for a while, so you decided to fuck with them. You need to be in trouble, so why not create a pack of vampire dogs to see if they'll finally put you inside the iron casket over the fire like you've been begging them to since you first became a vampire."

Jaret laughed at Brady's monologue. "Nah. They won't care. I control the dogs no problem, same as I do Darth."

Brady scratched his head. "Seven dogs? Seriously? Oh, not one or even two more, but let's add six. Come here, Darth." Darth ran to him, her stub of a tail spinning around and around. "You can live with me. Forget Jaret and these other dogs. I only have eyes for you." Darth gave him a big lick across his face.

"She likes her brothers and sisters. I think she's in charge," Jaret explained.

"I'd expect nothing less. In charge of you too, you know. If you're not trying to piss the Council off, what is this?" Brady waved his hand toward the dogs.

"I needed them. I don't know how to explain, but they're my pack. I want them in my life. They make me so happy."

"Good. That's what's most important to me." Brady fell to the floor and called all the dogs over to pet them.

CHAPTER TWENTY-FIVE

A SUMMONS FROM CHARON

9 APRIL 2019
Paris, France

Brady had remained a couple nights with Jaret, drinking and touring the French countryside, and Jaret stayed in the area afterward to embrace the peace and quiet as well as the freedom to learn more about his dogs' personalities. Staying away from the Council, Charon, and the tension in Paris kept Jaret in the Loire River Valley too. Having found a sense of calm, he had no desire to confront the vampire war until the fifteenth.

The sense of an approaching vampire ended those wishes.

Jaret sat at an outside café, early in the evening for a vampire but near closing time for the local establishment. He liked the company of the chatty young waitress and watching people while he waited for the dogs to go feed and return. His warning of another vampire tingled when a striking figure appeared out of nowhere, and soon enough the hot vampire sat across from Jaret, but Charon's expression spoke of something wrong.

"No smile?" Jaret asked Charon. "Can't be good."

Charon shook his head. "We have a problem."

"You aren't even going to try to seduce me first? I'm disappointed."

Charon smirked, a more typical reaction from him. "I can't take the continued rejection."

"I doubt you'll ever give up. Tell me what's going on."

"Take a guess."

"Styx. What else?"

"He visited me." Charon eyed the horizon.

"A social call? For dinner? What?"

"I'm not sure, which is why I came to you." Charon turned his attention back to Jaret and leaned across the table. "The boys and I moved after you left. Your flat felt creepy without you there. I could feel Council shit in the air. I didn't know what surveillance they had on the place. Plus, Styx knew about the location. When I tried to cast spells, Council bullshit magic blocked some of my power. Anyway, we created our own hideout and secured the place. A night after I finished placing my spells of protection, Styx found me in an alley. He interrupted the most gorgeous Frenchman I've ever seen giving me a glorious blow job."

"Thanks for the details," Jaret interrupted. "At least you sound more like yourself with your dick as the main character of your story."

Charon shrugged. "Since the guy didn't finish me off, blue balls might account for my confusion in the moment. Styx was pissed. But I don't usually worry about his being angry because he goes from crazy, happy lunatic to maniacal, mad scientist to normal in thirty seconds on an average day? This time his anger confused me because we agreed to meet on the fifteenth. I didn't expect to see him until then."

"What got his panties in a bunch?"

"He rambled on about loyalty and trust. I think, and he was all over the place so I'm not sure, but I think he was irate about my moving to a hideout and his not being able to find me. I pacified him by saying I wanted to get the fuck away from the Council. Which was actually the truth! He seemed placated, offered to go fetch the hot guy he had chased off, but said this before he left: 'I'm sure you'll appreciate how I must send a message."

Other than confirming Styx's consistent insanity, Jaret had no other way of interpreting what Charon had experienced. "Why are you here?"

"I need you back in Paris with me in case something happens."

Jaret sighed. "I like being out here. It's quiet. I made some new friends."

"Bring them along and let's go."

"You promise I can bring them all?"

Charon creased his brow. "Of course. I doubt you made a lot of fuck buddies."

Less than an hour later, Jaret had packed up his rental house, gathered his dogs, and arrived in Paris near the Louvre. Charon had refused to give him the exact location of his lair and arranged to meet him. A few minutes after Jaret got there Charon strode down the street with a look of horror.

"Um, I expected you made some vampire friends. Or came out of your shell and gathered hot Frenchmen to surround yourself with. I wasn't expecting a pack of hyenas."

Jaret punched him on the arm. "They're dogs. Domesticated dogs." The seven dogs, all on their own leash, wound around one another and pulled toward Charon with enthusiasm.

"*Vampire* dogs, and it's a little weird. No, *extremely* weird. I tolerate Darth visiting my pads because she comes with you. You'll have to kennel the rest of them."

"Nope." Jaret shook his head. "You want me to help, you get all of us."

Charon pursed his lips. "What do I get in return. A blow job?"

"My help!" Jaret proclaimed with mock exuberance.

"Oh, joy. Not even a kiss."

Jaret held the leashes to the side, hopped a step forward and pecked Charon on the lips. Then he kissed him on the cheek. "Deal. Now take me to your leader."

As they walked up the outer stairs of an apartment building, Charon wagged a finger at Jaret. "Someday I'll sneak in a request for more than a kiss, and you'll bound over even faster, ripping your pants off and begging for my cock in your ass."

"Will you go inside? At least you sound more like yourself."

They entered the building, walked up three flights of stairs, then went into a vacant apartment where Jaret unleashed the dogs. Inside a closet, Charon opened a secret door and Jaret realized they were passing from one building into another, where they came upon a concealed stairway that took them back down to the ground level and then below. A few seconds later, the vampire humans and dogs stood in one of Paris's many underground crypts. Instead of bones, rats, and spiders, Charon and his harem had transformed the place into an ornate living room in the style of Louis XVI. Jaret also sensed the magic protecting the perimeter to keep out unwanted guests: animal, human, vampire or otherwise. The dogs scampered around the room, sniffing and exploring.

"If one of them pees inside, I get to kill it."

"No, you don't. And they're house-trained. You do like hiding deep underground. Charming." Jaret swept his arm around the crypt. "Where is everyone?"

"They went to a club. And if you're going to make fun of me for hiding in the dirt, I can make fun of you for going insane and becoming part of a wolf pack."

"Domesticated dogs."

"Okay, part of a kennel. Jaret's vampire dog-sitting service."

"Why am I here?"

Charon grabbed Jaret's hand and pulled him to a couch, where they sat next to each other. "In case something happens, I already told you. I don't admit vulnerability very often, so I hope you appreciate what I'm about to say. I can't deal with Styx alone if he makes a move."

As he spoke, Charon's voice became a whisper. Jaret patted him on the thigh. "Then I'll stay here for you."

Charon grabbed Jaret's hand when he started to pull away. He held their hands on his thigh while peering straight into Jaret's eyes before sliding their hands up toward his groin.

Jaret squinted at Charon. "You're not even hard. You don't want me." Jaret spoke in jest, but an unanticipated quiver in his voice finished the last sentence.

Charon smiled, not his smart-ass-superior-than-thou grin but with the tender expression he always fought to hide. "Not true," Charon said. "But you're right." Charon released Jaret's hand. "I felt obligated to hit on you but couldn't get in the mood because I knew you'd rebuff me. I'm nervous as fuck about Styx, which makes it easier to ignore my sex drive."

Jaret chuckled. "I didn't know you ever shut your dick off."

"Good point." To demonstrate the turn their conversation had taken, Charon rubbed his crotch to show his growing excitement.

"That's better!" Jaret clapped.

Charon leaned back on the couch and sighed. "What do you wanna do? He may never act. But we need to do something, so I don't rape you."

"You mean play a game?" Jaret grimaced. "Plan a dinner party? What are you talking about?"

"Passing the time!" Charon yelled. "I don't feel like going out. You won't have sex with me, so recommend something else to occupy us. *Not* games."

"You know what? I have an idea. You showed a vulnerable part of yourself when you asked me to stay with you. I'll return the favor."

"How?"

"I should be focused on the war. We could fucking die on the fifteenth. But instead, I've spent a lot of time figuring myself out. I told Brady how I always lived to please others. When Anthony died, I didn't know who to please anymore. Then I realized I could just please myself from now on. As for my dogs," Jaret motioned toward where they had settled into a big puppy pile of sleeping canines, "I love dogs because I can be myself around them."

When Jaret stopped talking, Charon glanced at him with the

hint of a smile. Jaret braced for a smart-ass comment or rejoinder, but his heart fluttered at what came out. "Your sharing means so much to me. Thanks."

"I planned on you making fun of me to get us out of the seriousness."

"You always think I'm going to be an asshole." Charon frowned. "I'm not devoid of empathy. I don't take shit from anyone and think we should live to please ourselves. I know everyone thinks I imprisoned my boys but that's not entirely true. They like me. We love each other. I came to a mutual agreement about our situation."

An awkward silence fell between them.

Charon rubbed his face before he spoke. "We gotta get away from this heavy shit. Does finding yourself mean you released your puritanism and embraced fucking?" Charon's smile spread from one ear to the other.

"Who said I didn't embrace fucking before? Monogamous fucking is still fucking."

"I thought maybe your revelation included loosening up."

Jaret shook his head. "Nope. Not part of me."

"Oh, so instead, you want to be loyal to a group. A harem! You want to join us!"

Jaret laughed. "No. Not your bacchanal either."

Charon jumped to his feet and leapt over in front of Jaret before getting on one knee. "Will you marry me if I promise to convert to your monogamy?"

Jaret slapped Charon playfully upside the head. "You're teasing me. And lying."

Charon fell onto the floor and giggled. "I like you."

"What?" Jaret stopped laughing and stared at Charon.

"I like you." Charon leaned back on two elbows and grinned. "You're my friend. I haven't really had friends since Styx converted me and I had to leave my college frat buddies behind. I'm not sure what to call my boys and me, but they're different from friends. So I like you."

"Thanks. Despite your wicked ways, I like you too." Jaret reached out with his foot and ran his toes along Charon's stomach before tapping him on the leg. "You drive me fucking nuts."

Charon roared a laugh and began to respond when Jordan interrupted them by barreling into the room out of breath.

Charon and Jaret leapt to their feet at the same time when Jordan came to a stop in front of them, blood tears streaking down his face and his eyes wide in alarm. His entire body trembled as he shook his head. He reached a shaking hand up and ran his fingers through his hair, staring at the ground. Jaret had noticed the young vampire always took his cue from Charon with a bravado and flippant sexuality, but the war threatened to undo Jordan.

"Jordan, what?" Charon clutched him by both shoulders and hunched down to see him eye to eye. "You've gotta talk."

"You know you told us to stay close? At the bar you pointed

out? We did. Never left. Promise. Styx found us anyway. Made us all go into a room to show us something.”

“Did he hurt any of you?”

Jordan shook his head. “No. Told me to fetch you and show you his warning.”

Charon glanced toward Jaret with a grimace, then turned his attention back to Jordan. “Take us.”

Charon and Jordan headed down a dark tunnel. Before he followed, Jaret muttered a spell to keep the dogs in the crypt and then hurried after the vampires. In a zombielike trance, Jordan guided them on a different path than how they arrived, keeping them underground and moving through cobwebs, narrow passages, past skeletons and vermin until they came into a modern sewer and climbed a ladder to the surface.

A block away they came upon a club with a line of patrons waiting to enter, a young goth crowd. The trio hurried around back, checked to see no one watched, and leapt to a second-floor window. The three vampires rushed downstairs, past the entrance to the main club, and entered a private suite. Charon slammed the door shut behind them.

“Fuck,” Jaret muttered at the scene.

“Did any humans see this?” Charon asked Jordan.

Jordan stood near the door, his trembling returning as he looked straight down at the floor and shook his head. “No.”

“Where are the other boys?” Charon asked.

Jordan pointed toward the rear. "Separate room in the back. They're hiding."

Charon nodded. "How did Styx reveal this scene to you?"

Without glancing up from the floor, Jordan pointed toward the main club. "We were dancing. Mixed club, you know, so we had a competition to see how many straight boys we could seduce. We'd been at it for a while when Styx walked up to me and introduced himself. I turned to run but Styx grabbed my arm and told me we'd be safe if I obeyed. He had me gather the guys outside the doors, then flung them open and pushed us inside, telling me he had a message for my boss. He locked us in and disappeared. Once he left, I came to find you."

Charon pulled Jordan into a hug and kissed the top of his head. "Get the others and return to the crypt. You're safe. Promise."

Jordan took a deep breath and gave a slight nod before he left. A minute later Charon's entire group filed past Jaret and out the door, none of them looking at the carnage Styx had displayed in the room.

While they waited, Jaret studied the crime. Seven bodies lay displayed around the room, naked and posed as if they had passed out drunk during an orgy. In the middle, with his arms stretched in a Y-shape above his head and his legs spread-eagle, his penis stretched back and inserted into his ass, lay a dead vampire. Styx had removed the vampire's eyes and placed them in his mouth.

The human corpses appeared intact, each one reaching toward the vampire in the center.

"What the fuck?" Charon spat once Jaret and he had the room to themselves.

"I doubt I need to say this is demented." Jaret could not figure out Styx's motive.

"Styx is so scrambled in the head." Charon walked around too. "He likes to be sadistic for no other reason than to fuck with people. He told me he had to send me a message, and here it is. I bet he imagined he had created a new game show."

"Game show?" Jaret asked.

Charon nodded. "Yeah. Like when he made me by kidnapping three humans and forcing us into a competition with one another for the right to be converted. The remaining two died, at my hands. He saw the whole thing as a game show. Thought himself hilarious. I didn't give a fuck as long as I won."

Jaret snickered. "You never fail to charm me. What's the game here?"

"No idea. We gotta figure him out, though. One dead vampire, fucking himself. Seven humans worshipping him. Oh, fuck." Charon's eyes grew wide with recognition, and he pointed to the vampire. "Me. The eyes in the mouth because I failed to see something, the dick in the ass because I therefore fucked myself. And the seven humans? One for each remaining member of my army."

The observation left Jaret speechless because Charon had

nailed the macabre situation.

"Why a vampire? To show his power?"

"I assume so. To demonstrate he could kill me or more of my boys, and to show how he hides from the Council. He either suspects or knows I'm a double agent."

"Because you thought you could play around with a war you know nothing about." At the sound of another voice, Charon and Jaret whipped around in defense, not having sensed the approach of other vampires. Of course, the entire Vampire Council stood in the room. Xavier had spoken. Jaret stood straight and relaxed while Charon jumped back several feet.

Charon pointed an accusing finger at them. "Yeah, well, you've done such a bang-up job attacking Styx that four of my men already died."

No Council member moved or reacted other than glaring back until Harriet sauntered forward. "Looks like you got one of our own killed this time. We came when the magic alerted us. Styx was able to hide these killings for a while. You want to tell us about your double-agent role? Or keep going and getting in the way?"

"Fuck you." Charon flipped them off and ran out of the room.

Jaret wanted to follow.

Catherine held up a hand to block Jaret when he started to leave. "Stay."

"We won't be able to save this one." Thomas had knelt to inspect the dead vampire.

"What do you mean?" Jaret asked.

Harriet stepped directly in front of him. "You've done enough. Stay out of our business."

The gut punch hurt a second before Jaret got pissed, brushed off Catherine's hand, and stormed toward the door. "Charon was right. You four can fuck off."

He got outside before Catherine grabbed him from behind and whipped him around. She pulled him into a nearby café and headed to the back, where she thrust him into a secluded booth and sat opposite him. With nowhere else to go and bewildered, Jaret allowed her to command him.

"We're having an intimate dinner?" Jaret rolled his eyes. "Could you four start making some fucking sense?"

Catherine remained quiet until she ordered a bottle of wine and they each had a glass. "Fuck, fuck, fuck. I know when you're at the end of your rope because every sentence contains a fuck."

Jaret bit his lip to avoid smiling. "I say fuck *all* the time."

"True. You have a wonderful potty mouth. You *also* get worse when frustrated."

"Did you pull me in here to discuss my cussing?"

Catherine smiled and shook her head. "Do you remember my secret tutoring of you, when I disobeyed Xavier and showed you how to tour famous sites as a vampire?"

"Like when I ended up naked on top of the Eiffel Tower?" Despite his anger, Jaret laughed.

"Yeah." Catherine snickered. "You've always appealed to my sense of defiance. You understood me from the beginning, I swear as well as my brother does. You reminded me of my life in France, during a revolution and after, commanding a financial empire in a world of obnoxious men. Like you, I got so wrapped up in my own righteousness I could miss the most obvious realities around me."

"Like what? What does this have to do with the war?"

"Like when a warlock put a spell on me, controlling my lust and almost getting me to marry him. Not listening to my middle brother, Michel, until the Saint-Laurent home was invaded, and innocent people died. I relate to you because I learned the hard way too."

"I'm not learning anything except what it's like to lose everyone I love, over and over again."

Catherine reached across the table and cupped Jaret's cheek in her hand. "Please trust us. I don't expect you to comprehend. And you never need to forgive us or Anthony for his sacrifice." She paused, looking around the cafe. "Styx can read minds. We're not sure how much. Always? Some of the time? Only if he searches for specific information? No one's sure. If we tell you anything, no matter how hard you shield your mind, he can learn the information, or at least he might be able to. So we can't tell you the plan. Or Charon. We can keep him out of our own minds but can't risk more."

Jaret finished off his glass of wine and poured another.

"Wouldn't it have been easier to tell me from the beginning? What the fuck?"

Catherine shook her head. "Fuck again. Fuckity-fuck-fuck. Here's the problem: just in what I told you, he may have learned more about us. We have to keep him in the dark as much as possible. We want him to think you and Charon are combatting the Council."

Jaret squeezed his eyes shut and clenched his fists in his lap. "I'm frustrated."

Catherine leaned forward and reached across the table to grab both his hands. "Of course you are."

"And alone." Jaret wiped at a blood tear. "Though, I gotta tell you something." His story about finding his true self gushed out.

Catherine listened, as she often had, without interrupting. When he finished, she motioned for him to follow her outside, where they walked along the quiet Parisian streets.

"I wondered what was going on but didn't want to pry. And, despite what you and Charon think, we've been busy with the war." Catherine stopped and peered into Jaret's eyes. "We'll win. We're almost to the finish line. We'll tell you everything once this is over. Do me a favor? The Council needs to meet with Charon and you tomorrow. No recrimination or judgment. We need to coordinate about the war on the fifteenth."

"You know about the fifteenth?"

Catherine rolled her eyes. "Get the two of you to the top of the Arc de Triomphe tomorrow at midnight."

"I'll try. He trusts you much less than I do."

"Which is why I put you in charge. You have to succeed, even if you have to give him a blow job to get there."

Jaret's face turned bright red. "I'd never."

"Got you." Catherine pinched his cheek, spun around, and disappeared.

Jaret walked back to Charon's crypt. He spent as short a time as possible there to retrieve his dogs and leave, despite Charon's wanting him to stay. The vampires had stretched out on the ground to sleep for the next day.

Wanting time alone, Jaret returned to his flat and enchanted the dogs to remain inside with him for the rest of the night. He straightened things up from when Charon and his harem had stayed there, cleaning more to distract himself than from any great need. He wished for the sun to arrive soon.

The lab mix, Chewbacca, the tallest of his mutts, and he played with an orange bouncy ball for almost an hour, the dog running back and forth to fetch and return to Jaret over and over and over with his tongue hanging out the side of his mouth. The pure joy Chewy felt in the game lifted Jaret's spirits until a couple of the other dogs sought to curl up and go to bed when they sensed the approaching sun.

Jaret took his version of groupies into the underground cellar with the made-for-vampires bedding and secret rooms. He picked the largest one, with a king-sized bed, and crawled under the covers with seven dogs surrounding him. Lily snuggled between his legs, Mika sprawled out against one side, and Chewy laid on the other with his head on Jaret's chest. The others took their own spots until the sun sent them all to sleep.

PART TEN

END GAME

CHAPTER TWENTY-SIX

ROMEO AND JULIET

10 APRIL 2019
Paris, France

Per Catherine's request, Jaret woke the next evening and hurried to Charon's underground lair to get him to come to the Council meeting.

"Come with me!" Jaret exclaimed after he entered. "We're going to meet with the Council on top of the Arc de Triomphe!"

Charon flopped onto a couch and shook his head. "No."

"You have to admit, meeting on the Arc excites you a little, right?" Jaret asked Charon. "I mean, I get the shitty part about a vampire war, Styx fucking with you, and our having to rely on the Vampire Council. But also, who else but vampires would hold a secret strategy session high atop one of the most famous landmarks in Paris? Cool."

Jaret leaned his body into Charon, hoping to further entice him with proximity. "We'll have fun!" Jaret spread his lips into an exaggerated smile.

Charon glanced toward Jaret, a slight grin appearing at the corners of his mouth. "You'd make a horrible salesman. And I don't respond to being summoned like a dog. If I go, and I'm not saying I will yet, but *if* I go, then you have to promise to blow me after we win the war. Because you make me do all sorts of shit I don't want to do. So return the favor and suck me off. We both know you want to, anyway. I'm presenting a win win scenario for you. You get me to do your bidding and you get my cock in your mouth."

Jaret leapt to his feet and grabbed both of Charon's hands, yanking him off the couch. "You come along. No blackmail or agreement."

A minute later they found themselves walking along the Parisian streets in no hurry since the rendezvous was a few hours away. Charon never agreed to attend the summit nor had he refused, but he obediently followed Jaret.

"Where's the wolf pack?" Charon asked.

Jaret frowned. "Dogs. Normal dogs, no wolves. I left them at home so they won't get involved in the nonsense."

Charon giggled. "You worried the Council will enlist them as soldiers in the war?"

Jaret squirmed at the question. "I don't want to deal with the Council's reaction to my making them."

"They don't know about your hounds from hell?"

"I actually like that label. Funny, after your other multitude of unfunny attempts. As for the Council, I never told them. I mean, who the fuck knows what they learn? Seems like they spy on everything. Probably have a huge stash of vampire porn videos in their magical realm from every time we come. Bigger selection than a porn website. You can search by hundreds of key words and pairings. Solo vampires. Vampires eating come. Bi vamps. I wonder if any DILF vampires exist."

Charon laughed hard. "No worries on my part. I am hidden from them."

"Your vids would get a lot of hits. Lucky you, hiding from them. Because I bet they know about my dogs. Anyway, you should share the magic with me so I can hide from them too."

"I don't know if I can. Styx invented the ability to hide from them when he created me, remember? I'll look into the matter."

Jaret was surprised Charon had taken the request as serious. "I was kidding, but when all this shit ends, if you figure out how, let me know."

Charon's eyes gleamed with anticipation when he looked at Jaret. "I'll demand payment, *for real.* The transference of the concealing magic to you will come with a condition. I give you magic, you give me your ass."

"I might agree to your terms. You possess a pretty valuable commodity." Jaret turned bright red, trying to imagine a valid excuse for going to bed with Charon.

"I doubt you meant the double entendre, but your Freudian slip about my commodity spoke the truth."

Jaret turned his head from Charon to hide the blush. "I never denied my attraction. I'm glad we got back to flirting. I missed it."

Charon reached over and grabbed Jaret's ass, so he slapped the hand away and jumped forward.

The two vampires sauntered through Paris, as if friends chatting away on a casual walk or two guys on a first date. Jaret was both disappointed and relieved when the time came for them to head toward the Arc.

"We'd better run or we'll be late." Jaret hurried forward but Charon snatched his arm and pulled him back.

"Show restraint. We'll be fashionably late to show them we don't bow to their every demand."

They walked the remainder of the way at a slow pace and in silence.

Though he had visited the site several times, Jaret marveled again at the Arc. Pictures and videos failed to portray the magnitude of the war monument—the way the structure towered over the street level, extending high into the sky in tribute to France's military glory.

Leaping from one corner, across the street, then landing atop the Arc, Jaret wondered how the Vampire Council concealed themselves up here from modern surveillance, but he never doubted their safety. Harriet, Catherine, Xavier, and Thomas strolled around admiring the views of Paris, as if tourists, not a band of blood drinkers there illegally. They peered over at the new arrivals, turned, and stood together in a row.

Charon broke the serenity by speaking. "You've no idea how giddy I am for another drawn-out chat with you fine folks."

Thomas grinned, Xavier eyed Charon wearily, and Catherine stuck out her tongue. Harriet leaned forward and stared Charon into silence. She walked toward Charon and Jaret, followed by the others. "We'll keep our conversation short. We need you to obey, nothing more. Learn to listen to us, and we won't need much time." Harriet stopped a couple of feet in front of them.

Of the Council members, Harriet intimidated Jaret the most with her no-nonsense manner. She had shared her story with Jaret during his healing process after his family died, and he loved her because of her help. And she could be very funny and engaging. But, Jaret had no doubt she would immolate them with her annoyance alone if they stepped out of line tonight.

After several seconds of staring ice daggers, Harriet nodded.

"Good. You two already provided helpful resources. You're correct, Jaret, we needed an ideal vortex and your ability outmatched ours in pinpointing Notre Dame. We engage the battle there on the fifteenth, as Styx decided. And Charon, your affiliation with him will bring him to us. He knows we'll be there, but you paved the way for him to feel in control. You both must be there. No excuses. We'll need your magic because you two complement what we do as the Council. Bring your entire army, Charon. Bring the dogs, Jaret. Be prepared to follow our orders, and we can finish this. Good night."

Harriet spun around and walked away with the other vampires in tow.

"Wait a minute," Charon called out. The Council stopped and turned.

Harriet arched one brow. "I thought you wanted short and sweet. I doubt I could have gone any faster."

"Yeah, well, I'm not your fucking puppet."

Harriet tilted her head. "No? You'd rather help Styx win? I think you'd switch sides in a heartbeat. Your bravado hides a scared little boy inside who never learned to trust and love."

"Fuck you." Charon flipped her off.

"Are we done, then?" she asked.

"If you want us to help, you have to tell us more." Charon stuck out his chin though Jaret sensed Harriet's words had cut deep.

Harriet shook her head. "No, we don't. We're useful to each

other in a war. Once we win, we no longer need to play nice with each other. You either show up and help or assist Styx's conquest and die with him. 'The enemy of my enemy is my friend' brought us together."

Jaret stepped between them, holding up a hand in each direction to calm the two vampires. "We know." He looked at Harriet. "You're in charge, and we understand the Council has a way to defeat him. We're on *your side*. But you make working with you difficult with the secrecy and strangeness. The fact Anthony had to die. Then a grand meeting atop the Arc de Triomphe but instead of detailed strategy, you bark orders, stuff you could have sent in a magical little note. Come on." Jaret shrugged.

Harriet rolled her eyes as she spoke. "Such sensitive young ones. I was elected to speak because they," she motioned to the silent cohort behind her, "get too sympathetic and might cave to your demands. We've already told Jaret why we need to keep as much as possible out of your minds. I'm sure he told you in return. And if Styx could read yours," she motioned toward Jaret, "then your friend there would be like an open book. I'm being an asshole on purpose. We chose this location to make sure you came. And sending a magical message could be intercepted. Listen and obey. We'll see you in five days."

She finished and the four vampires vanished.

Charon peered at Jaret with an incredulous expression. "How are you friends with them? They're always a bunch of fucking assholes."

Jaret giggled.

"What's funny?" Charon asked.

"You. Them. Everything. I don't disagree with you. I've no defense for their behavior." Jaret waved his hand in the direction the Council had once stood. "I always admitted they drive me nuts. They care though. At an earlier moment in my life, they helped me and brought me over to being a vampire. I go both ways regarding them."

He got Charon to laugh. "I've known bi people, and you are *not* someone who goes both ways."

"Got me. All dick here. Let's go." Jaret jumped off the top of the Arc, moments later landing across the other side of the lanes of traffic and back on a sidewalk.

Charon followed him down, grabbed Jaret from behind, and raced along carrying him until they arrived under a tree with a fabulous view of the Eiffel Tower. Charon set Jaret on his feet, pressed him against the tree, and reached up to brush the hair out of Jaret's face.

Charon grinned. "I thought you'd resist my kidnapping you."

"Did you want me to put up a good fight?"

Charon shook his head, one hand lingering on Jaret's cheek. Their faces were so close Jaret felt the wisp of Charon's breath upon his brow. They remained in the same position for several minutes, staring into each other's eyes, neither breaking the spell nor taking further action.

"You do funny things to me," Charon whispered.

Jaret smiled. "Like what?"

"I'm not sure. If I could explain I would. I wish I could dismiss you as a prude asshole. But I'm drawn to you despite your reluctance to have sex. In a different time under different circumstances, we'd be together."

Jaret reached up on his tiptoes to press his forehead against Charon's. "I know." He kissed him lightly on the lips. Then Jaret stepped away from Charon and walked toward the tower.

Charon stepped next to him a second later. "Why is this so difficult?"

"Because we both have a fantasy with the other, but the fantasies don't come close to aligning. Neither can give in, but neither can give up." Jaret reached over and grabbed Charon's hand.

Charon halted and pulled Jaret to him, hugging him close and kissing the top of his head. When Jaret looked into his eyes, he saw the trickle of a blood tear at the corner. Jaret reached up and wiped it off, then licked the blood from his thumb. He thought of a thousand things to say, from the funny to the macabre to the serious, but nothing felt appropriate. Instead, he fell into Charon's arms and lay his head on his chest.

CHAPTER TWENTY-SEVEN

SURROGATE FATHER

14 APRIL 2019
Paris, France

The nights since Jaret had embraced Charon under the Eiffel Tower seemingly dragged on without end. His mind cycled through every imaginable outcome to the war with Jaret wishing he had a fast forward button to the April 15 end game, whatever the result. He had never been good at waiting, especially when faced with a crisis. One minute he believed the Council would triumph, the next he feared Styx had too much power and would win.

His only distraction came when he reminisced about being in Charon's arms. Eventually, Jaret kept his arm around Charon's waist and his head on Charon's bicep as they walked along the path. Unlike Charon, he never cried but struggled a couple times to keep himself under control. Neither one spoke another word the remainder of their time together. They walked through several neighborhoods until they stood outside Jaret's house. Charon kissed him on the cheek and left.

On the one hand, Jaret was grateful to have avoided another round of Charon pushing to have sex while Jaret wished for a monogamous relationship. He had meant the Romeo and Juliet analogy from the bottom of his heart. Yet so many unanswered questions remained.

As if on cue, a breeze blew through the open window and Jaret smelled Anthony's cologne. He shook his head but grinned. "I wondered what could make the situation more awkward and difficult? Of course! The ghost of my dead husband. Or was he just a lover since we never got married officially? I never liked lover because the term sounds like sex, which conveys part of our relationship, but one of many. Boyfriend is too high schoolish. Why are you here?"

Jaret scanned the room for further signs of Anthony but sensed nothing but his scent still hovering in the air.

At least Jaret could distract himself with the dogs. Lily and

Nosferatu had snuggled underneath his chair for a nap, while Chewbacca slept by himself a few feet away. Cher and Darth played, biting and running and spinning around. Dancin' Boy chewed a bone while Mika walked from one dog to another, sniffing them and wagging his tail.

At least Jaret had but one more day to endure until the battle. He tensed and felt his heart lighten when a vampire turned onto his street and walked toward his house. He peeked outside to see Xavier climb the stairs and knock.

"May I come in?" Xavier asked when Jaret opened the door.

"You four barge in whenever you want. I'm surprised you knocked." Jaret stepped aside and motioned for Xavier to enter.

Xavier stepped in. "The war has us on edge, making us forget our manners."

Jarret nodded and the two stood in awkward silence in the entryway. "Oh. I see. Come on." Jaret led Xavier into the living room. "Drink?"

Xavier shook his head and sat down. "I'm fine."

Jaret was nervous as he sat on the edge of a couch opposite Xavier. Xavier was the closest person Jaret had to a parental figure after Henrik killed Jaret's family, when Xavier saved Jaret from total despair. They'd remained close ever since, until the tension with the Council because of the war had drawn them apart. The separation had gnawed at Jaret.

"I feel better since we agreed to stop playing games." Xavier fidgeted with the cross hanging from his neck. His nerves appeared to be as frayed as Jaret's.

"Me too."

Another silence fell between them before Xavier chuckled. "Awkward. Since I came to you, I suppose I should tell you why I'm here."

"Okay." Jaret shuffled his hands together and bobbed his knee up and down.

"I should have been more direct in my apology after we agreed that neither of us has handled things well of late. I'm sorry for how the Council has to treat you. I love you as much as ever. I'm afraid, because of the war and shit, I failed you when Anthony died and sent you spinning out of control."

A blood tear trickled down the side of Jaret's cheek. "Thanks. I'm sorry for being an asshole too. I mean, like you, I think the climate deserved my 'tude but I hate how I lash out toward you. I think I'm harsher toward you because I feel closest to you. I felt you had betrayed my trust." Jaret held up a hand to stop Xavier. "Not anymore. I get it. I *do*. It means a lot you came today."

"Thanks for letting me in the door"—Xavier grinned as he spoke—"without my having to break in. I couldn't go into tomorrow with the shit between us. I've been worried I'd be distracted or thinking about you. So, I came."

"I'm glad."

Xavier peered around the room at the dogs. "I freaked when

I converted Darth into a vampire dog."

"I know you took a risk with the rest of the Council to transform Darth. You saved me when you gave her eternal life."

"About the dogs. Your explanation for making them vampires makes sense to the Council. We agreed to allow you to keep them."

A lump caught in Jaret's throat. "Oh, good. I wondered if you'd freak. My new pack already means the world to me."

"I know."

A surge of despair swept over Jaret as he thought about why he had sought to create his gang of dogs. "Has a being ever lost more than I? Don't answer. I need the self-indulgence. Imagine if you found Thomas after all your time alone, and then instead of having centuries together you had a few years before he threw himself into an inferno to save you." Jaret choked and blubbered, the words locked inside. "I didn't know what to do without him until they give me a purpose." He swept his arm across the room to indicate his dogs.

Xavier rushed over and held Jaret, rocking him. "Shh. I understand. I knew you lashed out because of your pain. Your spark of goodness burns so bright you could never extinguish it."

"I wish I could. I hate being good. I hate living up to expectations."

Xavier sat Jaret back against the couch. "The good I can't do anything about. I suffer the same malady. The expectations, well, those are on you."

"What do you mean?"

"You gotta let go. Be yourself without judging yourself all the time. Lean into yourself."

Overcome with emotion and needing to move forward, Jaret laughed. "Are you giving me permission to tell the Council to fuck off if I want to?"

Xavier roared a laugh. "We can deal with whatever you throw our way."

"I hope no one on the Council hates me."

Xavier shook his head. "We don't. We're concerned and can't wait to get past the war."

"I guess next you'll warn me away from Charon."

Xavier grinned wryly. "I warned you once about having a dangerous rebound. You can either hear me or dismiss my advice, your choice. I'm afraid some admonishment about his being an asshole would only attract you to him even more."

"I can't explain how I react to him."

Xavier squinted. "I think you know very well how you react to him."

"I want to be like him. I'm drawn to his disregard for any rules and his ability to please himself without concern for how others view him. Some part of me longs for the freedom because I'm spellbound to obey every rule. The defiance thing is so hot." Jaret blushed and wiped his hands across his face.

Again Xavier let out a hearty laugh. "See, you know the

situation. Good."

"You at least admit he's hot?"

"Eh," Xavier grimaced. "Not my type. Personality matters too much to me."

Jaret tried but failed to conceal his smile. "He's as hot as Anthony, in a different way. Sex on a stick. The bad boy confidence with the charm and good looks does me in."

Xavier held up his hands in surrender. "Enough! I don't want to know any more!" He shook his head but smiled. "Be wise and hang onto your true self. Don't do anything stupid."

Jaret calmed down. "I haven't. And I won't."

"Good." Xavier got up to leave. "I have to go. I didn't have time tonight until I realized you were the most important thing. I made the time but have to get back."

Jaret got up and followed Xavier to the door. "Thanks. Your visit means the world to me."

They hugged.

Xavier paused before going down the steps. "Stay with me. Okay?"

"I'm trying," Jaret answered. "If we win tomorrow, we can address my shit then."

"*When.*" Xavier asserted the word with a harsh accent. "*When* we win tomorrow."

Jaret gave a slight nod and watched as Xavier left, walking a few steps before breaking into a vampire run and disappearing.

Jaret turned the other direction and shook his head at the vampire standing under a tree. "Get up here."

Seconds later, Charon stood inches from Jaret, smiling down at him. "Another warning to stay away from the nasty vampire outside Council control?"

Jaret shook his head. "Xavier knows human nature too well to attempt a futile effort."

"You can't get enough of me, can you?"

"I get plenty of you, believe me. Besides, you came to me again. *You* can't get enough of me."

"At least I admit it," Charon retorted. "Until my tongue dives into your delicious ass I'll never get enough of you."

Jaret lowered his head to look at the ground. "No one makes me blush more than you. Every time I turn around you talk about one of my body parts. I don't like to think so much about my own body."

"Then think about me, naked and kissing you."

"Should we be flirting the night before a major war? Shouldn't we be getting ready to fight?"

Charon shook his head. "How? We know the plan. Show up at Notre Dame when summoned and obey the Council, hoping like motherfuckers they have a plan and not their usual bullshit of letting Styx murder everyone before he disappears. We have one more night of assured living. Celebrate and make sure you have no regrets if we depart this earth tomorrow."

Jaret walked into his living room laughing. "Let me guess. The one regret we might each suffer would be failure to consummate our relationship."

Charon, following behind, snorted. "Consummate. Like seventeenth century Puritans."

Jaret fell onto the couch and Mika jumped on top of him while Cher ran over and licked his face. "Quit avoiding the subject. Why are you here?"

"I'm jealous. The dog gets to lick your face when I should be the one." Charon licked his upper lip then flicked his tongue at Jaret before getting serious. "I don't know why I'm here." Jaret watched as Charon sat in a chair opposite him, not engaging his usual proximity and ramping up of their sexual tension.

Jaret grinned. "I know, even if you don't. You *did* want to see me. Nothing else."

Charon rubbed his chin. "Yeah. I've pretty much done whatever I want in life. I don't know if I've even picked to have a quiet evening inside. But here I am, staring at the only person I ever encountered who *didn't* want to go to bed with me."

"I never said I didn't want to. I said it's not a good idea for me. There's a big difference."

"Not according to my blue balls."

"We may survive, you know. I'm planning to do everything I can to beat Styx."

"You're right. I sound morbid. I plan to win too. If nothing else, I want to defeat Styx so I can continue pursuing you until I win."

Jaret's stomach fluttered. He petted Mika to keep him close because otherwise Jaret would run across the room and lunge into Charon's arms. A knock on the door saved him.

"Come in!" he screamed.

Brady walked into the room with a smirk. "You two playing hard to get again?"

"He is." Charon jerked his head toward Jaret. "I'm going to jack off and give you two time alone." Charon hurried away, holding his dick as if it might fall off.

"You sure you shouldn't fuck him and move on with life?" Brady asked.

Jaret rolled his eyes. "Ignore him and pour the drinks. We have a couple hours of guaranteed living remaining. If the vampire world implodes tomorrow, we don't want our last hours to be about him. Come on."

Jaret and Brady spent time drinking and wandering Paris. They laughed and dismissed the tension about tomorrow that lurked below the surface, until Brady had to leave.

"The Council has me staying in some dungeon to protect me tomorrow. I wanted to join the fight, but what the fuck could I do anyway?" Brady stopped and bit his lower lip. "I need you to win so this isn't goodbye." He choked on the last words.

Jaret yanked Brady into a tight hug, the two friends clinging to each other until Brady pulled away and ran. Jaret composed himself before he went to follow Charon.

CHAPTER TWENTY-EIGHT

CONFLAGRATION

15 APRIL 2019
Paris, France

Jaret woke disoriented in his coffin. His dogs surrounded him and he reached down to feel a raging boner because fantasies of sex with Charon had consumed almost every second of sleep. He had avoided any physical contact with Charon the entire night after Brady left until they retired below ground, where Charon grabbed Jaret into a hard embrace and forced the most passionate kiss Jaret ever experienced. Their tongues probed each other with desperation until Charon released Jaret and helped him into his coffin seconds before the sun sent him to sleep. Again, Charon shocked Jaret with his relative restraint.

Yet something other than sex dreams caused him to feel dizzy. He glanced around as the dogs roused themselves, each seeming as confused as Jaret. Some force was summoning him out of the coffin despite his body's resisting the call.

He opened the lid to find Charon standing above him, disheveled and yawning. "What the fuck?"

"What's going on?" Jaret asked.

Charon shrugged. "Not sure. I'm supposed to get to Notre Dame. I don't know *how* I know, but I do."

"Me too."

With sluggish movements they climbed the steps, Jaret compared this to how he felt as a human when he had the flu. But vampires didn't get sick.

When Jaret opened the door to the first floor, he flung himself back and covered his eyes. "Fuck!" he screamed. Squinting between his fingers, he peered out to see the sun blazing through the dining room window.

Charon had stepped into the room, shielding himself from the bright rays with his forearm. "No wonder I feel like the worst hangover in the world."

"You think Styx is behind this?" Jaret asked.

"Nope." Charon pointed at the orange glowing orb floating before him. "Council wants to fry us."

"Shit. Fuckers." Jaret glanced at the grandfather clock, chiming the top of the hour: 6:00 p.m. with the sun still up.

"Part of their strategy?" Charon stepped toward the front door as if drunk. "The orb is telling us not to worry. The sun will set soon and can't hurt us. Unless the Council decided to kill us. They might."

"Wait!" Jaret yelled. "I gotta get something." He tried to move fast, like a vampire in a hurry, but instead he could only go at a normal human pace as he returned to his crypt and unlocked the hidden safe. He took the entire chest of Bachmann Family Jewels and clung to them as he returned to Charon.

Without further discussion, the two vampires and dogs headed into the daylight. A couple of streets over Charon's boys joined them, appearing scared and sick but relieved to see their master.

As if infected humans in a zombie apocalypse, the throng of vampire beings made their way through Paris until they stood outside Notre Dame Cathedral, closed for the day but with tourists milling about outside. No one seemed to take note of the odd group. Jaret startled when he glanced at someone's watch to see they had taken two minutes to arrive when he felt like they had walked for hours.

"The Council want us to meet inside." Charon read the orb

for everyone.

They filed along, around the side of the cathedral to an un-guarded entrance surrounded by construction equipment. The Council must have orchestrated the area to allow them easy access to the building.

Jaret felt drunk from the sun as he followed behind Charon and his minions. The dogs stuck close to him as they meandered through the ancient structure. He wondered where they headed but trusted Charon's navigation and so concentrated on keeping himself moving. They ended in some medium-sized room on a top floor, empty of everything except a mass of furniture shoved off to one side and hidden underneath protective sheets.

Jaret slammed into the back of one of the most muscled boys when everyone ahead of him lurched to a stop. He could see between the vampires, his eyes growing wide with shock.

Had Styx won? He stood before them, smiling and confident. He meandered forward as if studying the throng and tutting while shaking his head. "You thought the Council brought you here?" He laughed. "To your enchanted vortex? I fooled them, as usual. I conjured the magic to summon you before they arrived. And you're stupid to believe you could hide your duplicity from me. You never dreamed of my power to attack during daylight!"

Charon held his hands up in surrender and began to talk.

Styx shook his head. He then screamed, "No! You will *not* speak! Time for my triumph."

Styx twirled a finger to create a force that shoved the vampires into a tighter and tighter circle. Jaret wondered if Styx intended to crush them together until they died and cursed himself for trusting the Council. But an energy suddenly tingled through Jaret's being, his gems jumped to life, and power surged into the room. The dogs let out a chorus of ferocious barking.

Styx's eyes grew wide with fright, and he shook his head. "No, no, no. Not again." He turned his head back and forth in search of an intruder before his face twisted in rage, his exposed skin smoldering.

Styx screamed at Charon. "Are you behind the magic controlling me?" Styx spat at Charon. "Traitor. How?"

On cue, the four members of the Vampire Council moved out from underneath the white cloth.

Harriet grinned. "We've been reading your mind, my friend. Game over."

Styx spun around. He slapped at his arms in obvious pain and glared at the Council.

Freed from Styx's spell, Jaret inched around Charon's boys, who remained tight together and behind Charon. His dogs followed him until he gained a better vantage point. He set his chest of gems onto the ground and opened the lid to see them alight with electricity, ready for the battle, despite Jaret never summoning them.

For the first time in months a pounding headache hit Jaret. This particular type of pain dated back to childhood and was a warning of supernatural visitors nearby. The presence of the vampires had awakened the giant vortex of magic housed inside Notre Dame. For a second, he marveled at how accurate he had been to choose the place. Despite the headache, Jaret was alive with power, the gems floating into the air and whirling around him and the dogs.

Jaret glanced to his side to see Charon surrounded by a golden sheen. Charon was commanding a different magic from Jaret's but with a similar potency.

The Council glowed orange.

And Styx smoked more than before as he writhed in pain and screamed. He patted at his arms, ripping his shirt off to stifle the burn, but black smoke continued to rise off him.

"How?" Styx forced through gritted teeth. His agony turned into a slight grin and his eyes lit with an idea. He snapped his fingers, stopped resisting, and stood still.

The glow from everyone disappeared, and Jaret felt his magic drain. A force seized control of him and the other vampires, lifting them a foot into the air and immobilizing them. Styx barked a laugh and walked at a casual pace from vampire to vampire, staring them in the eye and shaking his head.

Jaret struggled against Styx's power, to no avail. Terrified of dying, he wiggled and squirmed, chanted every spell he could imagine, but nothing released him or anyone else from Styx's grasp.

"Fucking Council," Jaret muttered. The years of insistence they had everything under control, the number of times they ignored Jaret's warnings, and their smug attitude came crashing down on everyone in Notre Dame. Styx was the master of the situation, despite their assurances to the contrary.

Styx moved to the center and closed his eyes. A burning sensation crept up Jaret, first on his toes, then his legs, and winding its way up his entire body. He screamed because of the pain, more than he had ever experienced in his human or vampire life.

"Doesn't feel so good to catch on fire?" Styx shouted his question to everyone. Jaret could barely hear him above the anguished screeches.

Jaret slammed his eyes shut and gritted his teeth. His only remaining recourse was to stop yelling and not give Styx the satisfaction of watching him wince and plead for relief before dying. So much for eternal life and the omnipotent Vampire Council.

Jaret was stunned when the burning dissipated, followed by his return to the ground. He opened his eyes as his feeling of magic came back and his gems regained their force. The spell he had been using before Styx took the upper hand engulfed him as the other vampires took turns scanning to see how each of them could command their ability again. They glowed with magic again.

Styx spun around, his eyes wide with alarm. "Where is he? This is impossible!"

"*No.*" Styx screamed. "*I* control *him*. I have since Anthony thought he won the war. Anthony has no power over me. He can't really be in my mind!" Despite his words, his skin smoldered and light smoke lifted off his body.

Jaret sensed his lover's spirit a moment before he spotted him. Anthony's ghost walked into their midst, his face set in concentration and his arms reaching toward Styx as if puppeteering him.

"Now!" Thomas screamed.

Charon moved first, closing his eyes and shouting for his men to surround Styx to keep him in place. He wrapped his boys in the golden magic, then sent rays out of each vampire that pulsated into Styx. Jaret's dogs ran in circles between Styx and the boys, lunging toward Styx and biting at him, then hurrying back before he could swat them away. Every item of Jaret's jewelry spun toward Styx's head, swirling so fast they created a rainbow of color. Last, the four Council members took positions at equal intervals around everyone while the entire time Anthony kept his outstretched arms pointed at Styx. All the vampires and dogs elevated into the air of their own accord this time and chanted. While nothing visible came from them, Jaret felt the might they added to the room. The vampires' effort had brought forth other forms of supernatural power. Good and evil forces alike were drawn toward the energy sources in the room and flowed into Styx's burning body.

Anthony, his power stronger than in life, had saved them. Jaret understood the necessity of his death, as he became more lethal than ever before and commanded the scene in a way Styx never envisioned.

"No," Styx screeched. "Anthony will *not* control me in his

death. I will not let him win! You fools cannot win!" Despite his words, flames shot from his arms.

Jaret believed they were back to defeating the worst vampire in history. The collective sorcery was too much for the self-professed master of evil. Even demonic spirits attacked Styx when they materialized, seeming to want to join the forces around them and feed alongside. Jaret marveled at how the powers combined and emitted more energy than Jaret had ever dreamed of. Anthony's aura extended into all of them to control Styx and mastermind the assault.

Too easy, of course. The vampires had succumbed to their overconfidence, and despite the concentration and hard work, Styx escaped their grasp. He shot straight up into the air, condensing himself into a slight round beam to slip from their grasp.

Charon's magic followed the Styx laser, the gems went straight through the roof after him, and Jaret spotted Anthony's ghost pursuing through the ceiling.

"Get up there!" Harriet yelled. "Into the rafters!"

Jaret wondered how to find a path up fast enough before Styx escaped because he knew nothing about the cathedral's architecture, stairways, or rooms. But like in a superhero movie, the four Council members rocketed upward and smashed through the roof, sending down plaster and debris. Sometimes Jaret forgot the force given to vampires—not to mention how the moment's urgency suspended any worry about concealing their actions from humans.

Jaret bent his knees and launched himself after them, with Charon and his boys right behind. Even the dogs leapt after Jaret.

Unlike the grand Cathedral below or the opulent room in which they started the fight, the rafters proved a forest of wood, low clearance, and a helter-skelter building plan. Anthony's spirit, visible at the roofline, created a purple shield over the ceiling to contain Styx in the building. Styx's line of energy fell apart and recreated his human form before their eyes, as he burned and flopped around the attic.

Jaret spotted an anomaly amid the form; Styx was not one individual vampire but rather a vampire encased in the spirit of a demon. At times the two clung together, the spirit invisible. But the fire jolted the demon outside Styx's body before it snapped back inside.

Charon and his men, Jaret and his dogs, the Council and Anthony reunited their combined magical assault to lock in on Styx and burn him.

Styx screamed in agony as his flesh disintegrated even more. He lashed around and batted at the flames, but nothing stopped the fire. In a torrid inferno, the vampire of malevolent design turned to ash. His ashes blew around the attic. With the vampire gone, the red glow of a sinister demon remained with several sets of glaring eyes casting about for another victim. The assailants persisted with their attack when the sprite started toward one of Charon's boys. The vampires altered their spells, causing the devil to break up and fizzle away before a large pop engulfed the room as he blew apart. The moment the demon disappeared, Anthony vanished and with him the force field at the ceiling.

Though he had used his energy often in both his human and vampire life, never before had Jaret felt depleted and unable to move. His muscles collapsed, his arms fell to the side, and he used every effort to step away from a burning beam. With what little strength he could muster, he summoned his dogs to stay near him and away from the flames while he called forth the chest from below and gathered the gems into it.

Charon had fallen across a rafter along with his men. He looked around but wasn't moving.

Jaret looked for the Council, hoping they could help, but everyone except Thomas appeared in the same condition. They stood limp and frozen.

Thomas frowned and gritted his teeth, his long black hair slicked with sweat. He held up his arms and shot beams of energy out of his fingers that engulfed each vampire and dog in shrouds of soothing magic. The pain left Jaret the instant Thomas's incantation hit him. He was lifted into the air and then descended through the holes in the ceiling and back into the building. He floated along with the others until Thomas lay them softly on a secluded part of the riverbank along the Seine, in view of Notre Dame but out of danger.

Jaret lay with his eyes open but unable to move. Thomas stood over everyone as one by one the vampires revived. First the other Council members stirred to life. Jaret came around soon thereafter and the same time as Charon, and next his harem of boys returned to their vampire forms. Jaret's dogs jumped to their paws and scampered toward him, wagging their tails and seeking his praise. Jaret collapsed back onto the ground with them, letting them topple him over as they vied with one another to lick his face.

Jaret was unable to tell how much time had lapsed since the battle commenced, but night had fallen. Despite the various vampire factions everyone remained together as each in different ways and at varying times came back to themselves. Once everyone appeared normal, and after Jaret took a deep breath and realized they had defeated Styx, he wrinkled his brow because an orange glow illuminated everything around them.

He turned around at the same time as Xavier to see the cause. Flames shot out the roof of Notre Dame. The ancient cathedral was in a conflagration that threatened to devastate the historic structure. Xavier lurched forward, toward Notre Dame, and Jaret followed to save the church.

Catherine and Thomas each grabbed one of Xavier's arms to stop him, while Harriet held up a hand to halt Jaret.

"Too late," Catherine said to Xavier. "We can't intervene."

"We caused the fire!" Xavier exclaimed. "We have an obligation." But his words grew faint by the time he finished speaking.

Thomas rubbed Xavier's arms and let him go. "It's been too

long. They're broadcasting the images around the world, and they initiated efforts to stop the fire. Too late for us, Xavier."

Xavier nodded and slumped to the ground. Everyone turned their attention to the fire.

As Jaret observed Notre Dame ablaze, he thought through the culminating battle. He had questions but kept them to himself to maintain the solemnity of the quiet vampire assembly. He noticed his chest of gems beside him. Thomas had somehow saved them along with the vampires and dogs.

Charon started the conversation for them, to Jaret's relief. "He's dead, right?" Charon never turned his head from watching the fire.

"Yes." Harriet answered from behind Jaret.

"Not to be rude, but you sure?" Charon clarified.

Thomas chuckled, alleviating a bit of the tension. "One hundred percent."

"And a sprite was there, one who possessed Styx." Jaret took his turn to gain clarity. "Did he appear because of the vortex? Or was he there from the beginning?"

"Now you see the complication of what we faced." Harriet spoke again, in her controlled way. "The demon took control of Styx during the first vampire war. Anthony learned of the possession when Styx reappeared with his new threat of war. Anthony was irate about how the demon had hidden from him for centuries. Anthony was observing the demon, but until Styx converted Charon, the truth remained elusive. The magic Styx invented to hide Charon revealed the anomaly in the Council's control and uncovered the demon. You see, the vampire who started the first war *was* defeated and killed. But Styx, enraged at the loss of his lover, summoned the vampire's ghost and allowed the spirit to possess him. The spirit and Styx worked together for centuries to get revenge. Thus was why Anthony thought at first Styx was the one to blame for everything of long ago. But, no. He was nothing more than an innocent pawn."

"And you kept this secret because as a demon he could gain information? Yes?" Jaret wanted answers.

"Correct." Catherine took her turn. "We had never faced a foe of his magnitude. Our delays and slow action were because we needed time to figure him out and plot our strategy. We also wanted him to grow overconfident in thinking he fooled us. Time alone gave us that advantage. Shall we tell them the good news?"

"Yes." The other Council members spoke in unison.

"Wait." Catherine exclaimed. "Let's show them instead. Turn around."

The vampires formed a circle at her direction.

"Before we begin," Thomas said, "Jaret, you need to listen to me. Don't get your hopes up. He had to die." Thomas stared at Jaret. "Do you understand?"

Of course he got the message. Whatever they planned to reveal, Anthony was dead. Jaret gave a slight nod, blood tears forming in his eyes.

The Council sat together in the circle and held hands. They closed their eyes, murmured a chant, and swayed back and forth. Charon gasped and his harem rushed into the middle of the immortals as the dead boys from their strange family materialized before them. They were alive and well even though everyone had witnessed their deaths at the hands of Styx. First Phil, then Travis and Alex. Charon lurched forward and tackled Kevin. The entire group shouted in joy.

The Council stopped and Thomas spoke. "The others who died over these years also came back to life. We had to make the demon think he wielded absolute power over us. We devised a Council magic for vampires to die for a brief time. Then we sent them to a hidden location and kept them there, safe and sound but unable to leave. They remained there until this moment. We've returned them to their previous lives."

The euphoria intoxicated the vampires. The moment even put the animosity between Charon and the Council on pause. Charon and his army of men jumped to their feet, dancing and hugging. The Council stood and stepped a few feet away to give them space. Jaret, surrounded by his dogs, remained on the ground. The revelry lightened his mood but a lead ball sat in Jaret's stomach. Everyone else had a little group while he sat alone.

Jaret grinned when he heard Charon whisper to his minions. "Go. Fast as fuck. Before they get any ideas." A split second later,

Charon's harem had disappeared into the Paris night. Charon wagged a finger at the Council. "I appreciate the cooperation, but you're not getting your fingers on me."

Catherine and Thomas smirked, while Harriet and Xavier stared him down.

Charon pointed at them. "Stay back."

Harriet held her hands up in surrender, and no one else moved as Charon backed away until he stood over Jaret. He reached a hand down and pulled Jaret to his feet, then turned so his back faced the Council and concealed Jaret from them. He muttered a spell. "So the fuckers can't eavesdrop."

Jaret giggled. "Fuckers."

Charon brushed Jaret's blowing hair out of his face before cupping Jaret's cheeks in his hands. "You okay?"

Jaret shrugged. "Being alive doesn't suck. We won. And yeah—I'm alive. I'm glad you got your boys back."

"Me too." Charon's smile hardly lit his face as he peered into Jaret's eyes in concern.

Jaret gulped back a sob and fought the urge to fall into Charon's arms. Jaret was drawn like never before toward his handsome face, the concern, and his powerful biceps. But Jaret knew he was looking at more fool's gold. Genuine love and support? Yeah. But of a Charon variety certain to crush Jaret's soul in the end. He chuckled. "I'm not fucking you."

Charon laughed and patted Jaret's cheeks. "You will

someday." He leaned over and kissed Jaret on the forehead. "I gotta leave before the Council gets any ideas. Come see me."

"I'll protect you from them," Jaret said.

Charon shook his head. "Besides, you've got a visitor." He pointed behind Jaret.

Jaret turned to see Anthony's ghost hovering nearby. "Just his ghost." Jaret spun his head back to look at Charon but he had vanished. The Council, too, had disappeared.

Jaret returned his attention to the ghost. His effort to contain his emotions failed as a flood of blood tears poured down his face. He slumped to the ground and fell into a pile of dogs who went into frantic efforts to comfort their master. Some licked him, others rubbed against him, and Mika jumped into his lap and lay down. Jaret clutched the dogs and let them attack, hiding in their love from the ghost standing before him. When Darth nudged the other dogs out of the way and smashed her snout into his stomach, Jaret gave her sole attention for a couple minutes. His eyes welled with tears of joy at their special moment. For a long time, he lost himself, allowing the accumulation of grief and change and revelation to pour out of himself as never before.

When he had spent himself, he kissed each dog on the top of the head and allowed them to settle in around him. He peeked up to see Anthony standing there. Jaret jerked his head to get Anthony to join him. The spirit ambled across the way, appearing more solid and almost human. Jaret glanced around to see that thousands of people had thronged to watch as the beloved French landmark burned.

"Surprised the Council let us carry on in front of these people. We were out in the open for everyone to see us." Jaret muttered, needing to talk because of the awkward silence. The first time since his death he and Anthony could communicate, and Jaret came up with small talk.

"You don't think they concealed you with a spell?" Anthony sat beside him.

"I needed something to say."

A long silence ensued but nothing came to mind except more stupid observations or deflections.

"I'm sorry," Anthony whispered.

"I figured."

"There was no other way. The demon had control. We needed power and information."

Jaret took a deep breath. "I need clarification. Can you be honest now?"

Anthony nodded.

"When did you know about Styx? How long? The Council said his conversion of Charon revealed the truth to you. Explain."

"You already know I'd kept an eye on him for a long time. The sorcery we put in place to monitor him alerted when he created Charon."

"Alerted?" Jaret raised a brow.

Anthony grinned. "I don't know how else to explain. There was a shift, as if a stone was tossed into our magical realm and created a ripple effect. When I investigated what happened in Key West, I saw how Styx had feigned his suicide. Then I noticed a magical anomaly, which I couldn't grasp until you revealed Charon to us. However, the energy left behind when the crypt exploded revealed two entities, not one. It was as if their shadows burned into the ether from the force. My charms worked to expose the truth of Styx's being two beings in one. We ramped up our effort from monitoring to preparing for war because I knew we faced the same foe who had started the first war."

"Can you tell me why you took so fucking long?"

"Because Styx or, I should say, the demon and Styx were watching us in return. We could hide Council business but not everything. We lured him into believing he hid from us and could conceal crimes while we ramped up efforts to counter him. We made him feel in control while making sure no one died. Our Council magic, however, kept indicating we needed a soul on the other side to get inside the demon's head. Of course, we attempted to summon spirits and other sorcery for help. Nothing worked. I concluded one of us must die to become like the spirit in Styx, to match the demon's ability and exceed his power when combined with the Council."

"You succeeded. You got him to murder you. And so you became the same as the demon."

Anthony sighed. "Better, actually. In addition to what he could do, I had brought Council magic to camouflage myself from him and then worked on a way to read his mind. You don't know how much I tried to find a way to stay alive with you. There was no other alternative. The other Council members wanted to trade places with me but, with all due respect, none compared to my capability. Which is why I acted without their knowing and became the bait."

"I think I get the rest." A tear trickled down Jaret's face. "On the other side you learned about his plan, tricked him more, and waited."

"Waited until he wanted to strike. And—" Anthony laughed, which seemed out of place but caused Jaret to smile. "I should tell you, I did *nothing* to guide your secret plan but I spied enough to keep track of you for myself and the Council. I hate to admit it, but you were right. We had to have what you and Charon did to win. You figured out to use Notre Dame. Ironically, Styx learned of your plot and saw the potential to defeat the Council instead. He believed he could overpower the Council and you. But Styx had relied on Charon obeying him and didn't know about me. He also assumed spirits would join him. However, spirits—especially evil ones—are very hard to control, as you know from your experience with Henrik. They arrived as Styx predicted but wanted nothing more than to feed on the magic. Styx and the demon were easier for them to attack because they were weaker than the rest of us working together. The energy I used to trap Styx inside the rafters came from my death, but the Council needed their strength combined with the unique abilities of you and Charon to annihilate him."

Jaret pointed toward the flaming cathedral. "You burned down fucking Notre Dame."

"Eh, it was French anyway."

Despite himself, Jaret laughed at Anthony's British dig. "That's not funny. I loved the place." Another pause made Jaret uncomfortable. "What are you and I supposed to do here?" Jaret asked. "No matter how many ghosts I see in my life, they always confuse the hell out of me. You're no exception. At least you didn't give me a raging headache before you appeared. And thanks for the apology. I accept. But you're still dead, and I'm still alone."

"Yeah, but you've learned about yourself."

Jaret rolled his eyes. "Do I have to keep losing fucking everything to get a lesson? Next time could I stop short of death consuming my loved ones so I could grow? I don't know, how about a mild case of anxiety followed by getting better?"

Anthony nudged Jaret with his shoulder. "You sound like yourself. Emotional but smart-ass."

Jaret glared at Anthony. He wanted to punch him in the face, but before he acted, Anthony reached over and, with surprising vigor for a ghost, pulled Jaret into a hug. Jaret relaxed his muscles and fell into Anthony's arms. Anthony ran his fingers through Jaret's hair.

"Do you believe me?" Anthony asked.

"About?"

"My dying."

Jaret blew out a deep breath. "Part of me wonders if you missed something. Why not keep searching for a different way to fight Styx? Then again, why ponder such questions because nothing will bring you back. Even if I figured out you could have won and remained alive, I'd feel even shittier because you'd be dead but for no reason. I *am* glad you've found peace." Jaret turned to look at his lover. "Maybe it's your being a ghost, but you feel more relaxed than I ever remember. Perhaps vampires can't really live forever, and you needed to go to find peace."

"Styx, the demon or whatever, had haunted me since the first war. Not anymore. Other than you, I don't miss being alive."

Anthony's honesty jolted Jaret. "Wow."

"I didn't mean to startle you. I think I would've thrived with you. But I don't know if that could beat being dead."

"Well, fuck. Instead of your committing suicide out of despair, can we stick with the narrative you had to die to defeat the demon? Makes things easier on my end." Jaret smiled. He was kidding and not kidding with his comment.

Anthony grinned. "Yes. Besides, it's the truth. I concocted a magic to defeat Styx that required my death and the combined magic of everyone else." Anthony jerked his chin toward Notre Dame. "Including the fire, I suppose."

Jaret sat up and scooted away from Anthony. "I don't want to get too attached."

"I'm not going to haunt you. Our souls can go someplace in death. And I want to."

"Good." Jaret tucked his knees up to his chest and clutched his legs to his body. "I want to apologize too. For being an ass about the Council and shit. I was learning about myself and never meant to hurt you."

"I know." Anthony whispered. "We're good."

"But I'm not sorry about who I am and what I believe."

Anthony cackled. "Also good. Very good."

"I'm keeping the dogs."

Anthony roared a laugh and held up his hands. "I wasn't going to say a word. Since you brought them up, six more does seem extreme."

"They needed me."

"Or you needed them?"

Jaret tilted his head. "Both?"

"Yeah. I think both." Anthony stood and pulled Jaret to his feet. "You good?"

Jaret pushed out a forced breath. "Yeah. I'm okay."

Anthony pulled him into a hug and Jaret leaned into the ghost. A couple of minutes later, Anthony evaporated and Jaret stood alone except for his dogs sitting around him.

CHAPTER TWENTY-NINE

THRIVING

JUNE 2019
Paris, France

Jaret had packed some belongings and souvenirs he wanted to take with him to Chicago, sending them ahead with a shipping service. He and the dogs would accompany Brady on a cruise across the Atlantic later in the evening. Instead of hurrying at vampire speed and using their ability to get home in one night, they decided to play human and return as if on vacation. Besides, unsure about keeping track of seven dogs swimming in the ocean, Brady felt better about being an eccentric rich American with too many hounds in a suite than traveling like vampires. As usual, vampire wealth came in handy when they paid ten times the fare to bribe the company into allowing the pack aboard. He was glad vampires could get around US customs to sneak his dogs in and out of America whenever he wanted without the mandated quarantine.

Jaret had time for one more walk around Paris. He hooked the seven dogs onto leashes, pretending he was a dog walker, and they headed out. The streets bustled with activity. A lot of people smiled at Jaret and his pack when they passed. More than anything, Jaret needed to say farewell to Notre Dame. The authorities had barricaded the cathedral to keep people from getting too close. With Jaret's vampire vision, he could see from afar the evasive action the French had taken already to secure the building, which continued to threaten to collapse in on itself. Heroic efforts by fire-fighters had saved the structure but its future remained at risk. For now, the building's integrity held, for which Jaret was grateful.

He blew a kiss at the church. "Adieu, good friend."

Standing where the vampires had congregated after defeating Styx, Jaret pondered the last couple of months. For the first time in years, since he found out about the impending vampire war, Jaret felt calm as his memory drifted back to his last encounter with Anthony's ghost.

He recalled the feeling of peace as he stood in Anthony's arms, the ghost clutching him and petting his hair. As Jaret's emotion subsided and Jaret relaxed, Anthony's ghost had faded away, leaving Jaret alone.

Jaret had glanced at his dogs, thankful to have them fill a void instead of solitude descending him into pity. The thought of the Council members having each other while Charon and his fuck buddies celebrated their reunion left Jaret feeling alone. As he had contemplated what to do with himself, a familiar presence came onto the scene, followed by the sound of one of his favorite laughs.

Brady had jogged over and picked Jaret up into an enormous hug. "Dude, we lived!"

Jaret forgot his loneliness, knowing he and his best friend in the whole world could venture out as single vampires and create whatever new life awaited them. They spent the next two months as tourists in Paris until they decided to head back to the United States. Brady decided to set up his own home for the first time as a vampire. Jaret wanted to begin the laborious process of doing the same except he now owned Anthony's empire, a network of wealth and property Anthony had assembled over centuries. The thought of figuring out how to manage affairs and the vast wealth and property threatened to overwhelm him, so he pushed the idea from his mind. For an unknown reason, he wanted to panic when he remembered some huge house Anthony once mentioned owning in Hong Kong. Jaret had never been to Hong Kong.

The recollection of Hong Kong snapped Jaret back to the present. He untangled the dogs and went at as casual a pace as possible when shepherding seven dogs. He returned to Anthony's Paris flat. He and Brady had agreed to meet there before heading to the ship.

"Dog man!" Brady shouted outside his flat. "Ready? Boat leaves soon."

Jaret nodded. "Do I get to know what kind of cruise you booked?"

Brady giggled. "A Lawrence Welk tribute cruise. I had to pay extra for them to waive the requirement you had to be eighty or older."

"Will you ever admit you are so *not* funny?"

Brady pointed to Cher. "She thinks I'm hilarious."

"She loves all people, as long as they fawn over her. She's not an accurate gauge about your humor. She'll give you a dog smile in return for letting her lick your face."

Brady wrinkled his nose. "Sexy. But we gotta hurry. Come on," Brady instructed. They started walking toward the outskirts of Paris. Once there, Brady shouted at Jaret as they raced through the French countryside with the dogs following. "Of course, I booked us on a gay cruise! Ever been on one?"

"No."

"Me, neither. Two singles on a gay cruise. I'm planning on serious coming. As vampires, I bet we can shoot multiple times a night."

"You bet? Or you know from practice?"

Brady grinned and opened his mouth to talk but they had arrived at their destination, so he gave no answer. Brady assisted Jaret in getting the dogs aboard ship and into the largest suite on the vessel. They followed official channels here so Jaret could have the dogs on their private balcony without worry of someone discovering them.

"I'm gonna get a drink. Want to come?" Brady asked after they settled into their quarters.

Jaret leaned against the balcony railing. "Not yet. You go. I wanna make sure they're okay." He motioned with his head toward the dogs.

"Don't hook up with some man and make our place smell like hot sweaty man sex while I'm gone."

Jaret laughed. "I thought that was the point?"

"Only when the aroma includes my smells." Brady slammed the door shut with both of them laughing.

Jaret would have followed his friend except he saw the vampire lurking along the port. A moment after Brady departed, jumping from a distant sidewalk to land next to Jaret on the balcony, Charon grinned.

"Did you think I'd let you leave France without saying goodbye?"

"I haven't seen you since the night we won. I figured you and the boys were enthralled with a never-ending celebration of parties, drinking, and fucking."

"We did plenty of all of the above!" Charon laughed. "But I stayed away from you because I've been working on something."

"Do I want to know what?" Jaret frowned. "I don't trust you."

Without answering, Charon reached into his pocket to pull out a handful of multicolored glitter. He threw the concoction at Jaret without warning. Jaret closed his eyes. At first, he felt nothing but the glitter landing on his face and in his hair, wondering how he would ever get it out. Jaret laughed and began to scold Charon when a more powerful sensation took over.

Jaret's skin tingled, his senses went numb, and he blacked out for a second before returning to his normal self. He opened his eyes and glared at Charon. "What the fuck did you do? You did some kind of magic."

Charon lunged forward and grasped Jaret in a bear hug, picking him off his feet and twirling him around. "The Council has no idea where the fuck you are or what's going on!" Charon laughed.

Jaret went limp in Charon's arms, the statement sinking in. "Are you talking about the concealing spell?"

"Yeah!" Charon set Jaret down but kept his arms around him. "It took longer than I thought to isolate the magic so I could share with you. I spent extra time to infuse the potion in glitter to make the celebration more fabulous." He picked out a few pieces of glitter from Jaret's hair. "Aren't you excited?"

Jaret smiled. "I appreciate the gesture. I do. I doubt the

Council will share your enthusiasm."

"Fuck 'em." Charon shrugged. "Oh, you know what this means?"

"What?"

"We get to fuck!" Charon jumped up and down in excitement.

Jaret shook his head and laughed. "We never made an agreement. I said I'd consider the exchange, but in your impatience you gave up the magic without sealing the deal."

Charon pouted but could not stop the grin from spreading across his face. He grabbed Jaret by both shoulders and yanked him forward until their lips smacked together. His tongue probed deep inside Jaret's mouth and their cocks ground together. Jaret allowed Charon to pick him off his feet as they kissed and held tight to each other. Holding Jaret up with one hand, Charon rammed his other hand down Jaret's pants, bursting his belt and ripping his jeans until he was able to get a finger probing inside Jaret's ass. Jaret ground back and forth as he tore open Charon's pants and grabbed his dick, jerking him but making sure Charon never came.

A loud horn blasted and startled Charon, who set Jaret down and stepped away, snapping his underwear back into place but discarding his destroyed pants. Jaret clung to what remained of his own jeans to cover himself.

"Your ass is so tight. How am I supposed to go anywhere with this?" Charon pointed at his boner straining for release from his underwear.

"I got my own problems." Jaret motioned with his head toward his exposed groin.

"Anyway, I gotta go. Promised the boys we'd visit Amsterdam before returning to the castle. High and drunk vampires should be interesting. Otherwise, I'd stay on the cruise to seduce you."

Jaret squinted at Charon. "You're leaving without more protest? And I should add a thank-you. Your giving me the magic means the world to me. But you gave up the spell so easily. I get to go on my way without fighting you off just as you had your finger in my ass?"

"Oh, I won't forget about you." Charon winked. "Two can play hard to get."

Jaret knew he had a big silly grin plastered on his face as he stared toward the shore to watch Charon disappear as the ship sailed out of port toward the ocean. A second later, he saw nothing but a vampire blur and bright pink underwear vanish into the night. He plopped into the chair behind him as the dogs scampered over and settled around him. He leaned over and picked up Charon's pants, resisting the urge to smell the crotch. The breeze blew through his hair, and he smiled again. Jaret adjusted his erection and used what remained of his own clothes and Charon's pants to conceal his cock as he rubbed himself to visions of Charon.

About Damian Serbu

Damian Serbu is an author of gay horror/speculative fiction. After over twenty years of teaching history at the collegiate level, he now writes full time. He lives in the Chicagoland area with his husband and two dogs.

Email
DamianSerbu@aol.com

Facebook
www.facebook.com/Damian-Serbu

Twitter
@damianserbu

Website
www.damianserbu.com

Other NineStar books by this author

The Realm of the Vampire Council
The Vampire's Angel
The Vampire's Quest
The Vampire's Protégé
The Vampire's Witch

Santa's Kinky Elf Simon
Santa is a Vampire
The Bachmann Family Secret

CONNECT WITH NINESTAR PRESS

WWW.NINESTARPRESS.COM

WWW.FACEBOOK.COM/NINESTARPRESS

WWW.FACEBOOK.COM/GROUPS/NINESTARNICHE

WWW.TWITTER.COM/NINESTARPRESS

WWW.INSTAGRAM.COM/NINESTARPRESS

www.ingramcontent.com/pod-product-compliance
Lightning Source LLC
Chambersburg PA
CBHW060305100726
47907CB00002B/294